BETWEEN

AND REAL

Dannie M. Olguin

To the Survivors,
You are loved. You are not alone. You are fierce.

Dear Reader,

Stop! I know Author's Notes can be dull, but please take a moment to read this one.

This is a book about love and friendship. About siblings and found family. About strength and courage and learning to trust yourself. This book is positively bursting with love, and I'm so excited for you to experience all of it. But first, some housekeeping.

Content or trigger warnings can be a controversial topic, but I care about you and your mental health, so I want to let you know that it's one-hundred percent okay if you decide to set this book down before turning to page one. It's okay to set this book aside for a little while if it gets too hard for you. And it's absolutely okay for you to stop reading this book entirely if that's what you need to do to protect your mental health. You, sweet reader, are my priority and I'm sure we can both agree that getting triggered when you're not expecting it is an awful feeling. It's one I dealt with time and again as I wrote and rewrote Between Safe and Real.

Although this book is a love song to siblings and found family, it's also a song that touches on child abuse, neglect, addiction, parental mental illness, poverty, and self-harm. If you've experienced any of these things, please, *please* listen to that little voice inside you and step away if you need to.

One more thing, dear reader, before you either turn to page one or set this book down. If you have a history with any of the above-mentioned topics, please know that I believe you and I love you. You are good. You are worthy of love. And one day, you'll understand that what happened to you was in no way your fault.

Wrapping you in a fuzzy blanket and surrounding you with all my love,

Dannie

REAL 1

This may be a new journal, but nothing much ever changes. Mama's yelling at Daddy again—big freaking surprise. The moment she raised her voice, Bobby and Leesh took off, and I can't say I blame them. If I weren't grounded to my room, I'd have made myself scarce, too. Bobby's under the back porch, probably trying to dig a hole to the center of the earth. I know because that's his favorite spot to hide whenever Mama yells. Besides, I dare anyone to show me a six-year-old who doesn't love the idea of digging a hole to the center of the earth.

I'm pretty sure Leesh is under the tree behind the house. Lately, she's been spending a lot of time out there, lying on the grass and staring up at the leaves. I should probably ask her again if something's bothering her, but the last time I asked, she told me to go away, huffed off to her room and slammed the door. I wonder if she's about to get her first period. After all, I was twelve when I got mine, and she just turned thirteen. If that's what's going on with her, it makes sense she's crabby.

Does it make me a bad person that I don't even want to know why Mama's screaming? All that matters to me is she's not screaming at me. I know I'm ugly, but she makes it sound like I'm some kind of disgusting mutant. Sometimes, when I accidentally see myself in the mirror when I'm brushing my teeth or putting my hair in a ponytail, I think she's right. My nose is crooked, and my eyes always have raccoon circles so dark you can't even tell my eyes are brown. Not that it matters, since Mama says my eyes are the same color as Sammycat's poop. She can be mean to all of us, but she only says crap like that to me. Until the day I die, I'll never understand what I did to make her hate me so much.

Get out of my sight, Zoe. Looking at you makes me sick. No wonder you don't have a boyfriend. What boy would ever be caught dead with you? I swear to Jesus on the cross, your hair's the exact same color as old dishwater, and for the life of me I can't understand why you don't shave it all off. You're so skinny, if you did shave it, everyone would think you had cancer. We could set up one of them online fundraisers and rake in the cash.

Honestly, I think Daddy's gone so much because he figures she'll yell at him the same as me if he's home. I get so mad at him for being gone all the time, but he has a family to support so I can't stay angry too long. I just wish he had a job where he came home every night like he used to instead of driving a semi and being gone for a week or more at a time. I wish I could disappear, too, but someone's gotta take care of Leesh and Bobby. Besides, like Mama says, *if wishes were fishes, the sea would be empty*. I don't even know what that means, but it seems fitting, somehow.

Mama doesn't know I found out she's been reading my old journal. I took care to hide it some place I thought she'd never find it—way back on the top shelf of my closet, wrapped up in my favorite shirt from three years ago. When I came home from school one day last week, the diary wasn't in the right place, and the shirt was jumbled around the diary instead of folded around it the way I do. It had to be Mama, because

Leesh is too honest to snoop. She's serious about her privacy and would never violate mine.

Bobby doesn't even know about my diary, but if he somehow found out about it and got it in his head to look for it, he couldn't reach the hiding spot. When I look back on how Mama acted between when I found the journal in the wrong spot and when I made my last entry, I realize she had been asking all sorts of nosy questions that fit with my entries. Do I have a crush on anyone—that kind of stuff.

She never asks me how school was or why I don't invite friends over. The only time she shows any interest in me at all is if she wants something or is screaming at me, so why in the world did she bother looking for my diary? What a stupid question, Zoe. Duh. She went looking for it to find proof I think she's a shit mom, so she doesn't have to feel guilty about the way she treats me. I'm glad I listened to my instincts that my diary wasn't safe, and I never wrote about her in it. Thankfully, it was just full of stupid boring stuff, like what I had for lunch or that we had a substitute teacher in English.

There's no way she'll ever get her hands on this one. Every time I leave the house, it'll come with me. I carry my backpack everywhere anyway, so she won't even notice I have another notebook in it. It's a relief to finally have a place where I can be honest. I'm still gonna write in my old diary now and then, though. Now that she knows about the first diary, I know she'll check it every chance she gets and if I stop writing in it, she'll become suspicious I have a new one and will tear my room apart to find it.

I swear, I'm not being all dramatic with this kind of talk. It seems like at least once a month she gets mad and goes through my room, trashing it worse than a tornado ever could. With luck, she'll get bored by all the pointless entries in my old diary and will stop snooping. Maybe then I can go back to hiding my journal in my room like a normal fifteen-year-old instead of having to sneak it out of the house under my shirt or in my backpack every time I leave.

If wishes were fishes...

———

SAFE 1

Dear Diary,

There's this girl in History, Cheryl, who's been trying to talk to me. I seriously can't think of a single reason she'd want to be nice to me, because she's the exact opposite of me in every way. Smart as hell, blonde hair that bounces when she walks, unlike my nasty dishwater hair. She's popular and nice, and I can see why everyone likes her, but what's the point of making friends with the popular girl? Keeping to myself is lonely, but it makes all the moving easier. I mean, it seems like such a waste of time to make friends when we'll probably move again before the end of the year.

Man, seeing it written out like that makes me sound so ungrateful, when that's not how I feel at all. Yeah, moving a lot is really, really hard sometimes, but it's also worth it. Kids like Cheryl have been stuck in the same small town their whole lives and, honestly, I feel sorry for them. Me and Bobby and Leesh have seen so many interesting things and have more experiences in one year than they have in their whole lives. I wish I could take credit for that point of view, but all the credit goes straight to Mama.

She's the one who helped me learn to love being what she and Daddy call a *nomad*, which is someone who's truly free. Nomads don't feel bound to any one place but jump around from place to place whenever they want. Mama says sometimes she and Daddy get wild hairs up their butts and they just know they'll die if they don't pack us up and chase a new adventure. I can't say I understand that feeling, but I don't care where we live as long as we're together. And I'm all about doing whatever makes Mama happy.

Now, I could never imagine any other kind of life. It's not that I wouldn't like a group of friends, or heck, even just one friend, to hang out with, but even if I knew we'd never move again, I know I'd never fit in with the kids here. They're all swimming in money and have been in their friend groups since preschool. They could never understand going to ten schools in ten years like I have. I learned years ago to say yes when kids ask me if my dad's in the military because it's easier than explaining how some families just like the way the wind pushes their backs and encourages them to explore new places. Well, it's not like we're living on the streets, but we don't have money to spare, either.

But if I'm being totally honest, I have to admit out of all the houses we've ever lived in, I adore this one best and can almost imagine staying here until I go away to college. For the first time in ages, Leesh, Bobby and I don't have to share a room, but that's not what I love so much about it. I love how different it is. It has to be at least a hundred years old, and it's no McMansion like so many other houses around here. It's old and drafty, and you can't even roll over in bed without the whole house creaking. I like to pretend I'm living in a haunted old house in the mountains. Don't get me wrong, diary, I'm not complaining at all.

Who cares if we don't have a swimming pool, or the hot water only lasts long enough for one shower? This old house is pure perfection, drafts, and all. Plus, I could get used to having my own room, even if I do get a little scared all alone sometimes. I don't believe in ghosts, but it's fun imagining what kind of ghosts would haunt our house and I end up scaring myself. I read once that ghosts don't like to be in the same room as cats. Even though I *know* there's no such thing as ghosts, I'm still glad Sammy likes to sleep with me.

Anyway, when Cheryl from History tries to talk to me, it's easy to let my imagination run wild, especially since I have my own room now. I like to think about how awesome it'd be to invite a group of girls over for a sleepover. I'd tell them all about the ghosts that wander the house at night, and we'd eat entire mountains of popcorn and scare ourselves silly. But that's just a fantasy, not reality. The reality is, even if Cheryl really is a nice person trying to chat with the new girl, I don't have time for frivolous things like sleepovers.

Like Mama says, I need to keep my head on the ground and my shoulders out of the clouds. I think she's mixing up two sayings there: *Keep your feet on the ground* and *head in the clouds*. But even mixed up, it still makes sense. I need to focus on the things that are real, like making sure the kids finish their homework, and helping Mama with the chores, especially when she has one of her headaches. There will be plenty of time for the extras, like going to the mall or a horror-movie marathon when I'm older. Plus, who knows how long we'll stay here? The wind has a way of changing directions and taking us with it. As interesting as it is to move around and experience new places, it makes it hard to have friends.

Okay, enough stalling. I have English to do. Luckily, that's all I have for tonight, so maybe I'll get a jump on stuff that's due later in the week.

SYNT (see ya next time!)

REAL 2

I'm exhausted. All I want is to close my eyes and float into sweet darkness, but every time I try, my brain replays what happened, over and over. I wish sleep could steal my memories. Or I could drift off and when I wake up, I'll discover I've been living a nightmare for the last fifteen years. Dream on, Zoe. Dream on. Since I can't sleep, I'll write.

We were at Ikea, and Mama lost her damn mind. I don't even know what happened. Well, that's not totally true. I felt the tension building in her all day. She woke up with all this nervous energy, and she sort of buzzed around the house trying to do things, but not really focusing on anything. She plugged up the sink and ran the faucet to do the dishes, then got the vacuum from the hall closet.

When I walked into the kitchen, the mountain of fluffy, white bubbles covered the spout, and water flowed to the floor. I ran to turn off the water, rolled my sleeves up, and winced as I plunged my arm into the sink to pull the plug. She ran it on pure hot. When I finally yanked the plug, little wisps of steam rose from my arm like wildfire smoke. I grabbed a dirty towel from the hamper to sop up the mess on the floor. Sometimes I wish we had a laundry room, but today, I was glad the laundry room and the kitchen are in the same place.

The vacuum roared to life as I dropped the towel into the washer and topped off the load. After I started the washer, I noticed even though Mama turned the vacuum on, it wasn't making the usual back-and-forth sound it makes when it's moving. Instead, it had that high-pitched sound it makes when it's standing still. Mama hates that noise. She hates pretty much every sound except her own voice, but the vacuum standing still is one of her most hated.

If I leave the vacuum running without pushing it for even three seconds, she always says the same thing, *Zoe Dawn Wilkes! If I have to endure the screeching of that vacuum, it damn well better be moving.*

When I came into the hall, sure enough, the vacuum was on, but Mama was nowhere to be seen. A little ball of cold dread plunked down to my stomach. I turned off the machine and debated whether or not to go looking for trouble... I mean, Mama. In the end, I decided it'd be best to leave things alone. Whatever she was up to, I was damned sure I didn't want to be involved. I went back to the kitchen and rinsed the leftover bubbles down the sink.

Shit, she's awake for some reason. I'll write more when I can.

SAFE 2

Dear Diary,

Cheryl invited me to sit with her at lunch today, and guess what? I actually did! Instead of making up some stupid excuse and hiding in the library or bathroom, I took her up on her offer and sat with her. She waved at her group of friends as she led us away from her usual table to a less crowded one. I think I love her for that. It was hard enough to come up with things to say to one person, forget about a whole table full of her friends.

I know I don't fit in with her crowd—the McMansion kids. The beautiful, smart ones. The ones who run for Student Council President and actually win. Not like the time I ran for secretary and got a grand total of four votes. God, how humiliating. I've never been more relieved to move to a new school than I was that year.

I usually enjoy my quiet lunches. Nobody bothers me while I look at the world and people around me. Today was interesting, though, because sitting with Cheryl gave me a front row seat to the Hormonal Teenager Show. I've concluded that teenagers are weird. I know, I know. I am a teenager, but most of the time, I feel more like an alien scientist, beamed down and given the body of a fifteen-year-old girl so I can blend in with the local wildlife and study them without being observed. I once read an article that said when someone is being observed, they change their behavior, even if they don't realize they're changing it. That's why I'm incognito, in teen-girl form.

Now, before you go calling the ambulance and having me committed, obviously, I don't really believe I'm an alien scientist. I just think it's a fun thing to imagine. Then again, maybe you should consider having me committed. After all, I'm talking to some imaginary "you" as if anyone will ever actually read this and worry about my mental health. I guess sometimes, it's easier to write like I'm telling a story to someone rather than relaying a bunch of boring facts about my day.

Speaking of which, I gotta run. Algebra won't do itself. SYNT!

REAL 3

I'm back. Not two minutes after I stopped writing, Mama came into my room. My light was off, and I pretended to be asleep, so she'd go away, but she didn't. She sat at the foot of my bed for a few minutes but didn't talk to me or touch me or even check to see if I was really sleeping. It was weird. No, not weird. Creepy. She just sat there, her head in her hands, for like five minutes. Then, she got up and left. I'm sort of freaking out about it.

How often does she come into my room at night? What the hell did she want? Of course, I can't ask her because then she'd know I was awake, and she'd yell at me for ignoring her. Mama hates to be ignored. When she says, "jump", I'm not even allowed to ask, "how high?" She expects me to jump without question and all I can do is hope I'm jumping right. And do it immediately, or she assumes I'm ignoring her, and she goes bat shit.

Anyway, back to what went down at Ikea. After I turned off the vacuum, I left it where it was because I figured she'd probably come back for it and would get mad if I moved it. Maybe I should have vacuumed for her, but I didn't want to mess up her plan. It's like that a lot. Somehow, I magically need to know what she wants me to do, like I'm psychic. I went back to the kitchen to do the dishes, then curled up on the couch to catch up on my English reading. After a while, Mama came buzzing in with her nervous energy bubbling over like a pot of rice over too much heat.

She'd been getting cleaned up. Mascara clumped on her lashes and bright red lipstick screamed on her normally naked lips. Her from-a-bottle blond hair, which she hardly even remembers to brush most days, was styled and wavy. And I'd never even seen the tight jeans and black boots she had on. Her attempt to get all dressed up made her look like she was on her way to some hole-in-the-wall bar, and between you and me, it embarrassed me.

"I'm bored! Let's go do something."

Oh, no. Going out with her when she has this kind of energy is always a bad idea.

"Wow, Mama! You look so pretty! But it's so hot. If we drive somewhere, your hair will fall." I hoped she'd remember the van still doesn't have working AC, and how she hates to be sweaty. And more than that, how much she hates driving. No such luck. Storm clouds gathered to make her dark brown eyes almost black, and she stomped one foot on the floor like Bobby used to when he was a toddler.

"You're ashamed of me, aren't you?" She stepped toward me, and I jumped up from the couch.

"Of course not! All the girls at school are jealous their moms aren't as pretty as you." I knew exactly the right lie to tell.

She smiled and twirled her brittle hair around her finger. "Really?"

"Totally." There was no way to avoid it. If I didn't want her to go all Mt. Vesuvius on me, I had to go along with her plan and go out. "Let me round up the kids."

And that's how we ended up at Ikea, even though I knew it was the worst idea ever.

Of course, traffic was bad. Traffic is always bad around Dallas. For the life of me, I'll never understand why she sometimes gets it in her head to drive on the highways when even driving on surface streets makes her freak out. By the time we pulled into the ginormous parking lot, Mama's hair was a smooshed down mess from the humidity and the wind.

Mascara and eyeliner smeared around her eyes like the raccoon's mask she always says I have. Her face shimmered with sweat, and her hands trembled as she pushed her damp hair off her forehead. She barely looked like the same person who stood in the living room an hour earlier. It's a miracle she didn't either cause an accident with her erratic driving or pull over and demand I drive the rest of the way, even though I don't even have my learner's permit yet.

I shivered and wished I'd thought to bring a sweater when we walked into the air-conditioned store. People swarmed around us, and I grabbed Bobby's hand to keep him from wandering off. Mama's eyes glazed over, and she sort of disappeared inside herself, right there in the entryway.

I took a deep breath and tried to keep my voice light. "Where to?" I asked, hoping to pull her back from herself. She's the one who wanted to come to Ikea in the first place, and when we get here, she shuts down. Typical. "How about we get the kids something from the cafe?"

Bobby smiled his missing-teeth smile at me. "I'm hungry! Can we get a cinnamon roll, Zoe?" How do you say no to a kid who pronounces cinnamon "thinnamon"?

Mama yanked Bobby's hand from mine. "Why are you asking her? Is she your mother?"

He stuck his thumb in his mouth and looked down at the floor.

"Didn't Zoe feed you and your sister breakfast? No, of

course Little Queenie didn't feed you. I have to do everything myself!" Her voice bounced off the polished floors, but nobody looked at us. Or, if they did, they did a good job of pretending they weren't.

I ignored the bit about me not feeding the kids breakfast. Of course, I did, but it's best not to contradict her.

"It's okay, Mama. Cinnamon rolls are only a dollar, and I found five dollars on the way to school yesterday." Finding five bucks felt like winning the lottery, but I'd gladly give up a million dollars to keep her from flipping out in public.

The hardness dropped from her face, and she smiled like a little girl looking at an expensive doll in a toy store.

"You have money, Zoe? Maybe I could get a roll, too?"

She's always acting like she's the kid and I'm the mom. It's weird, and it makes me feel gross in a way I don't understand, but what could I do? If I told her I was trying to save every penny I find for an actual emergency, she'd throw a crybaby fit. I bought two cinnamon rolls. Leesh and Bobby shared one and Mama had the other.

"Don't you want any?" Leesh asked.

"No, my stomach's a little wonky. Thanks though." A harmless enough lie to cover up the truth. I can't stand sharing food with Mama. Once, when I was maybe seven, she brought me and Leesh cups of bright green Kool-Aid on a hot summer day, which was totally not like her. As I was about to take a drink of mine, I looked down and noticed a little island of white foam floating at the top of my cup. I snuck a look into Leesh's cup and didn't see the foam. My stomach did somersaults as it occurred to me Mama might have spit in my Kool-Aid to punish me for having the TV up too loud earlier that morning and I claimed it was an accident when I spilled it. From that day to this, I've never completely trusted anything she touched again.

Mama laughed and shoved a forkful of gooey cinnamon

roll into her mouth. "Aleesha, we both know Zoe doesn't need any of this. She's packing on the pounds as it is." She swallowed and threw eye daggers at me. "Zoe, Zoe, two by four" she chanted while stomping her feet. "Couldn't fit through the kitchen door. Kept on saying, 'mmm mmm I want some more.'"

She always does that, too. One day she tells me I'm so skinny nobody could see me if I hid behind a stop sign, and the next day she tells me I'm fat. I know I'm too skinny, so I'll never understand why she says the opposite so often. It's almost like she's trying to make me develop an eating disorder.

My stomach lurched, and I silently thanked myself for not eating any of the roll. No matter how often she sings that horrid song, it always makes me feel ashamed and sick. Leesh gave me a sympathetic look and shoved a big bite into her mouth to avoid joining in. I know Mama hates me, but I'm so grateful my sister doesn't.

After the snack, Mama perked back up and she, literally, took off running through the store before I could even make sure Bobby's hands and face weren't sticky. She says run, and we can't ask how fast, we just take off after her. I'm sure we looked like a bunch of wild dogs tearing through the store, trying to keep up. Bobby's sandal slipped off his foot as we chased her, and I stopped to help him put it back on.

"Stay there," I told Leesh while I tried to slip the too-big sandal onto his squirming foot. By the time I fixed it, Mama had already been swallowed up by the maze.

We wandered around looking for her for what felt like an hour but was probably closer to ten minutes. Leesh suggested we split up, but I nixed that idea real quick. The last thing we needed was for all of us to end up separated and lost. Finally, we found her. Or heard her, anyway.

"Oh my God," she wailed from a far section of the area rug

department. "Somebody took my babies! FUCK! Someone, help! Call the police! My babies!"

The three of us looked at each other and ran toward her voice.

"Mama," I shouted. "Mama, we're here!"

We turned a corner and there she was, sitting on a pile of area rugs, surrounded by helpful employees in blue and yellow striped shirts. She cried hysterically as a worried-looking woman gently rubbed her back and a security officer talked to her.

Bobby wrenched out of my hand and flew straight into Mama, knocking her backward. She wrapped her arms around Bobby and laughed as they rolled around on the stack of rugs like two out of control toddlers. Curious eyes bored into us as if we were a freak show instead of a family. All at once, almost like someone flipped a switch, everyone realized we hadn't been kidnapped and went back to their shopping. No longer the center of attention, Mama really lost her shit. She pushed Bobby off her and stood up, hands on her hips.

"What are ya'll staring at? Haven't you ever seen a mother play with her baby before?"

I put my hand on her arm, trying to calm her down, but she shoved me, and I fell flat on my ass. My cheeks burned as strangers gasped in shock. She didn't even glance at me as I picked myself up off the gross floor. Her fiery eyes jumped from one startled person to the next, looking for a victim to consume.

"Why don't you take a fucking picture? It'll last longer."

A woman pushing a baby in a cart tried to maneuver around the commotion, and Mama found her target. "And you! You better enjoy your little bastard while you can. Before you know it, she'll be lying to you and avoiding you. She'll be saying you should have killed yourself years ago, and you're gonna wish you'd listened to her father and had an abortion after all!"

The woman's hand darted out to touch her baby—an instinct to protect her. Mama read the woman's move as weakness and took two steps toward her. The security guard stepped in and put his hand on Mama's shoulder.

"Ma'am," he said simply.

"Get your filthy hand off me, you rapist!" She pushed his hand away and made to smack him in the face when I jumped between them.

"Mama, stop," I shouted. Her hand froze midair. "Let's go home now, before traffic gets bad. Okay? I'll make us some dinner." I looked the guard in the eyes and silently pleaded for him to let us go. Hopefully, he'd realize he doesn't get paid enough to deal with our kind. He blinked slowly, shell-shocked, and nodded his head one time.

I looked back to Mama and took her hand. She had left herself again, which was a blessing this time. Her eyes had a glassy look and her mouth hung open. She squeezed my hand and made quiet whimpering noises as I pulled her through the building. When she's gone like that, at least it's easy to direct her where I want her to go. There was no way in hell she'd be able to drive us home in her state, so once again, it was up to me to be the adult in the situation.

Most kids get a learner's permit and months and months of driving practice before their parents let them get behind the wheel, but I didn't have months and months. I'd be driving for the first time through Dallas traffic with two siblings and a mother who was as likely to jump out of the moving van as sleep the whole way home.

Whatever. I had to get all of us the hell out of there before someone called the cops on us. I didn't have to tell the kids to keep up. Leesh took Bobby's hand and followed close behind me and Mama. People parted for us, as if our crazy was a disease they could catch. Every single person pretended not to stare as we passed.

I looked behind me, just to make sure Leesh and Bobby were keeping up, but someone else looked back at me.

Nate Evans. His perfectly pink lips were all scrunched up and he crossed his muscular arms over his chest. At school, I could watch him talk to his friends all day and never get bored. But this was Ikea, not school, and I had a quickly vanishing mother and a brother and sister to focus on. When his eyes met mine, my entire soul ignited—like someone firing a flame thrower inside my body. I immediately turned around and focused on finding the damned exit.

Why did it have to be Nate? Last month, I would have given my left big toe if he knew I existed. Now, I'd give my right arm if he didn't.

———

SAFE 3

Dear Diary,

Yesterday, Mama decided we should all get out of the house and go on an adventure. At first, I didn't want to. I wanted to stay home and try and get caught up with all the laundry, but Mama insisted.

"Girly, I'm a lot older than you, so take my advice. You can't stay at home doing chores all day. Sometimes, you gotta get out and have an adventure. The laundry ain't growing legs and running away anytime soon."

Even though I didn't feel like going, she's always right about this kind of stuff. I mean, she is older than me, like she said, and I'm glad she loves me enough to share her wisdom with me. Besides, she had on new pants and boots, and even did her hair and makeup. She looked so pretty! It would have been a total waste to stay home, so I got the kids ready and off we went.

At first, Mama didn't know where we should go, but we eventually ended up at Ikea because she said it was a perfect place for an adventure. I'll be the first to admit Ikea's not my favorite place in the world. It's always way too busy, and the whole store is so overwhelming. I had to keep a super close eye on Bobby so he wouldn't wander off, but I'm happy to watch him if it helps Mama relax and enjoy herself. She works so hard for us, and it's the least I can do to make her day a little better.

Right away when we got there, we decided to go up to the cafe and get a couple of cinnamon rolls. You know, treat ourselves after the long, hot car ride. As much as I don't like going to Ikea, I have to say, their cinnamon rolls are pure heaven. After we ate, Mama couldn't wait to go exploring. One of her favorite things to do there is try and pronounce the Swedish names of all the products and try to make us guess how to spell them.

We followed her around for a while until she settled on the section filled with area rugs. At one point, Bobby hugged her hard, and she fell onto a pile of rugs and the two of them rolled around, play-wrestling, for a few seconds. Eventually, a security guard came over and asked if everything was okay, and after telling him we were fine, we decided to leave. It was an uneventful trip.

Well, except for one thing. I saw Nate from school there. I don't think he saw us, though. He was looking down at his phone when we walked by. But still, it's always a bit shocking to see someone from school in public, and I almost didn't recognize him. There's this psychological thing where you can go to the same store every week for a year and have the same cashier every single time.

You could even be friendly with the cashier and have whole conversations about their dog, but the minute you run into them at Costco or at the movie theater, you don't recognize them because they're out of context. If Nate had seen me, he probably wouldn't have recognized me, even though I just sat with Cheryl at lunch. It's just as well. I don't know if Cheryl is into him or not. Treading the social waters of tenth grade is tricky enough without a misunderstanding about boys.

REAL 4

If it's not one thing, it's your mother. I think some famous actor said that, but maybe it was a psychologist.

She's horrible. No, she's worse than horrible. She's evil. I don't mean evil like a serial killer or evil like the devil. She's a different kind of evil. There's no way to describe it, and there's no way to understand it unless you live with her.

I had an algebra test today, and I've been stressing out about it all week. After her freak-out at Ikea the other day, she's been strange. Crying a lot. More withdrawn than usual. Hell, not even getting mad at me if the kids are too loud or if I leave dirty dishes on the counter. It's like she's depressed or something—I don't know. I've been trying to perk her back up because Bobby's getting scared. I have this algebra test to study for, and I've been trying to make sure everyone has their lunches and homework and dinner and all that jazz. Like, I've just really been busy trying to make things better for her on top of studying.

Anyway, algebra is second period and I've been almost sick to my stomach over this test because I don't know what I'm doing wrong. I do fine on my homework. I take careful notes. I study as much as I can at home, even though I don't have nearly enough time to study the way I need to. But when I take the tests, everything I knew vanishes. It's like a spell comes over me and I make tons of stupid mistakes.

Halfway through first period, Ms. Thomas is talking about Shakespearean insults and I'm trying to enjoy what should be a fun lesson, but I'm stressing about the test the next period, and my phone vibrates. Luckily, I remembered to turn off the sound, or I would have gotten in trouble. I peeked at my phone and saw a text from her.

Strange. She never texts me, especially so early in the morning. I don't think she even gets out of bed before ten most days. My heart dropped down to my stomach and I opened the message.

Zoe, I thought you should know your cat died. You can bury it when you get home if you want. It's in a Wal-Mart bag in the freezer.

What the hell kind of mother texts her daughter her cat died in the middle of school and doesn't even say what happened? There was nothing wrong with Sam when I left. She slept with me all night. I fed her breakfast. It didn't make any sense. Cats don't up and die for no good reason.

I texted Mama back asking what happened, but she didn't reply. I asked if I could come home, but she didn't respond to that, either. All I could do was sit there, thinking about my poor Sammycat and trying not to cry in English while stressing out about a damned stupid algebra test. I'm about to cry again, just thinking about it.

Needless to say, I probably failed the algebra test. I also failed at keeping my tears inside my eyes. I didn't sob or anything, but I couldn't stop the tears from spilling. Nobody asked if I was okay, and honestly, I don't know if anyone even noticed me.

I texted Mama a couple more times. At lunch, I called the house at least twenty times. She never answered.

What could she be doing that she wasn't answering? I didn't think she cared much about Sammycat, but maybe finding her upset her so much, she climbed back into bed and cried herself to sleep. It's the only explanation I could come up with, because what else could it be? I couldn't stop thinking about Sammycat. Every time I closed my eyes, I saw her small, orange body, frozen stiff, in a garbage bag in the freezer. I don't even know how I made it through the day without screaming.

Leesh noticed right away something was wrong with me after school. I tried to stay strong, but I cried when I showed her the text. Sam was more my cat than anyone's, but Leesh blinked back tears, hugged me hard, and told me she was so sorry. I had to let go of her or I'd burst like an old pipe in winter. She took charge of Bobby on the way home so I wouldn't have to deal with his questions.

Walking up the four steps to our front door felt like walking to the moon. Sam almost always greeted me at the front door when I got home. I think she was always genuinely happy to see me after being stuck at home with Mama all day. I couldn't imagine my sweet girl never greeting me again.

I turned the key and opened the door. Sam came running full speed down the hallway and wound herself around my legs, like always. What the hell? I swooped her up and ugly-cried into her fur. Leesh gave me a quick hug and sad smile before she sent Bobby off to wash his hands for a snack.

Then I heard the laughter. The crazy, evil, maniacal laughter. I wiped tears and fur off my face and looked at Gynger. How could she? What kind of mother would do something so cruel to their own kid? I swear to God, I'm never calling her my mother in this journal again. She just sat on the couch, pointing, and laughing at me. Tears streamed down her face, and she wiped them with the back of her hand. After a couple of heartbeats, it hit me. She'd been home all day, ignoring my calls.

"Girl," she said. "You should have seen the look on your face. Holy shit, that was priceless!" The whiskey and ice sloshed in her glass.

"Huh?"

Her voice sounded far away, like she was talking from the other end of a tunnel. Her words bled together, and I couldn't understand anything she said for a moment.

"Oh, my God, that was so funny. I nearly died from excitement waiting for you to get home, but the look on your face made the waiting worth it."

Everything snapped back into focus, and I looked at her. I didn't know what to do or say. I didn't even reply to her. I just walked to my room hugging Sam all the way.

Like I said, if it's not one thing, it's your goddamn mother.

———

SAFE 4

Dear Diary,

It's been a while, hasn't it? I guess I've been in some kind of giant funk lately. I don't know what to write about since my days are all pretty much the same. School, home, homework, chores, dinner, more homework, and bed. My life is dull, dull, dull, and I have a hard time convincing myself it's worth writing about. Maybe hormones are making me feel so...I don't know. Flat. I'm sure I'll pull myself out of this rut soon enough.

Exercising would help. Maybe if I get up an hour early and

go for a run or do some stretches, I'll start to feel more like myself. The thing is, it's hard to find the motivation to get up and do anything extra when I'm already so drained as it is. Mostly, I'm writing this entry as a placeholder. A promise to myself that I'll get back to writing again. Today, though, I've run out of things to say.

REAL 5

Jesus, this having two diaries thing is stressful, but I'm so glad I'm keeping up the other one—or trying to, anyway. After Gynger's pathetic attempt at a joke, I was so angry, I couldn't even come up with anything fake-happy to write about, for the sake of keeping up appearances, but I have to get back to it. And I've got to be more careful not to mention Nate. She's been checking for updates and keeps finding ways I'm sure she thinks are sly to ask about him. It's annoying and it reminds me how careless and stupid I've been. Not only by mentioning him to begin with, but by not keeping up with the entries in my Dear Diary.

Since her stupid stunt with Sam, I've been thinking a lot about Gynger and what her perception of reality is. When she read the *Happy Family* version of our day at Ikea, did she believe it? Did she forget what really went down and thinks I wrote the actual truth? Or, maybe on some deep level, she knows how it really went and feels embarrassed and ashamed, so she's choosing to believe fiction is fact.

Or, shit, I just thought of this… What if she knows what really happened but she's hoping I don't. Maybe she thinks if she doesn't contradict what I wrote, then that'll change what happened. Or at the very least, my memory of it. I swear, living in this family is like living on Mars and having to pretend I'm a Martian. I can't even tell which way is up anymore.

What I do know is if I don't make more regular entries in *The Other Diary*, she's sure to get suspicious. Of what, I'm not entirely sure. I'm operating from a place of pure instinct, but I wouldn't put it past her to ransack my room, looking for evidence of some crime I can't even begin to imagine. Whether or not I want to, I'll keep plugging away at the other one, just to stay on the safe side. If she decides to snoop through my notebooks for school, this journal will be toast. Hell, I'll be toast. I definitely need to find a real hiding spot for this journal. A hiding spot she'll never find.

If she ever reads what I really think about her, she might literally kill me. I don't mean "literally" in the stupid figurative sense, like "I literally coughed up a lung." No. I think she might literally beat me to death or stab me in a fit of rage. A woman who jokes about her daughter's cat dying the way she did is capable of anything. There is something seriously wrong with her. She's not a little eccentric. She doesn't have a wild temper. She's scary and dangerous.

How messed up is it that I even have to think about this kind of thing? I'm fifteen years old, I shouldn't be afraid my mother could actually murder me. It shouldn't be like this. I should be allowed to write whatever I want and have my privacy respected. I shouldn't feel afraid for my safety all the time. Sometimes, I feel like I live in a prison. No, that's not quite right. More like I'm being held hostage, and if I slip up, I'll get hurt. I'm not even entitled to my own thoughts.

Whoa. This entry got dark quick, and I should probably rip this page out. Some thoughts should never be allowed out of my head.

REAL 6

I can't believe how different everything is now. Not a month ago, I was sneaking around behind Nate, memorizing his schedule, and following him to class. I spent a ridiculous amount of passing period time trying to devise a way to bump into him just so I could have the chance to maybe mumble a quick "sorry" to him. Looking back, I can't believe I didn't get in trouble for low-key stalking the guy. I'm not sure if I should be embarrassed for myself or relieved he never filed a restraining order on me. Now, everything's flipped upside down.

Since Ikea, I've gone out of my way to avoid him. I don't know how much he saw, and I don't want to know, but I think it must have been a lot. If it wasn't, why does *he* keep trying to run into *me*? I should charge him a quarter so he can gawk at the freak show that is my life. When I was into him, he didn't seem to know I even existed. Now, he's always right there. If I happen to look at him, he opens his mouth like he wants to say something and waves at me before I run in the ass-opposite direction. It doesn't even matter if I run the opposite direction of where I'm going, I just want him to leave me alone.

Wanna know how I know there's no God? Because Nate was at Ikea. I know how cringy I sound, but it's true. They say God always has a plan, and there's a reason for everything and we lowly humans can't understand those reasons—which doesn't even make sense since humans were supposedly created in God's image or whatever. They say when a kid is born in a country that's suffering from war or famine, it's not God's fault. Mankind caused the suffering in the first place. When a baby's born into a family who tortures and abuses it, again, not God's fault.

Some poor babies go through more suffering in their short lives than many truly rotten old people experience in theirs. But don't blame God. Blame society. Blame the parents. Besides, maybe that child had to go through all that terrible stuff so they could grow up and be a social justice advocate or find a way to stamp out child abuse. Maybe the kid whose little brother died of cancer will be the one who finally cures it. *God's ways are mysterious.* What a load of crap. It's nothing but a way to explain why bad things happen to good people.

There was nothing mysterious about Nate being at Ikea. Maybe it's ironic, and it's definitely unfortunate as hell, but it's not part of some divine plan. If I believed there were a God, I'd ask her one question. How am I supposed to walk around acting normal when Nate knows my biggest secret—my mother is batshit and my family is a mess?

I just re-read this entry and the one before it, and now I'm panicking. I said some awful stuff about Gynger. Thinking those kinds of things is bad enough, but to write them down? How stupid can I get? I need to stop this. I need to tear out these pages and burn them, but I can't. I'm alone. There's nobody for me to talk to about how bad things are. The only thing I have is this stupid composition book. Well, that and my Sammycat. She's purring next to me on the bed right now, and having her near makes me feel better, but I'm afraid I'll go as crazy as Gynger if I don't get my thoughts out of my head. This journal stays—for my own sanity, it has to. I just have to be beyond careful and not ever let anyone find it

———

SAFE 5

Dear Diary,

A placeholder isn't a placeholder if you never pick back up where you left off. Instead, it's nothing but a sad reminder that you couldn't commit to doing what you said you would. A reminder that you can't stick with things and have no follow through. So, even though I'm not sure what I want to say, I know I have to say something before I end up ashamed of myself for letting this journal get dusty.

"You know," Cheryl said, setting her Diet Coke and bag of Takis next to my free-lunch tray of mystery slop. "You keep sitting alone, and I'm starting to think I smell bad or something." She lifted her left arm and sniffed a couple of times. "You're the first new kid I've ever met who avoids making friends. You're a challenge, and I like challenges."

"Hi, Cheryl." I pronounced her name carefully, with two syllables, the way you're supposed to. People around here always smush their words together, so Cheryl comes out more like "Shurl."

"Scooch over. My ass needs more room." She nudged her way between me and the geek next to me. The boy slid over without looking up from his phone, as if he were immune to her charms.

"You don't stink." I poked at the mass on my tray. "And

I'm not even that new anymore. I've been at this school for three months."

"Girl, you'll always be *The New Kid* to these troglodytes." She laughed her high, chittery laugh and the other kids at the table looked up to see what was so funny. But she didn't seem to notice all the eyes on her. I don't know if Cheryl's that confident or if she's really good at pretending. Either way, it's one thing about her I admire. I wish I could pretend to be even one one-hundredth as confident as she is.

"Well, if you're not avoiding me because I stink, why don't you ever try to find me at lunch or between classes? I feel like I'm always chasing you down and you're always running the other way, and I can't even begin to wrap my head around that. I'm awesome."

The thing about Cheryl is she doesn't mince words. More like she takes the biggest machete she can find and chops away like a maniac. As usual, I couldn't think of anything good to say, so I shrugged like an idiot instead. Another thing about Cheryl is she doesn't dwell on things. She could have kept on about how I never seek her out, but instead she crammed spicy chips into her mouth like she hadn't eaten in three days. She obviously didn't have a weird hang up about eating whatever she wants in front of people. I like that about her, too. Turns out, there's an awful lot to like about her.

I guess there's a lot more to like about her than not, and I honestly don't know why I try so hard to push her away. Why the hell don't I want to be her friend? Sure, partly it's because we move practically every year, so what's the point. But mostly, I think I'm not the kind of person who makes friends. Leesh always makes friends easily, but I never figured out how I should act around people. I'm the most socially awkward person I've ever met.

"Here." Cheryl slid a folded slip of paper over to me.

"What's this?" I unfolded it and tried to make sense of what I saw.

"What's it look like? My number. I totally don't expect you to since you barely even acknowledge my existence, but if you ever wanna talk or hang out, hit me up."

Ouch.

I slid the paper back to Cheryl without opening it. "I'm not allowed to use my phone except for emergencies. My mom says if I want to chat with friends outside of school, I need to get a job and buy my own phone. I'm so grateful to have a mama who tries to teach me responsibility."

She gave me some serious side-eye and raised her eyebrows at me. "I feel like you're avoiding me."

"I'm not avoiding you, Cheryl. I just…I guess I don't know how to people. We've never lived in one place long enough for me to make friends, and I learned a long time ago that moving hurts a whole lot less when I don't have to leave behind people I care about."

"Still sounds like some avoidant bullshit to me. Haven't you ever heard of the Internet? It's easy to stay friends with people you never see. Hell, some of my best friends are people I've never even met, but you do you. All I'm saying is I'm here and I'm available." She took her number back and put it in the empty chips bag. "Who knows? Maybe you'll stay this time. Or, if you do move again, you can at least have fun while you're here."

When I looked up from my plate of gloop, I expected her to look at least a little annoyed, but she didn't. She smiled at me and changed the conversation to how Jason Bortles got busted trying to steal a copy of an English test and now his parents are threatening to sue the school for kicking him off the football team. It was as if we've never been anything but BFFs since kindergarten.

Like I said, Cheryl's not one to hold a grudge.

REAL 7

Okay, so I was talking about Cheryl in my other journal, but I had to stop myself so I wouldn't spill things I don't want Gynger to know. Like the fact I kept Cheryl's number.

She's seriously wearing me down. I don't know why I keep trying to push her away, but I think at least part of it is I'm ashamed of my family and our practically condemned house. Sure, Cheryl acts like she wants to be my friend now, but the minute she saw how we live—saw the cockroaches climbing up the walls in broad daylight, felt the rotting floor literally sag under her feet, she'd head for the hills before I ever noticed she was running.

Even if she never came over and always met me at the mall or the park or something, eventually she'd meet Gynger, which would be a disaster of epic proportions. One way or another, eventually Cheryl will figure out I'm really trash, and she won't want anything to do with me anymore. Or worse, we'll end up moving as soon as I start to get close. Why bother?

Cheryl is the most stubborn person I've ever met. She's told me before she's more stubborn than a mule, and I didn't believe her. I sure as hell do now, though. Every day, whether I look at her or not, she sits with me at lunch. When I tried to blow her off by asking if her friends won't get jealous, she just waved her hand and said she doesn't see the point in having one group of friends. I think she knew I'd never have joined her if she invited me to sit with her group, so instead, she came to me.

Even on the days I kept my nose buried in a book and pretended I couldn't hear her, she chattered away like we've been BFFs since preschool. Do you know how hard it is to keep pushing someone away who keeps coming at you, cheerful and friendly as a preacher's daughter on Sunday morning? I don't know why she's glommed on to me like this. She's so pretty, so smart, and has incredible taste in clothes. Absolutely everyone adores her, but at the same time, she's not one of those snobby popular girls.

Today, as soon as she sat down across from me, she kicked me gently under the table.

"So, what's going on with you and Nate?" she asked as I looked up from the chicken potpie spreading across my plate.

"I don't know what you're talking about."

"You're a shitty liar, Zoe. There is most definitely something going on. It couldn't be more obvious if you two made out during the Pledge."

"I swear, nothing's going on between me and Nate. Like, at all." I looked into her hazel eyes and tried to project confidence. "I seriously have no clue what you're talking about."

"Are you for real right now? You're trying to tell me you haven't noticed he's following you around like a puppy? Dude. You've been practically stalking him since you moved here, and now that he's trying to get your attention, you expect me to believe you didn't notice? Forgive me if I think you're lying out your ass."

I wanted to tell her everything right then. Not just about Gynger's painfully public freak-out, but about everything.

How there's never enough food at home. How I'm afraid my mother will straight up kill me someday. About her evil joke about Sam, and the way she hits us, and tornadoes through my room, leaving it a disaster zone. All of it. Cheryl clearly wanted to be my friend, and for a moment, letting her seemed like heaven. Everyone deserves at least one friend, right? Even me. But I'm a damned coward.

"I have noticed he seems to be everywhere I am lately, and I've seen him looking at me, but do you think I'm insane?" I tried to keep my voice light, but the words felt like pills stuck in my throat.

"What do you mean?" Cheryl shoved a handful of Takis into her mouth and followed it with a dainty sip of her Diet Coke.

"Earth to Cheryl. He's the hottest guy in school. Why would he want anything to do with me? Not a single girl in this place would turn him down."

"One, he's cute but he's definitely not the hottest. And B, did you just admit something is going on with you two?"

Aren't whispers supposed to be quiet? "Shh! Absolutely not. I saw him at Ikea a while ago, but we didn't even talk. I was with my mom and the kids, and Bobby threw a fit. Nate saw the whole thing and started following me around the next Monday. Probably to tease me or something." I scooped up some potpie and watched it drip back down to the plate.

"How can you be so stupid, Zoe?"

An icicle stabbed my heart at the insult. "Don't call me stupid."

"Then don't be stupid, dummy. He doesn't want to tease you any more than I do. Why do you assume everyone who's nice to you is out to get you? Has it ever occurred to you people might actually like you?"

"Whatever. It's not like I have chronically low self-esteem. I just know my place in the pecking order." I covered my uneaten lunch with a napkin and pushed the plate away from me. Looking at it made me want to puke. "Nate's out of my league. You are too, only you don't seem to care. I seriously don't get it."

Cheryl sighed ridiculously loudly and shook her head. "You don't give yourself enough credit, girl. You're awesome, smart, and sweet." She punctuated each word by raising a finger like she was counting. "And you're a hell of a lot more interesting than most of the kids around here.

"Thanks, but I have a hard time believing that."

"Well, the great thing about truth is it doesn't care whether or not you believe it."

I wanted to tell her how confused I am that Nate's always there. It flatters and terrifies me how hard he's trying to get my attention. If I wasn't such a wuss and could open up to her, I'm sure she'd be able to help me figure out what to do, but it seems I'm completely incapable of saying any of the things in my head.

The way Leesh makes friends so easily depresses me. Why isn't she afraid to open up? Now that I think about it, though, she talks about friends from school, but they never come over, and she never goes out with them. None of them has ever met Gynger, so she must be as embarrassed as I am. Maybe it's possible to keep my school life and my home life separate, like Leesh does. Maybe Cheryl would never ask about my family or want to come over. Maybe I'm making a big stinking deal over nothing. And if she did want to come over, I could find a way to blow her off. Maybe tell her we're remodeling the living room and the house is a mess or something.

"Okay." I decided to trust her just a little. "I have no inten-tion of acting on anything but..." I lowered my voice as if the kids around me give a shit what I say. "When I first noticed him following me, I couldn't believe it. In my wildest fantasies, maybe we go out for burgers or something one night. But that's never gonna happen. It's best to ignore him."

"Why?" She dabbed the corners of her mouth with a napkin.

"He must think my family is a freak show after the way my brother acted, and I have zero interest in trying to convince him I'm not like them." It was as close to the truth as I could let myself come.

"Um, you do know everyone's little brother acts like a jerk in public, right? Trust me. My parents have been fostering kids practically my whole life. At this point, I probably know more about kids throwing tantrums than most child psychologists. Why would Nate judge you for your brother's fit, anyway?"

The bell rang and our conversation drowned in a sea of last-minute shouts.

Saved by the bell.

SAFE 6

Dear Diary,

Daddy's home! He got in at about two o'clock this morning, and he's still asleep and I don't blame him one little bit. If I had to drive all night just to get back home, I'd be exhausted, too. I wish he'd wake up already, though. I know it's only been a couple of weeks, but it feels so much longer. I wish he could stop driving his giant, loud semi all over the country and get a job that lets him come home at night.

I know how selfish I sound, but I liked it better when he worked construction. Sure, he came home exhausted, and we couldn't afford such a nice house back then, but at least I got to see him every day. I'd rather be rich in love and poor in money than to have more money but not get to see Daddy as much.

No matter how much I wish, I don't think he'll ever give up trucking. He says the money he makes is too good to give up, and he even says maybe he can convince the landlord to sell us this house after he saves a little money.

Awesome as it would be to get to live in this pretend-haunted old house forever, I'd rather live in a tent if it meant Daddy got to come home at night. I should quit whining and count myself lucky to have a dad who actually works for his family. We might not have a lot of extras or expensive things, but at least we have a nice roof over our heads, and we have everything we need. I really, really miss him, because he's gone more than he's here. But it's not my decision to make is it, Diary? It's an adult decision and all I can do is soak up every minute with him when he is home.

You know the phrase, *ants in your pants*? Well, I guess Bobby woke up with crickets in his pants. He was practically climbing the walls within ten minutes of getting out of bed. For our own safety, we're not allowed to go outside if Mama or Daddy isn't up, so I couldn't even send him out to run laps around the yard like I usually do when he has extra energy built up. When he gets like this, he won't even sit still to watch cartoons. I don't know where the idea came from, but as soon as it hit me, I knew it would work.

"Hey, Bobby. Want to help me build a pillow fort? I bet if we use all the couch cushions, we can make it big enough for all three of us."

"Heck, yeah," he shouted.

"Shh! Not so loud." I took the first cushion off the couch. "Mama's still asleep. Hand me another pillow. Listen, Bubs," He always listens better when I use his nickname for some reason. "Daddy came home late, late last night."

He beamed at me and took a deep breath that I knew meant

he was about to whoop for joy. I lowered my voice to an exaggerated whisper and tiptoed over to the couch to grab another cushion.

"We have to be super extra quiet, though. He drove a long time to get home to us, and he needs to rest so he has the energy to play. You want him to play with you, don't you?"

He nodded, pulled up the middle cushion, and brought it over to me.

"I'm sure he'll wake up in a bit, but until he's up and has coffee, you have to use your quietest voice, okay?"

"Okay, Zoe," he whispered back.

I put the final pillow wall in place and draped a big sheet over the fort. "Voila. Your fortress awaits."

It wasn't impressive, but the way Bobby's eyes lit up, he seemed to think it was a magical castle instead of a sagging couch cushion tent.

"It really is big enough for all three of us," he exclaimed. "It's like a mansion fort! Leesh, you gotta come in here. You too, Zoe! It's awesome!" Even though I literally told him to be quiet two seconds ago, he was already on the verge of shouting down the roof.

"Bobby," Leesh snapped. "What did Zoe tell you? Be quiet or I'll pull your fort down." She looked at me and raised her eyebrows. "I'll do it, won't I, Zoe?"

"Yep. And that would suck big time because if you pull it down, I'm not gonna put it back up, and then Bobby will just have to watch cartoons in a boring old living room instead of a cool fort."

"Sorry," he whispered.

"Okay, then." I handed him the remote. "Here's your magic wand. Don't turn up the TV any louder than it is right now, but you can pick whatever you want to watch."

He took the remote from me and hurried into his fort. And, since he begged us, Leesh and I came in, too. Right now, she's drawing something in her sketchbook. I wonder if Leesh uses her sketchbook like I use this diary. Does she draw out her feelings? I should ask her sometime.

Daddy started coughing a few minutes ago. He always coughs himself awake, so I know he's about to get out of bed. It's time to put you away now, *Dear Diary*, and see if I can't find something to make for breakfast. I think we have a few eggs and some milk left. Maybe I can make a big pancake breakfast to celebrate Daddy coming home. Squee! I can't wait to give him a great big hug!

As Tigger always says, TTFN! Ta-Ta for now!

REAL 8

Stupid! Stupid, stupid, stupid, STUPID!

What the hell is wrong with me? I know how jealous she gets when Daddy gets attention and she doesn't. I should have never talked about him like I care about him in my other diary. I should have damn well known she'd flip if she read it.

Here's what happened. I'm not putting all this down for any other reason than to remind myself never to be so careless again. Plus, if I write it all down exactly the way it happened, maybe it'll help me feel less crazy later, when I try to tell myself I made things out to be worse than they were—which I always do. I need to be able to come back to this and remember I didn't make it all up or blow it out of proportion.

We had barely enough eggs to make a double batch of pancakes. Daddy spent another few minutes hacking up a lung, which I knew Gynger couldn't sleep through, so I gathered everything I'd need for our breakfast. We only had enough ingredients to make a single batch instead of a triple batch like we needed, but if I skipped breakfast, and Leesh only ate one pancake, we might make do. In the fridge, I found a couple of mushy apples, so I decided to make some sort of cinnamon apple topping type thing to help make breakfast more filling. Plus, we don't have syrup. I asked Leesh to try and keep Bobby quiet and got to work.

Even though I figured Gynger was already awake, it's always best to keep quiet and out of the way until she's had at least two cups of coffee and something to eat. Daddy wandered in as I was about to flip the first batch of pancakes. He had on his favorite pair of old jeans—the one with the ancient oil stain down the left side—and his big, bare belly hung down low over his belt. Daddy isn't fat, but when he's not wearing a shirt, you can tell he's not skinny. His black hair, which he usually keeps in a low ponytail, was down and oily, like he hadn't washed it for a few days.

"Morning, ZuZu. What'cha up to?" Daddy is the only one who calls me that. I asked him once where it came from, but he just tapped the side of his head and winked, like that would mean anything to me.

"Wow, you made coffee, too?" He poured a mug for him and another for Gynger.

I took the three pancakes off the griddle and poured three more in their place. Daddy came up behind me and put his hand on my shoulder.

"Those look mighty fine, ZuZu. Thank you for taking such good care of your mama and the kids."

It feels good when he notices and appreciates the things I do—like cook breakfast for the family—unlike certain other parental units, who shall remain nameless. Of course, the pancakes looked mighty fine, though. I had to learn how to cook simple things for Gynger and Leesh when I was like six. Daddy would cook dinner when he came home at night, but if we wanted to eat during the day while he was working, I had to do it. Even when I think about it until smoke comes out of my ears, I can't remember Gynger ever cooking more than a microwaveable bag of popcorn.

I turned around and hugged him, glad he was home, even if it would only be for a couple of days. My workload doesn't get lighter when he's here, but somehow everything seems a little easier. I guess it's because he keeps Gynger distracted. And when she's distracted with him, she's not focused on finding every little thing wrong with me. For no reason at all, tears burned my eyes, so I squeezed them tight and hugged him a little harder.

"Hey, little girlie, what's this all about?" His gentle voice wrapped me in a cloud of his coffee and old cigarette breath. It was equal parts comforting and gross. He put his hand on top of my head and sort of smoothed out my hair.

I wanted to tell him how much I missed him and how I wished he'd never go away again. I wanted to tell him Gynger's getting worse. Her temper is more unpredictable. She's meaner than ever and disappears into herself more often. I wanted to spill it about Ikea and how she told me Sammycat died, and she put her in the freezer, but I was too afraid. If I tried to say anything, I knew the only thing that would come out would be stupid sobs. God, I'm such a baby.

The pancakes smelled almost burned. As I pulled myself away from Daddy's safe hug to flip them, *she* came in.

"What the fuck is going on in here? First you write that filth about your father, and now you're hanging all over him like some cheap whore?" Her acid words burned little holes in my heart.

Before Daddy could let me go or I could pull completely away, she was on me. It was like she teleported. One moment, I heard her behind me on the far side of the kitchen. The next moment, she's literally on my back, screeching like a stray cat, pulling my hair with one hand, and hitting me with the other.

I don't know if I screamed or if I was stunned silent. What filth was she talking about? It all happened too fast. Everything jumbled together and even as I write this, I'm starting to doubt it even happened at all. If it weren't for the lump on my fore-head and the raw, burning spot where she yanked out a handful of hair, I might believe it was a super vivid nightmare.

What I do know is she screamed the worst things any mother could say to her daughter. She shouted at me, called me a *disgusting, fucking slut.* I remember losing my balance and somehow hitting my forehead on something. Was it the counter? The floor? I don't know. I remember the smell of burning pancakes. Daddy's Welcome Home breakfast—the only food we had in the whole house—was ruined.

Somehow, I ended up on my stomach, and she climbed on top of me, still pulling my hair, still hitting me. Still accusing me of sleeping with my own father. Pancake smoke filled the air and I realized I was crying. She pulled my head back and I caught sight of Daddy. His eyes were sad as he set his coffee on the counter. He didn't rush. He didn't shout. He casually sauntered over and squatted down beside us like he saw his wife attack his daughter every day. Like he was squatting to look at an interesting bug or pick up a lost quarter.

"Morning, Darlin'," he said softly to her. She loosened her grip on my hair and whimpered a little. "Hey, Ginnie. I'm so glad you're up, babe. I was about to bring you coffee in bed, but it's a nice day to sit out on the porch. What do you say?"

Now that she had stopped hitting me, the world looked all tilty, like in a fun house. Something woosh-wooshed in my ears, and I thought I might throw up. I tried to hear what he said to her, but I couldn't make anything out. All of a sudden, I could breathe again. I don't know if she got off me herself or if he pulled her off, but it didn't matter. All I cared about was not getting hurt anymore.

I stayed right on the floor until I knew for sure they weren't in the kitchen. When I thought it was safe, I rolled over and looked up at the cracks in the ceiling. A cockroach scuttled down the wall and I closed my eyes and considered falling asleep on the spot until the smell of burnt food pulled me back from the edge of darkness. I pulled myself up, leaned against the counter, and pulled the griddle's power cord from the outlet.

Bobby stood in the kitchen entryway. He must have been crying because a clean line streaked down each dirty cheek and big green eyes were big as silver dollar pancakes.

"Zoe, when's pancakes?"

Leesh came up next to him and took his hand. "Not right now, Bobby. We're gonna let Zoe rest, and maybe we can finish the pancakes for her. We can bring them to her room, okay?"

I didn't wait to hear how Bobby responded. I just pushed past them and came straight to my room to write this all down. I'm taking a risk by doing this now instead of waiting until Gynger and Daddy leave, but I don't want to forget even one detail of what happened. Besides, when she does this kind of thing to me, she usually can't stand the sight of me for at least a couple of hours. I'm safer now than I will be later.

Thank God, Daddy was here to help me. She really might have killed me this time. I have to be careful not to say nice things about him. If she honestly believes all the disgusting things she accused me of, I have to be more careful than I've ever been before. What would the kids do if she hurt me so badly, I had to go to the hospital? Or if she killed me?

Why is she like this? Who did I piss off in a past life to deserve this? I must have been a horrible person for this to be my punishment. Forget about past lives. I must be a horrible person now. Or I will be in the future. Somewhere, in a time-line I don't remember or haven't lived yet, I must have been a grade-a asshole. What other explanation is there? My own mother doesn't love me. Clearly, she sees the same rot in me the universe sees but I can't see for myself. My head hurts so much. I need a nap.

REAL 9

The house is quieter than Christmas Eve in a movie. A plate of blob-shaped pancakes, cold and rubbery, is on my desk. Leesh obviously cooked the rest of the batter and brought them to me while I was asleep. I don't know how long I've been out. Maybe an hour, maybe five. When I first woke up in my bed, I tried to convince myself none of it happened. A nightmare, that's all. Sammycat's warm body pressed deep into my belly, and she stretched and jumped to the floor as I wiggled around a little, looking for the pain I knew I'd find.

When I sat up, my head pounded in the usual way it does when she hits it. It kind of throbs, but that's not the right word. It's like my whole heart is in my head and every single heart-beat is like someone inside is hammering to get out. My hammering head proves the attack in the kitchen wasn't a dream, but maybe it hadn't really happened the way I think it did.

Slowly, quietly, I got out of bed and crept to the door. I opened it a crack and listened for a long time. I couldn't hear the TV or anyone talking, so I thought it might be safe to go to the bathroom. Or I hoped so, anyway. Maybe I need to keep a bucket in my room for emergencies—for when it's not safe to leave my room, but I'll have an accident if I don't. I know how gross I sound, but better gross than dead.

My throat felt scratchy, and I realized I was so thirsty I could drink an entire gallon of water. When I finished in the bathroom, I made my way toward the kitchen, still trying to separate out reality from nightmare. The remains of Bobby's fort was scattered all over the living room.

The kitchen looked even worse than the living room. Gummy bits of leftover batter covered the counter and the rim of the pancake bowl. Stacked plates teetered dangerously close to the edge of the counter, and for some reason, the fridge door stood wide open. Nothing had been put away or cleaned up. I slammed the refrigerator door and considered doing the dishes, but I didn't have it in me to keep myself upright. Anyway, the last thing in the universe I wanted was to be out of my room when they got back from whatever family outing they went on with Daddy.

I grabbed a cleanish looking used cup from the counter, filled it at the sink, and gulped down the water in one long drink before refilling it to bring to my room for later. With luck, she'll think I slept the whole time. Her words keep coming back to me, and they hurt almost as much as the beating. A little bit ago, I reread the entry in my Safe diary, looking for whatever triggered her rage.

All I can figure is she must have gotten up at the same time as Daddy, and while we were in the kitchen, she had been reading my diary, which I stupidly threw on my bed instead of hiding like usual. Was she just being nosy, or looking for proof that her sick thoughts were justified? I don't know how she could have interpreted anything so gross from what I wrote, but she sure as hell found a way.

Maybe it's time to stop writing all together. It's too danger-ous. If she wants to find something to hate me for, she'll find it. And she'll kill me if she reads what I write in this one. I'm stupid and selfish. I cannot keep writing.

I know this shit isn't normal and I could probably report her. I I'm too afraid to report her myself, so maybe I could tell someone. But who? Mrs. Thomas seems to like me. She's always so encouraging in English. She's the one who first put it in my head that maybe I could be a writer someday. If I stayed after school one day and told her about Gynger or even showed her my two diaries, maybe she could help get us out of here. She could report her for me.

No. It's too risky. Daddy's always warning us how family stuff needs to stay in the family, and if we tell anyone, we'll end up separated and never see each other again. How could I protect the kids then? I wouldn't be able to make sure they have food and clean clothes. What if I ended up in a good home but Bobby ended up with someone like Gynger? Or what if Leesh ended up in a home where she gets raped?

I absolutely, one-hundred percent can never tell anybody what happens here. The only way I can even attempt to keep everyone safe is by keeping my fool mouth shut and doing my best not to piss Her Highness off. I'm trapped. Like it or not, this is my life until I grow up and move away. I only have to hang on until graduation.

As soon as I do, I'll get a job somewhere, I don't even care where, and get a small apartment. Leesh and I can share one of the rooms and Bobby can have the other. I *will* get them out of here and give them the chance at a normal life that I never had. This won't be my life forever, it's my life for now. I can get through anything if I remember an end is in sight.

REAL 10

She flat-out told me she read my safe journal when she attacked me in the kitchen. I don't know if she remembers or not since she usually blacks out when she goes off her rocker like that. Not knowing is what's so hard. I know I said I wouldn't write in either journal anymore, but I don't think I can hold myself to that. If I can't talk to anyone about what's happening, I need a way to process all this shit on my own. I have to find a way to get it out of my head. When I write things down, I can make some sense of them. I'm afraid if I stop writing in both diaries, I might lose my grip on reality, and then how will I be able to keep myself from becoming exactly like her?

I'm stuck. It's too dangerous to write, but too dangerous not to. I might consider giving up the safe journal, but I'm too afraid of losing myself to stop this one.

REAL 11

When I was in kindergarten or first grade, I drew a stupid little picture for Daddy. I don't remember why, but maybe for his birthday or Father's Day. Anyway, I made a crappy stick figure little girl holding hands with a stick figure man and wrote "To Daddy" on the front and gave it to him. I remember how proud I was when I handed it to him as he sipped on his coffee. I still remember the way he smiled and scooped me into his arms made me the happiest kid in the world.

Then *she* came into the living room. She picked up my drawing as Daddy set me down, and I'll never forget her face when she looked at the picture. Her lips squeezed together, her nostrils flared wide, and her eyes flashed like black lightning. She looked at me like I was two-day-old roadkill in July.

"To Daddy," she read in a childish voice. "Forget about Mommy. Nobody cares about Mommy, even though I'm the one trapped here while your precious daddy is off doing God knows what all day.

"Calm down, there, Ginnie," Daddy said. "She didn't mean to upset you. It's nothing but a child's picture. Hell, I bet she draws you pictures all the time." He looked at me and winked.

"Don't you, ZuZu? You draw your Mama lots of pictures when I'm not here, right?"

The thing is, I didn't. I only drew her a few pictures before I stopped because she never seemed to care about them. If she looked at a drawing at all, she'd give it a quick glance, then leave it on the couch or table until something eventually spilled on it and I had to throw it away.

I don't remember how I responded to Daddy, but from then on, any time I drew a picture for him, I always put "To Mama and Daddy" on it, which was a complete lie. Those pictures were always for him, but it was easier to add her name than to deal with her rage.

A couple years later, I drew him a picture for Father's Day. and I didn't put her name on it. Why the hell would I? She pulled the exact same shit then, too. She went on and on about how nobody appreciates her and the sacrifices she makes, about how he can be gone sunup to sundown, but when he comes home, she suddenly becomes invisible.

"He gets to go off all day every day, and I'm stuck here having to be Mama and Daddy, and does anyone appreciate me? No! I'm only the poor servant, here to clean up everyone's messes." She rushed over to Daddy, who sat on the couch, and lifted his feet onto the old trunk we used as a coffee table. "Here, Master," she said in what I assume was her best *genie in a bottle* voice. "Put your feet up. Relax! I'll take care of everything, Sire!"

I never made another card addressed just to him again, not even for his birthday.

I can't even pretend I'm surprised by her reaction when she came into the kitchen the other day. How stupid am I? I know better than to give him affection without giving her a dose, too. Now that I'm getting older, her jealousy has turned darker and more twisted. I think the best thing I can do is keep my distance from him when he's home.

REAL 12

Holy crap. I, Zoe Dawn Wilkes, had a real, honest to God conversation with Nate freaking Evans! It's like, just when I think my life can't possibly get any more complicated, BAM! Nate chats me up in the hallway.

Sometimes, I question if the things that happen to me really happened at all, so I want to write it all down here so when I question myself, I'll be able to reread this and know it was real.

I was sitting in English, wasting time since I finished the book last week, as usual. I hate finishing books early, but I hate putting a good book down even more. Everyone was supposed to be finishing the last three chapters, but I didn't have anything to do so I asked Mrs. Thomas for a bathroom pass. I didn't really have to go, but I wanted to stretch my legs.

As soon as I was alone in the hallway, my shoulders relaxed. There's something about being completely alone in a building boiling over with kids that feels so peaceful. I wandered through the hallways, lost in my own thoughts, as I made my way to the furthest possible bathroom. When I turned the corner, I nearly ran smack into Nate. What was he even doing out of class? I looked down at the floor and tried to pretend I didn't recognize him as I edged past him.

"Zoe, wait," he called.

I didn't want to wait. I wanted the floor to open and swallow me whole. Obviously, that didn't happen, so I stopped and looked at him instead. I wish I could tell you I had something cool or funny to say, but no such luck. Instead of showing him my sparkling personality or sharp wit, I stood there like I've never spoken a day in my life.

"Why are you avoiding me?" He reached his hand out to touch my shoulder but pulled it away when I flinched. What is wrong with me? Why the hell did I flinch?

"I'm not avoiding you. I have to take a leak." *Take a leak?* Jesus, I'm such an ass. I walked toward the bathroom again and hoped he couldn't see the red I felt in my cheeks.

His thousand-kilowatt smile was almost too much for me, but I forced myself to keep my head up as he fell in step beside me.

"I've been trying to talk to you for ages, but you run the other direction every time you see me. Why won't you talk to me?"

"What are you even talking about, Nate? You never wanted to talk to me before." We were almost to the bathroom. "What are you doing out here, anyway? Shouldn't you be in class?"

"Lucky timing, I guess." Oh, that smile! "Or maybe it's fate finally giving me the chance to talk to you since you won't give me the time of day."

I stood there like a fool, mainly because he was right, but I didn't want to acknowledge it.

"I saw you and your family at Ikea."

And there it was, the head-dive into the one thing I didn't want to talk about.

"Really? I didn't see you." *Liar, liar.*

We finally made it to the bathrooms. Before he could say anything, I pushed through the swinging door of the girls' room and sighed as it swung closed behind me. I made sure to take my sweet time, hoping he'd go back to class before I came out. I splashed water on my still-red face and tried like hell to avoid my reflection. I did *not* need to see how awful I looked before dealing with him if he waited around for me to finish. The scratchy, brown paper towels smelled like old, wet boxes. When I thought it had to be safe, I came out of the bathroom.

"I thought maybe you fell in or something." Nate's foot was up against the wall, and he smirked as he looked up from his phone.

"Well, since you obviously can't take a hint," I snapped, "why don't you tell me what you want so we can both get back to class before we get in trouble."

He dropped the goofy smile from his face, shoved his phone into the back pocket of his expensive jeans, and squinted at me like I was a dangerous snake. As soon as the words came out of my mouth, I regretted them. Gynger reacts out of anger, not me. If I don't want to end up like her, I need to be way more careful.

"I'm sorry, Nate. I didn't mean to be a jerk. Why did you wait for me?"

He shrugged off my apology and smiled again. I guess *The Nice Guy* act isn't an act after all.

"What choice did I have? You won't talk to me. Did you really not see me at Ikea?"

"I saw you, but I wish I hadn't." Heat burned my cheeks, but the honesty felt good.

"Why?" He sounded so sincere, I couldn't even find it in myself to be annoyed at how stupid the question was.

"You saw first-hand how my mother is. You could destroy me if you talked about it. My only hope is I'm too insignificant to bother with."

He slowed down and I matched my pace to his, even though I one hundred percent did not want to be having this conversation. "One, you're not insignificant. And two, what kind of creep would I have to be to talk shit about your mom?"

"Look, no offense to you personally, but why wouldn't you talk about my nightmare family? If I weren't related to them, I bet I'd find the whole story pretty entertaining."

"Pretty much every time someone says, 'no offense,' they're about to say something extremely offensive." His fingers gently brushed against my left hand, but I was too terrified to even feel excited about it. "What do you know about me, Zoe?"

Hmmm…what did I know about him? You mean other than he's unbearably gorgeous? Other than he's Student Council President, in all honors classes and on the honor roll, and, despite his social standing, he still seems like a decent human?

"I only know what you want anyone to know. You're smart. You're funny. You're cute—" I clamped my hand over my mouth as heat raced up my neck and burned my face. *Idiot!*

"The first thing you said is exactly it. You only know what I want people to know. When I saw you at Ikea, I realized it's the same with you. The thing is, I think we have a lot more in common than you think we do."

We were almost back to my class. I should have been relieved to make my escape, but I wanted to stand in the hall and talk to him until Christmas—as long as the topic of conversation wasn't the unhinged Wilkes clan.

"Your mother's something else, too?"

"My mom? No. But my dad's a real bastard. I don't talk about him with anyone, and sometimes that seriously sucks. I walk around acting like my life's so perfect when everything's really shit at home. Know what I mean?"

"Yeah, I do. And as much as I'd love to play *Whose Family Sucks More* with you, I don't think that's such a good idea. You should worry about your reputation instead of ditching class to follow me to the bathroom."

"I actually don't give a shit about my reputation, but even if I did, being your friend wouldn't do it any harm. It's not like I'm asking you to be my girlfriend." He swallowed and looked down awkwardly. "Shit." He ran his hand through his dark brown hair, and I almost melted into a puddle of goo right there. "I mean, it's not like being your boyfriend would hurt me any. It wouldn't, but if it did, I wouldn't even care. You're—"

"What's your point, Nate?" I interrupted.

"I'm just offering you my friendship. If you're interested, you know where to find me."

I nodded like one of those stupid bobblehead dogs.

"Okay." He flashed his high-beam smile at me again. "You better get back in there before Mrs. Thomas calls in the Coast Guard to find you." And just like that, he sauntered back the way we had come.

————

SAFE 7

Hi, Diary,

Sorry it's been so long since my last entry.

Daddy's gone again. It was nice to have him home, but honestly, I like it better when he's on the road. When he's home, he doesn't want to be the bad-guy parent, so Bobby always acts up. Don't get me wrong, Diary. I don't blame Bobby. Heck, sometimes I push things too far, too, just because I know Daddy won't do anything about it. Then Mama has to come in and keep us in line because someone has to be the adult around here, which is totally not fair to her.

That's what happened on Saturday. I planned on making pancakes to celebrate Daddy's homecoming, but instead, I goofed off and built a pillow fort with Bobby and Leesh, which wrecked the living room. Plus, I picked a fight with Leesh for no good reason. Basically, I acted like a grade-a jerk all morning. When Mama came out and saw what a mess I'd made of the living room and that I hadn't even started cooking breakfast yet, she got upset and grounded me to my room. I'm not even mad about it anymore. Like I said, when Daddy's around, we all act up more and it makes her life so much harder.

At first, I was furious nobody else got in trouble. I mean, Bobby could have woken the dead with his screaming and Leesh fought right back with me. But after a while, I realized Mama did the right thing to punish me and not the kids. I'm the oldest, so it's my job to keep them in line when she's not around, but instead of doing what I should have, I riled them up. I should have known better, and I got exactly what I deserved. Mama can seem harsh sometimes, but she's always fair.

As much as I hated being stuck in my room, it turned out to be a blessing in disguise. I got my history report on Middle Kingdom Egypt done, and it's not even due for another week. I also read a super good book called *Daddy Long Legs*. It's about this teenager who's about to be turned out of the orphanage where she was raised.

She's called to the headmistress's office, and she finds out she has a secret benefactor who offers to pay for her college and give her a monthly allowance. In exchange, she promises to write him one letter a month to tell him about her studies and to work hard and become an author.

Oh, and she's not allowed to ask about his identity. One thing about this book is it was written over a hundred years ago. It's kind of hard to read because people wrote so differently back then, which made it a little slow at first, but whatever. I basically had all the time in the world, and now that I'm done, I'm so glad I stuck with it.

Did you know women couldn't even vote when *Daddy Long Legs* was written? That's so hard to believe? The girl changes her name from Jerusha to Judy, and even though she owes everything she has to some mysterious man, she's strong and stubborn and makes her own decisions. Considering what the world was like when it was written, it's quite a feminist book.

I'm so in love with the idea of someone sending me to college because they see my potential, but I bet everyone wishes for a secret benefactor sometimes. Will I ever be able to go to college? I don't know how much college costs, but I do know it's a whole lot more than we pay for rent. There's no way I could expect Mama and Daddy to pay for it, so if I do go, I know it will be all on my own steam. I'll have to work harder in school than I already am. I'll need scholarships and a job, and I'll have to be extremely careful with my money and my time, but I've never been afraid of hard work.

I feel sorry for people like Cheryl. People whose parents can send them to college and buy them a car and everything they need for a dorm room. Those people might have financial advantages over people like me, but what they don't have is what Mama and Daddy call "street smarts." I have street smarts to spare, though. I know how to stretch my resources and how to improvise when I need to. I'm tough, so when things get hard, I know how to dig in and get through it. Plus, I have way more appreciation for the little things in life. I don't need a hundred-dollar pair of jeans to make me happy. Just listening to Sammycat purr as I'm curled up with a good book is all I need to remind me happiness is everywhere if you know how to look for it.

Even though it wasn't the most exciting thing to be stuck in my room all weekend, at least I was productive.

REAL 13

When I came out of my room earlier, Leesh was sitting cross-legged on the couch, attempting to paint her nails a seriously amazing bright blue. "Since when do you paint your nails?"

"Since now. Meagan gave it to me because she said it clashes with her hair." Leesh didn't look up, and her left hand trembled as she tried to paint her right pointer finger.

"She's blond. Her hair goes with everything."

Leesh tilted her head to one side and shrugged. Electric blue clumped along her cuticles in a horrifying mess.

"Your nails look like a Smurf murder scene. Let me help you." I lowered myself to the middle cushion, trying to avoid making things worse than they already were.

"I don't need your help, Zoe. I'm thirteen, not six, you know."

I picked up the remote. "Suit yourself. I guess you could always tell everyone at school you let Bobby paint your nails. At least then you'd have an excuse." I channel surfed until I found a British cooking competition. After a few minutes, Leesh sighed and held out the bottle of blue.

"Thanks." Her voice didn't sound right, and when I looked

at her, I was surprised to see her holding back tears. My sister has never been the emotional type.

"No wonder you're doing such a crappy job. How can you even see your hand through the waterworks?" The sisterly thing to do would have been to ask what was bothering her, but I got a serious *don't even ask* vibe from her. I took the polish instead. "Do you have remover? I think it'd be better to start with a clean canvas."

She pressed her lips together and shook her head. A couple of tears ran down her cheeks, and I didn't know what to do. Should I pretend I didn't notice so she wouldn't feel embarrassed? Should I ask her what had her so upset?

"You might be in luck," I stalled. "I think I have an old bottle in my room somewhere. Let's go find out." I stood up and pulled her off the couch. She didn't help, but she didn't resist, either. She shuffled behind me and flopped down on my bed while I dug out the long-forgotten bottle of pink acetone and a small stack of cotton rounds.

"You take off the polish and I'll put it back on for you, okay?"

Leesh sat up and got to work, but didn't say anything.

"Wanna tell me what's going on with you? You're not one to mope around the house all dramatically. That's more my thing."

She snorted and a small snot ball shot out of her nose. We both laughed as she wiped herself with her sleeve.

"You don't have to talk to me about whatever's going on, but I'm here if you need me."

"I—" her voice sounded so small and broken. "I can't handle it anymore." She scrubbed so hard at the nail polish, it seemed like she was trying to erase herself.

"Handle what?"

"I'm sorry, Zoe." Her broken voice cracked even more as her words turned to sobs. "I'm such an asshole."

I put the lid back on the remover and set it on the floor so I could put my arms around her.

"You're not an asshole. Why do you say that?"

She was full-on ugly crying at this point and couldn't get words out, so I held on to her helplessly until she calmed down a little.

"I don't understand why she hates you. Why she comes after you the way she does."

"Who? Mama?"

"Yes, Mama. I don't get it. You do everything for her. Hell, you even do everything for us. It doesn't make sense how she treats you like an abused dog. But—" her voice squeaked again, but she swallowed and got control of it. "I'm a coward. I should try to distract her, so she'll leave you alone, but I'm too afraid. And even worse, there's a part of me that's glad it's you and not me."

She pulled out of my hug, curled into a tight ball, and cried like someone just died. Like she'd never stop.

Leesh and I have never talked about this. It's the lion in the room nobody wants to admit is there. Everyone in this messed up family knows I'm the one who gets it worst. I wonder if the phrase *black sheep of the family* is really about people like me. People who will never belong, will never fit in, and will always be the ones to get in trouble, no matter how badly other people screw up. Sometimes, I'm so jealous of the attention my sister gets, I want to scream and punch things. It never once crossed my mind how hard this crappy situation is on her. Still, seeing her break down just about broke me.

"Hey," I whispered as I curled up next to her and cradled her in my arms. "Calm down, Leesh. It's okay. You're not a coward, okay?"

"Yes, I am. I shouldn't let her hurt you. I should have done something, anything, to make her come after me instead last weekend. I should have helped you." She grabbed a fistful of her hair and pulled so hard I heard the roots snapping from her scalp. "I hate myself, and you have every right to hate me, too."

I took her hands in mine and massaged them until she relaxed her grip. "Stop it, Leesh," I begged. "I don't hate you any more than I could ever hate Bobby. I'm your big sister, it's my job to protect you. Honestly, I'd take a beating from her every day of my life if it meant she never laid a hand on you or Bobby."

She lay there and cried, and I wracked my brain for a way to take her pain from her. In the end, all I could do was keep holding her tightly and whisper soothing words in her ear. Like whispering a bedtime story to a crying baby. My poor sister thinks I hate her, when the truth is, I hate myself for so many things, including not protecting her better when Gynger goes after her. True, she doesn't get it nearly as often as I do, but she doesn't deserve it when it does happen.

Plus, seeing her big sister punished the way Gynger punishes me must take a serious toll on Leesh. If I weren't such a screw-up in the first place, she wouldn't have to see Gynger hurt me again and again. The thing I hate myself for most, though, is not knowing the right words to say to make her pain go away. I can sure as hell find all the words when I'm writing, but the minute I need to talk, I forget every word I know.

"Hey," I said after she calmed down a little. "Want to hear something absolutely horrifying?"

"I don't know. Does it have anything to do with our effed-up family?"

"Well, yeah, but no. Do you want to hear it or not?"

She rolled over and nodded. Her eyes were puffy and red.

"I can't believe I'm about to tell you this." I took a deep breath to steel my nerves. "Someone from my school was at Ikea."

"Really?" She wiped her eyes with the back of her hand. "Do I know them? Who is it?"

"Nate."

"Nate, Nate? The guy you've been crushing on since we moved here?"

"Yep."

This humiliating revelation had the exact impact I hoped for. She sat up and settled into a pretzel-legged *let's gossip* posture. The things you do for sisters.

"Oh. My. Gawd. Tell me he didn't see it." There was no need for her to clarify *it* was Gynger's meltdown.

"Like anything is ever so easy for me." I shook my head and smiled at her. "He saw the whole thing and now he's following me around like a lost puppy. He went from not even knowing I exist to practically stalking me. He even followed me to the bathroom today."

"What did he want?"

"Beats the heck out of me. He *said* we have more in common than I think, and he wants to be my friend, but who knows. I mean, it's not like he'll get anything out of hanging out with me, so I don't get it." I flopped back on the bed and stared at the cracks on the ceiling. "I think my best bet is to be polite but keep him at arm's length."

She gave me a gentle shove. "You're so dumb. What do you have to lose? You've been dying for his attention forever, and now that he's giving it to you, you're blowing him off? Don't do that. If he wanted to make fun of you, your life would already be hell. And anyways, you deserve something good to happen to you for once. Who knows? You might start off friends and end up together. Stranger things have happened."

Maybe she had a point, but the last thing I need to do is obsess over some guy—either as a friend or a possible boyfriend. Right now, my only concern is making sure Leesh and Bobby stay safe. In no version of the story of my life does Nate Evans play even a minor role.

SAFE 8

Dear Diary,

Something downright incredible happened. Yesterday, Leesh was on the couch trying to paint her nails but doing a terrible job. After I teased her for a minute, we came back to my room, and I helped her get the old stuff off and put new stuff on. That's not the incredible thing, though. The great thing is that we talked. Like really, really talked. For the first time in probably years, we opened up and shared our most private thoughts with each other.

Of course, I love my sister, and I know she loves me, but it seems like we never have a chance to hang out and chat anymore. She goes off and does her own thing after school, and I'm so busy helping Bobby and working on dinner and after-dinner chores that before I know it, it's ten o'clock and I'm about dead on my feet. I didn't realize how much I miss Leesh, and I hope we can spend more time like we did yesterday.

Okay, diary. I really didn't have anything else to say, so TTFN!

REAL 14

Even though I told her I don't, Leesh still thinks I hate her, and I don't know what to do. Nothing in the world could ever be further from the truth. Telling me Bigfoot moved in next door, or the Loch Ness Monster spends summers with her girlfriend at the crappy public pool by the library would be way more believable than me hating my sister. I could never, ever hate my sister.

How can I find the words to tell her how I feel? Since her confession, she's avoided me like I'm covered in raw sewage, and even if I can get her in the same room as me, she won't talk to me. Is she embarrassed about opening up? Does she regret it? I need to find a way to tell her it's not her fault. Hell, I'm actually glad she's not the gleam of hatred in Gynger's eyes. Sometimes, yeah, I wish I could be loved like Leesh is, but I don't hate her for it. She can't help the way Gynger treats her any more than I can. It's a cold hard truth that not everyone gets to feel loved and safe, but what kind of big sister would I be if I wished my pain on my sister? I'm glad it's me and not her or Bobby.

But then again...I'm a little jealous, too. It's not jealousy like I wish we could switch places. It's more like, why can't Gynger be the mom to me she is to Leesh and Bobby? Yeah, sometimes she freaks out and smacks Leesh around a bit, but she's always quick to get over it and she always tries to make it up to her in some way. I know she's not a complete monster because she can love them. So why doesn't she love me?

Maybe I'm bad. Rotten as an Easter egg on the Fourth of July. It's the only thing that makes sense. If Gynger can love, but she doesn't love me, then it must be because of who I am, down at my core. And if that's the case, I'm not doing anyone any good at all. I'm not really protecting Leesh or Bobby, which is the one thing I always believed I was good at. Now, I can't help but wonder if everyone would be better off without me.

Oh, God. When I go back and read that, I feel so stupid. I sound like such a drama queen. In case anyone ever finds this journal, I'm not suicidal, okay?

REAL 15

I'm starting to doubt my sanity. How did I get myself stuck in such a stupid situation? Keeping two diaries is the dumbest idea I've ever, ever had. I thought I was sooo smart. Thought I could trick Gynger with the safe diary and still be able to write about the things I want, but it's all so confusing. The fake entries are so over-the-top happy, they don't even sound a little bit true to me. I mean, come on! I was grounded to my room for being too loud while building a fort, but it's okay because I read what could have been the first feminist book and I finished a report a week early? Puh-leeze.

On the other hand, the bad things I need to write about are so over-the-top bad, even though every word is true, I wonder if those things really happened at all. Is it possible I've made everything up? Or at least made it all out to be worse than it is? If Gynger really does the things I say she does, then she's a monster. A real monster, not a legend like the Babadook or Slenderman.

And if she's a monster, what chance do I have of surviving long enough to get out of here? What chance do Leesh and Bobby have? In fact, if she's the way I say she is, how could any of us have survived even this long? A monster can't take care of babies. Can't change diapers or give wiggly toddlers a bath. Caring like that requires putting someone else's needs ahead of yours, and monsters can't put others first. Thinking logically, what does that mean?

It means I'm wrong. But does it really?

Gynger cut Grams and Papo out of her life years ago, and they don't even know where we live anymore, but I remember spending weekends with them sometimes when I was little. When she cut them off, the weekend visits stopped and suddenly it was up to six-year-old Zoe to feed Mama and little Leesh while Daddy worked whatever job he had. At first, we ate lots of peanut butter sandwiches, but it wasn't long before I learned how to make toast and to badly scramble some eggs. When I sit down and really think about it honestly, I know the truth. I raised myself and my brother and sister.

I don't understand why I get most of her rage. Bobby is spared from the physical stuff because he's the only son and the youngest, so can do no wrong. He can be a brat, but he's also a good kid, overall. And Leesh, well, she's the favorite daughter. Sometimes I can't help but wonder if Leesh was born first, would Gynger hate her the way she hates me? I don't think so. I think there's something in my blood that makes my own mother hate me. Even though I do a lot for Bobby and Leesh, like cooking, laundry or making sure their homework is done, Gynger still loves them and cares for them in her own strange ways. She'll sit on the couch and cuddle with Bobby, or she'll tell Leesh how pretty she is. A monster couldn't do those things, right?

What's wrong with my brain that I insist I'm a victim? Why do I believe she's awful when there's no real evidence, other than my own memory or the tender spots on my head? Maybe I'm a nightmare of a kid to raise, and Gynger does the best she can. But since I'm so bad, and clearly battier than a dark cave at high noon, sometimes she loses her temper. When she does, I change everything around in my mind and even go so far as to make things up. Why? I still haven't figured it out, but maybe it's so I don't have to take accountability for my own actions when things go south. Like they say, it takes two to start a fight.

That must be it. Nothing else makes sense.

REAL 16

Nate left a note in my locker today. Don't ask me how he managed to even get into it in the first place, because I have no freaking idea. Goes to show that popularity is serious currency in high school, I guess. Not that being Mr. Popular gives him the right to break into my locker, but it's the only thing I can figure out.

> *Zoe,*
>
> *Hey, I know it's weird and maybe even creepy to leave this in your locker, but since you won't talk to me, I don't know how else to get your attention.*
>
> *I'm not going to beg you to be my friend. I just want to put it out there one last time that if you need someone to talk to, I'm here. You can trust me, Zoe. God, that sounds so bad. Like something a corny villain in a bad movie would say. But lame as it sounds, I'm serious. Like I said in the hall, I don't give two shits what anyone might think. Not that anyone would think anything, anyway. You seem to believe you're some uber-weirdo, but you're not, trust me! I have no idea where you even came up with such a thing. Since you moved*

here, you always kept to yourself before you and Cheryl got close. I've never seen anyone treat you crappy, and believe me, I see everything.

Anyway, I really hope if you can't trust me, you find someone you can open up to. Selfishly, I hope it's me because I could use someone to talk to, too.

Later,

Nate

What am I supposed to do with this? God, I want to trust him so badly, but what if this is some sort of sick joke? Why is everything so hard?

REAL 17

I see a pattern, but I don't know what it means. Cheryl tries to be my friend, and I blow her off. Nate left me a note and stalks me outside the bathroom, trying to convince me to be his friend, and I blow him off, too. Why? I don't mean why do I keep pushing them away. Why I push is more obvious than a hundred-dollar bill taped to a windshield. I mean, why are they chasing me? It's not like either of them is hurting for friends. And don't even try to convince me their reputations wouldn't be hurt by hanging out with a loser like me. But they keep pressing. I'm so confused!

How is it possible to have so many contradictory things in my head all at once? The way Nate and Cheryl seem to truly care about me makes me wonder if maybe I'm not such a worthless loser after all. But if they're right, then what about Gynger? If Cheryl and Nate are right about me, then Gynger must be wrong. And if she's wrong about me, then I'm not making all of this up, and she really is god-awful. My head hurts from trying to figure out what's real and what's not.

I saw a boy walking down the hall yesterday. He had on a black shirt with a picture of a UFO on it. *I want to believe* was written under the UFO. Me, too, guy. Me, too. I want to believe Nate and Cheryl are sincere, but this paranoid part of me is convinced it's a cruel trick. I want to believe my mother isn't really so bad, but the rational part of my brain tells me not to bet my last dollar on it. Ugh, I spend way too much time in my own head. None of this is so complicated.

My mother doesn't love me. She never has. She isn't exactly the most affectionate parent, but at least she has something to give Leesh and Bobby, but for me...all I get is her wounding words and hammer hands. Mothers are biologically programmed to love their kids. Her not loving me tells me everything I need to know; something inside me is bad, and I don't deserve to be loved. I can't trust Cheryl or Nate. They have no reason to give the pathetic *New Girl* a second thought.

How do I keep on living when I'm not worth loving?

Don't worry, I'm still not suicidal, just confused.

REAL 18

I've been thinking a lot about my question from last time. How do I keep living if I'm not worth loving? Well, I think I'm on to a kind of answer there. Love is the most important thing, and love keeps me from giving up all together. Not the hope I'll ever be worthy of my own mother's love, but my love for my sister and brother. I want, no, I *need,* to survive to make sure they're okay. The way I see it, my entire job is to make sure they never feel the way I feel.

I learned how to take care of Leesh when I was little because I loved her so much, I couldn't stand to see her cry for food. When Bobby came along, it was the same thing. Gynger held him a lot when she was in a good mood, but there were times where she didn't touch him for days. Even on her good days, the minute he cried, she'd either shove him into my arms and tell me to shut him up, or plop him to the floor, stomp to her room, and slam the door. What could I do? Not make Bobby a bottle? Let him sit in a gross diaper until either Gynger snapped out of her *whatever* or Daddy came home to change it?

Leesh is still in a bad place, and I'm so worried about her.

Yesterday, I walked into the living room to find her sitting on the couch, pinching her arm with her chipping blue nails. Little red valleys ran up and down her arm in intricate spirals. Some of the pinch marks had gone deep enough to bleed and others must have been there for a few days because they looked blue-green. Old bruises trying to heal.

"Leesh, what the hell are you doing?" I ran over to her and smacked her hand away from her arm. I tried to talk sense into her, but she got up, shuffled to her room, and slammed the door like she wasn't even worried about getting in trouble for it.

I'm so worried about her I can barely think of anything else. The thing is, I have so much to worry about, like you know, staying alive. I can't stand the thought if something happened to me, Gynger could turn around and treat one of them like she treats me. I can't let that happen. I may not be good at much, but I know I'm a damned good sister. If I listened to the voices in my head and killed myself, I'd be abandoning them. Abandoning them means the voice in my head was right all along—I'm worthless. I refuse to let Gynger's voice in my head be the only true thing in my life. Or theirs.

I need a plan when the voice gets to me. It might be good to talk to someone about it, but who? And the million-dollar question is, how do I talk to someone without sounding all dramatic or irrational? There has to be a way to avoid blurting out something like *Oh, by the way, I hear my mother's voice in my head telling me to put my brother and sister out of their misery and kill myself already*. If I said those words out loud to someone, I could end up in some kind of psychiatric hospital for kids and then anything could happen to Leesh and Bobby, and I wouldn't be able to help them.

Or maybe I'm already too far gone, and I need to be locked away for my own good.

SAFE 9

Oh, Diary!

I messed up bad and almost forgot to make dinner! I came home from school, fixed Bobby a snack, and settled him in front of the TV, same as always. Then, I sat down to work on my English project. I'll admit I let time slip away and I worked longer than I meant to, but I swear it wasn't on purpose. Before I knew it, it was nearly dark and Bobby wandered in, orange Cheezie Pops dust stuck to his fingers and around his mouth and asked what was for dinner. I tried to pull my head out of Puck and Oberon's Forest and back into reality. Why didn't I set a timer? I know better than to let myself get so distracted. It's no surprise Mama got so upset with me.

"What's taking dinner so long?" She came up behind me as I dug through the fridge.

"I'm sorry, Mama. I got caught up writing my paper. It's due tomorrow, and I lost track of time."

We had some eggs, cheese, and a few slices of bread. I could make cheesy eggs and toast. I wasn't even hungry, so there would be plenty of food for Mama and the kids.

"You know it's your job to be sure those kids are fed. I work hard all day, keeping a clean house and all I ask is you take care of dinner. Keep your priorities straight. No English paper's ever gonna do you as much good as learning to cook will."

"Yes, Mama. I know you're right." I put the heavy skillet over the electric blue flame and cracked eggs into a bowl. She's always right.

REAL 19

Okay, Zoe. Breathe. Stop your hands from shaking and breathe. Tonight's fight was no different from any other. God, it's frustrating to keep up two diaries. Why can't I have a normal mother? One who doesn't snoop through my things. One who doesn't call me useless for doing my homework. One who makes sure we have more than a few eggs and some cheese in the house. She has three kids! Why is it always a surprise when we run out of food? She's selfish and irresponsible, and I hate her. I. HATE. HER!

Three kids eat a lot. She makes such a big deal about staying home all day and keeping the house clean, and I'm supposed to act like every word is true. All she does is sit on the couch, watching her shows and sleeping off hangovers. Does she honestly believe she's the one who does the laundry and dishes? Is she so messed up she believes she's the one who keeps this house from rotting out from under us? There's no way she could be that delusional, is there? Then again, she seems to think she's the one who helps with homework or who stays up all night when Bobby's had another nightmare. It must be nice to believe you deserve credit for someone else's work.

Obviously, everything I wrote in my other journal is a load of crap. Gynger didn't come out, chat with me a few seconds, and then wander off. Nothing's ever so simple with her, is it?

I really did lose track of time working on my essay. As I stood in front of the open fridge, panic burbled around my stomach. I didn't know what to make. All we had was half a dozen eggs, a couple slices of American cheese, and a few pieces of bread. I moved to the cupboard, hoping to find oatmeal magically appeared since this morning. Hell, I'd settle for flour and baking powder to make pancakes again, but the cupboard had even less food than the refrigerator.

"Zoe, what the hell is taking dinner so long?" She stumbled into the kitchen and slammed her empty glass on the counter. The sour smell of whiskey hung around her in a thick cloud.

"Sorry, Mama. I have this important paper in English tomorrow, and I lost track of time trying to finish it up."

"An English paper? What's it about?" Her voice softened, but the hairs on the back of my neck raised and goosebumps prickled down my arms. She might be able to fool everyone else with her fake sweet voice, but I knew it meant she wanted a fight.

I yanked open the fridge and grabbed the eggs while trying to keep my voice steady. "One of Shakespeare's plays. *A Midsummer Night's Dream*. It's about a fairy king and queen who—"

"One of Shakespeare's plays," she repeated, all singsong like.

My mouth went dry, and my stomach muscles clenched as I waited for the other shoe to drop. I didn't have to wait long.

She came up behind me so close I could feel the heat radiating off her. "Look at you, Miss High and Mighty. Reading Shakespeare like it makes you better than me."

My heart hammered at her razor-sharp words, and my brain raced to find a way out of this conversation.

"Of course, I don't think that, Mama." I set the cheese slices on top of the egg carton and pulled them both out of the fridge. "I'm making breakfast for dinner tonight. Sound good?"

Before I could close the refrigerator, she grabbed me by the shoulders and spun me around. I tried to stop the eggs from smashing on the floor, but there was nothing I could do to stop gravity.

The look in her eyes made me want to die. "I'm sorry, Your Majesty. Is our peasant food not good enough for you and your Shakespeare-loving ass? Do you want me to run out and get you a filet mignon?"

I knew there was no way I could talk myself out of what was coming, but I had to try.

"I don't think I'm better than you, Mama, it's only an assignment—" She slapped me hard across the face and I fell backward into the refrigerator.

"Look what you did, you stupid, stupid girl!" She grabbed my face in her hand and forced my head to turn so I looked at the only food we had in the house, smashed all over the floor.

I didn't mean to, but my body betrayed me and let the tears fall. "I'm sorry, Mama. I'll clean it up."

"Damn straight you will." She shoved me again, and this time I fell to my knees and braced myself for her signature rib kick. "And stop crying before I give you something to cry about. Do you understand me? Do you? Answer me." Her voice rattled the kitchen window, and I wondered if the neighbors could hear her. If so, why didn't they do something? Why doesn't anyone ever do anything?

I curled up on the floor to make myself as small a target as possible and prayed she wouldn't kick me hard enough to break my ribs. I've heard they can't fix broken ribs. If I did end up with something broken, especially something she couldn't see, she'd call me a lazy drama queen and accuse me of trying to get out of chores.

I closed my eyes and tried to disappear into myself. To think about anything but the pain my own mother rained down on me. The thing my mind grabbed onto was the fridge. I was right in front of it, and the cool air spilled down on me. I imagined the cool air was a fog wrapping me up to protect me, even though God himself can't protect you when Gynger sets her sights on you.

My head still hurts. It burns and throbs, like a flaming heartbeat in my skull. Somehow, not all the eggs smashed when I dropped them. Must have been a guardian angel or something. Ha. What a laugh. Guardian angels are about as real as the tooth fairy. If guardian angels were real, I'd have a different mother. I can't count on angels or anyone else to protect me, and if I get hurt, it's my own fault. In a dream world, I'd have a mother who cares about my grades and wants me to do well in school, but I don't live in a dream, do I?

When she finally stormed off, I pulled myself to my knees and tried to make the world stop spinning. A small pile of brown hair lay on the floor near where my head had been. My hair. I scooped it up, put it in the trash, and made toast and the last couple of eggs for dinner.

One thing is certain, though. I'm not crazy or making things up. The clump of hair in the trash proves it.

REAL 20

Talk about a time when you felt truly happy.

That's what Mrs. Thomas had on the board when we filed into English today. After the bell, she handed out notebooks and had us put our names on them. We're not allowed to bring them home, and every day when we come in, we're supposed to grab our notebooks from the bookshelf and spend the first ten minutes of class writing about the prompt.

I love the idea of writing prompts. Sometimes it's so hard to know what to write about, but if I have a topic, it's like my brain can hardly wait to start writing about it. Only why did she have to choose such a hard one right out of the gate? I can't remember the last time I felt real happiness. Most of the other kids started working right away, but I had to take a second to think about what I could possibly say.

Even though Mrs. Thomas promised never to read our journals, how can I trust she won't? It didn't seem wise to write about how I never feel happy because I'm always busy putting out Gynger-shaped fires. I suppose I could have written about the awful "joke" Gynger played on me. Seeing Sammycat run to me when I expected to find her dead in the freezer is the closest to happiness I've felt in a long time. I didn't know a person could feel crushing grief one moment and over-whelming joy the next. When I opened the front door and Sammy twisted around my legs and meowed up at me, it took me at least twenty seconds to realize I hadn't hallucinated her. The world melted away, and Sam was the only thing I could see.

Everything about that moment is crystal clear in my memory. Her fluffy, orangey-gold fur, her gold-green eyes, and the way she crinkled up her nose as she meowed up at me. All of it so clear, I couldn't see anything else in the world. Until Gynger's cackling. The ice in her drink clinked against the glass and broke through the fog of clarity—*Fog of Clarity*. What a cool name for a band, or maybe a book.

No flipping way could I write about that. Instead, I created a memory out of nothing. I wrote about an imaginary Christmas vacation at the mountain house in Colorado where Daddy spent summers as a kid. With all the hustle and bustle of getting packed and making sure we had everything we'd need for two weeks in the mountains, we forgot to pack the Christmas presents. At first the kids and I were so heartbroken, but then Mama reminded us how the best gifts of all are the gifts of family and time.

"But," Mama said, "If you really want presents, there are woods and a big, old house to explore. Surely, somewhere under the snow or in a corner of the attic, you can find presents for each other."

We spent days scouring inside and out for the perfect gifts. By Christmas morning, presents of all shapes and sizes crowded under the tree, wrapped in pillowcases, and yellowed funny pages from a lifetime ago. We drank homemade hot cocoa and laughed until our sides ached, and we couldn't breathe as we unwrapped our presents. In the end, none of us missed the makeup or the gadgets, because Mama had been right. The best gift of all was each other.

What's the word I'm looking for here? Oh, yeah. Barf. But hey, a cheesy-ass story was better than nothing.

I'm so tired and confused from always hiding the way my life is. The thing is, I have to go through the effort of keeping up the safe journal, in case Gynger reads it. I also have to make sure this journal never leaves my sight, and now...now I'm faking more entries for English. I don't know how much longer I can keep pretending everything is okay.

———

SAFE 10

Hi, Diary!

English was the absolute best part of today. Mrs. Thomas passed out journals and told us we'll be doing writing prompts the first ten minutes of class every day. Today she had us write about a happy memory, and I wrote about the day we found Sammycat under the porch and she snuggled into me like she's been my cat since the day she was born. It's hard to describe how much I love Sam, and I wonder if the way I love her is even close to the way Mama loves us. I doubt it. I've heard no love is bigger than the love a mother has for her kids, but I bet a girl's love for her cat comes in a close second.

I don't have anything else to talk about today, Diary. The rest of the day was nothing but the same old stuff and not even worth writing about. Anyway, I have algebra to do, so I have to run.

TTFN!

REAL 21

What if I fall? Oh, but my darling, what if you fly?

Today's prompt damn near made me roll my eyes out of my head. I expected more from Mrs. Thomas. What'd she do, head over to Pinterest and search *inspirational memes*? I can't imagine how hard it is to come up with prompts every day, but I like to think if I were in charge, I'd at least get a little creative. Isn't tapping into your creativity the whole point of writing prompts? Maybe I'm being too hard on her, but for some reason this one rubs me the wrong way. I wish I had been able to say so in my class journal, but instead I wrote some stupid thing about not letting fear hold you back. It was probably the exact same superficial crap everyone else wrote.

But that prompt has been bouncing off my brain all day. I have this image of a girl standing on the roof of a skyscraper. I see her from behind. The wind blows her long hair around her head, a miniature, brown tornado. It must be slapping her in the face, but she doesn't brush it away. She just stands there, looking down over the edge for a moment before taking baby steps forward. She's not so close that her toes are hanging off, but she's stupid-close to the edge. If she gets dizzy, if the wind gusts and she loses her balance, she'll fall.

Is it normal to see things in your head so clearly? Is it normal to be afraid of those unreal things? Just when I get to thinking I might be okay, along comes a tornado-haired girl standing on a ledge. I could say it's my imagination, but what if it's my way of covering up my crazy? They say mental illness runs in families, so I'm probably totally screwed. Daddy must be a little crazy to stay with Gynger, the way she treats him and us. Between the two of them, my DNA is stacked against me.

I'm afraid for the girl on the ledge, but part of me wants her to step off. What if she does fly? If it were real, of course she'd fall straight down and burst like a watermelon when she hit the ground, but since I'm only imagining her, anything could happen. And if she stepped off the edge and discovered she could fly, where would she go? Maybe up, up, and up into the clouds. Into the atmosphere. Up past all the reasons she climbed up to the roof in the first place. Maybe she keeps on flying, further and further, until she finds a new place. Another planet like Earth, but better. And if she's incredibly brave, she finds her way to a new home where nobody hurts her. Where there is enough food to make her feel like she'll burst.

I'm writing this and I realize I'm describing where I'd fly. If it's my imagination, and I'm describing where I'd go, then it must be my own brown hair making a tornado around my own head.

The girl looks down, and suddenly, I'm looking down with her. The cars on the street below are beetles. People are ants. I'm on top of the tallest building in the world. The wind gusts and I sway. My throat burns, and I swallow. I inch forward—hang my right foot over the edge.

What if I fly?

REAL 22

I need help, but I don't know how to get it. I don't know how to say what's really happening. How to explain how dangerous she is without sounding like a hysterical kid. We have a roof over our heads. We have a bit of food in the house. And except for her meltdown at Ikea, Gynger is so good at pretending to be normal in public. What would I say, and who would I even say it to? Should I talk to Mrs. Thomas?

Stick together, Gynger always tells us. *Y'all watch out for each other. If one of you gets hurt, you're all gonna get hurt when you get home.*

"Bobby, Aleesha, you kids know better than to go talking about our private family stuff to anyone, don't you?" she says after she explodes. "What happens in this house stays in this house, and you're not to tell anyone." Here, she always stops for dramatic effect. "Unless you want the cops to come in and take you. They'll take you away from me and they'll separate you. You'll *never* see each other or me or your dad again."

Sometimes, if she's yelled at Bobby or hurt Leesh, she hits a terrible low and begs them for forgiveness. "I'm sorry, my baby. I'm so sorry. I don't know what happened. I didn't mean to hurt you. It won't happen again, honey. You know it won't. Promise me you won't tell anyone about this. They'll take you away from me and I'll never see you again. If they do, I'll die. You don't want your mama to die, do you baby?"

Blah, blah, blah-bitty blah. It makes me sick. She used to include me in her tearful apologies, but she stopped years ago. I'd like to think she knows I won't say anything, but I'm betting she legit doesn't give a damn about me.

How do I ask for help, and what can I do to make sure we stay together? Maybe there's nothing I can do. Maybe the simple fact is, if I want to keep the kids safe and together, I need to keep my mouth shut. At least here I'm a shield. If we're separated, I won't know if something bad happens to them. And I don't even want to think about what Gynger might do to herself if Bobby and Leesh left. I know I shouldn't care about her, but she's my mother and I can't help it. I hate myself for still loving her after all she's done.

REAL 23

I'm sitting here with my heart hammering in my chest and I'm trying my damnedest to keep myself together. Breathe, Zoe. Slow down and breathe. You got us all out. Everyone is okay. Even if it's not forever, at least for tonight, we're all safe.

Okay, backing up a little so I don't forget anything.

Bobby, Leesh, and I were almost to the house when we saw the front yard. You know those pictures you see after a tornado hits a small town? Things that should be inside, nice, and tidy, are all outside. It looked like the house got sick and barfed all our stuff into the yard. Couch cushions, clothes, books, and photo albums were strewn everywhere. We all slowed down, trying to delay walking into who knows what, for as long as possible.

Bobby stuck his hand into mine and squeezed. "Zoe, why's all our stuff in the yard?" he asked.

"I don't know."

"Are we moving again?" His voice was small and quiet.

"I don't know, Bub." I set my backpack down and turned to Leesh. "You two stay here," I told her. "I'm going to see if I can figure out what's happening. Don't move until I come and get you."

Leesh nodded and threw her arms around me. "Be careful."

"I'm always careful." I pulled out of her hug. "Besides, it's not like I'm going off to war. I'll come back to get you when the coast is clear, but I'm serious. Do *not* come in unless I come and get you. Like, even if I call you from the front porch and tell you to come in, don't do it. Promise me you'll stay put."

"Yeah, you're really reassuring me now." She smiled a weak smile that didn't make it all the way to her eyes. She was worried, and I could tell she was struggling to hold herself together. "We'll see you back here soon."

"Bobby, stay here with Leesh, okay? Make sure no bad guys try to kidnap her."

"Don't worry. If they want to take her, they have to go through me first." He kicked and karate chopped an imaginary bad guy a few times to prove Leesh was in good hands.

"All right, then. Remember, I'm counting on you. I'll be back in a few minutes."

The few hundred feet to our house felt like a thousand miles. I'm used to coming home and finding my room wrecked, but Gynger has never trashed the house like this before. It's times like this when I really wish we had an auntie or uncle to call for help. Or a grandparent, or hell, even an old family friend. But there's no one. Never has been, never will be. So, it's up to me to pull on my big girl pants and figure out what's going on.

A green garbage truck rumbled down the street and, for a moment, it drowned out the sound of my blood rushing through my head.

A soft mewling came from the far corner of the porch and Sammycat ran down the porch steps and wound around my legs. My heart soared when I realized that whatever Gynger did, at least she left my cat alone.

"Good kitty." I picked her up, kissed her head, and set her back down.

At the front door, I paused and looked back at Bobby and Leesh. Every muscle in my body burned to turn tail and run back to them, but what good would that do? With nowhere to go, we wouldn't last one night on our own. Eventually, we'd have to come home. Bobby smiled and waved enthusiastically, as if he were in the audience, and I was up on a stage for some stupid school play. Leesh put her arm around Bobby's shoulders and gave me a thumbs-up. I took a deep breath, stood up tall, and stepped into the house.

It took me a full thirty seconds to wrap my head around the scene I walked into. When it all came into focus, my stomach did somersaults, and I had to fight my throat to swallow down the barf that demanded release.

The blinds had been pulled off the windows and thrown to the other side of the room. Somehow, Gynger had managed to flip the couch upside down. The back of the couch sagged in the middle, where a support board had been broken. The television lay face down on the floor and the power cord had been ripped clean out of the back. The plants in the windows had been thrown across the room. Black soil and shattered terra-cotta dotted the always-dirty brown carpet. Leaves and stems tangled in macramé hanging nets. As awful as all of that was, it wasn't even the worst of it.

Gynger had dragged the dinner table over to the wall where the couch had been and, apparently, stood on it while she spray-painted the ceiling and walls black. Black paint had fallen from the ceiling and landed like raindrops on the table-top. Parts of the wall were sprayed a deep and even black. Other parts were lightly misted with squiggly lines. "WHY" was sprayed in huge diagonal letters across one side of the wall.

I was thirsty. Thirstier than I've ever been in my entire life, but whatever was happening, the last thing I had time for was a nice glass of sweet tea. My legs coiled tight and screamed to run. Run far and fast, until this house, this town, this life was smaller than a fly on a horse. Run and never look back. But running was impossible. I couldn't run and leave my brother and sister behind. My number one priority is to keep them safe, no matter what, and that meant I had to find Gynger. Until I found her, I couldn't come up with a plan, and without a plan, we'd be as good as dead living on the streets.

Something thudded in the back of the house. Her bedroom. Once again, I ordered the bile to stay in my stomach where it belonged, straightened my back, and walked slowly toward her room.

"Chin up, shoulders back, tits out. No fear. Chin up, shoulders back, tits out. No fear," I whispered for strength. A character in some cable tv movie said those exact words to a friend right before she went onstage to give a speech. It worked and the audience gave the woman a standing ovation. If those words could make her brave enough to face an audience, maybe they could make me brave enough to face my mother.

Her bedroom door hung from one hinge. I knew she was strong, but I had no idea she was strong enough to yank a door from its hinges.

Go! My legs urged. *Run far and fast. Run now.*

"Chin up, shoulders back, tits out. No fear." I took one more deep breath and stepped into the lion's den.

"Mama?" I called quietly. "Mama, are you in here?"

A sound like a muffled sob came from the other side of the bed. She sat with her back against the wall, hugging her knees and swaying gently side to side. I squatted down in front of her, even though every synapse in my brain told me to get the hell out of there. I reached out and touched her shoulder gently.

"Why?" she asked thickly. "Why would he do this to me?"

"Who, Mama? What are you talking about?"

"Your father, you idiot! Can't you read?" She shoved me and stood up. "Your good for nothing, stupid, dumb shit father. He's been cheating on me. Didn't you see it when you came in?"

"I—I don't know. See what?"

"I don't know, I don't know," she mocked back. "The writing on the wall, Zoe. God, keep up, will you? He wrote all about *her* and his affair on the wall. He even drew disgusting pictures of the two of them going at it like wild animals. Are you really so blind you didn't see it?" She stood up and stepped toward me, and I backed up.

My world is never safe, but at least I can pretty much always anticipate when the worst will happen, and when it does, at least it's only a handful of predictable things. Nasty words. Hair pulling. Kicking. Hitting. Spitting. These are all part of the things I've come to expect when I know I'm not safe.

But this...this was different. And different is most definitely not good. In my fifteen years as Gynger Wilkes's daughter, I've never seen her act like this, which means there's absolutely no way to predict what she'll do next. No way to keep myself safe. And if I can't keep myself safe, I can't keep the kids safe. And then what?

"I saw something on the walls, Mama." Was my voice as smooth and calm as I'm remembering it now? Surely not. "But I was so worried about you I didn't stop to read it. I thought burglars broke in, so I came running back here to make sure you were okay."

"Oh, I was robbed, all right. Robbed of your father's love by some stupid heifer." She grabbed my arm and pulled me after her. "Come here. Let me show you what your precious father's been up to."

"Look at this." She pointed up at the splotchy wall. "Do you see this smut?" She picked up the spray paint can and shook it. The clacking marble inside hurt my ears, but I forced myself to stand perfectly still.

Chin up. Shoulders back. Tits out. No fear.

"I know there's more here. I don't know how he did it. What kind of magic pen he used, but I know there's more. Everything he wrote is invisible until the spray paint shows it. It's like that movie where there's a map on the back of the Constitution or some shit. Look." She talked faster than I ever heard her talk before. The words practically tumbled out of her mouth, and I had to concentrate hard to catch all her words.

She climbed onto the table and sprayed wildly at the wall. "See. Here's another. I *told* you so. Read it and weep. Your precious daddy has a whole 'nother family and he never even loved you." She pointed to the freshly sprayed section and read words only she could see. "Today I took my real daughter to the zoo and bought her ice cream. She's way better than stupid old Zoe. God, I hate her."

"I don't see anything, Mama. Why don't you come down off there before you fall and hurt yourself?" I held my hand out to help her down.

"No." She threw the can across the room hard enough to dent the wall. "You're blind as a bat if you can't see what's right in front of your face. Blind and stupid." Veins throbbed in her forehead. Spittle flew out of her mouth, and she screamed, "Get out of my sight! I never want to see you again, you hear me. If you're too blind and stupid to see what's right in front of you, then you're no good to me. Go."

I took a step backward. My legs burned to run, but maybe this was a trick. Maybe she'd stab me in my back as soon as I turned around.

"Go! Leave. Now!"

So, I did. I finally let my legs have their way and I bolted. By the time I hit the front door, her screams had turned to sobs. Part of me wanted to turn around and comfort her, but the more rational part of my brain took over. I scooped up Sam from the yard and kept moving.

As soon as Leesh saw me, she picked up my backpack and held it out to me.

"Let's go." I handed Sam to her, slung the backpack over one shoulder, took Bobby's hand and headed back toward the bus stop.

"Where are we going, Zoe?" Bobby demanded. "I want to go home. Slow down. You're walking too fast. You're hurting my hand."

"Hush, Bobby," I loosened my grip but didn't let go. "Mama's really sick and she told me to take you and Leesh somewhere else tonight, so we don't get sick, too. Okay?"

"No-kay," he replied. It's what he says every time he was willing to do something he really didn't want to do. For some reason, it broke my heart when he said it this time.

"What the hell happened back there?" Leesh asked.

"I'm not really sure. I can only handle one thing at a time right now and I've gotta find us a place to stay the night. I promise, I'll tell you everything later."

We walked past the bus stop all the way to the 7-11. It wasn't an ideal place to gather my wits, but at least it was public, so the odds of someone snatching us were low.

"Let's sit here a second so I can think." I threw my backpack against the red brick wall. My legs wobbled under me, and I slumped to the ground. Sammycat pulled out of Leesh's arms and climbed into my lap. I scratched her gently behind her ears as I tried to come up with a plan.

"I'm hungry," Bobby whined. "I didn't get my after-school snack."

"I know you didn't, Bub. I promise I'll get you fed, but you have to give me a minute, okay?" Instead of responding, he stuck his thumb in his mouth, and sighed.

"Zoe," Leesh said. "You have to call Dad."

"I know, but it's not like he can do anything. He's God knows where and probably doesn't even have a signal." I dug my phone out of my backpack and called him anyway. Just like I thought, he didn't answer.

"Daddy? It's Zoe. Sorry to bother you, but this is an emergency. Something's wrong with Mama and we need you to come home. Okay? Please? Call me."

I hung up and wracked my brain to come up with somewhere for us to stay for the night, but I kept coming up empty. Well, except for one thing, anyway. It was the absolute last thing I wanted to do, but I didn't have any other options. I pushed back my tears and dialed.

"Hey, Cheryl, it's Zoe. Listen, I know this is a huge favor, but do you think your mom or dad can pick us up and let us spend the night with you? My mom is super sick, and she thinks it'd be better for all of us to stay away from her for a while. Call me when you get this, okay? Bye."

———

SAFE 11

Dear Diary,

I've been so worried about Mama. When we got home from school the other day, she was lying on the couch looking kind of gray. She said she'd been throwing up all day and didn't want us to get sick, so she told me to ask Cheryl's mom if we could spend the night. Lucky for us, Mrs. Dwyer agreed, and she came to pick us up right away. She even let us bring Sammycat so Mama could get total rest without having to worry about anything.

A big part of me feels bad about it. I don't want to be a bother to Mrs. and Mr. Dwyer, and I feel like a jerk for abandoning Mama when she's too sick to take care of herself, but when I tried to convince her to let us stay home so I could help her, she put her foot down and said she'd recover faster if she didn't have kids underfoot to worry about. Hopefully, she'll be better by tomorrow and we can come home then, but in the meantime, I'm going to do all I can to help around here. Taking in three kids you've never met with no notice is a big deal, so I want to make things as easy for Cheryl's mom as possible. Starting with setting the table for dinner.

TTFN!

REAL 24

So, this is what a family is supposed to be like, huh? It's warm here. Not warm like hot or muggy. Warm like cozy and safe. It's clean and bright. There's food. At dinner, Cheryl's dad put on some music by a guy named Miles Davis. It was jazzy and relaxing at the same time. No words, just some mellow horns, deep bass, and some drums. I've never heard of Miles Davis before, but I think he might be my new favorite artist in the whole world. His music feels like Christmas morning. Or what I imagine Christmas morning would feel like in a regular family, anyway.

"Thank you so much for setting the table, Zoe." Mrs. Dwyer put a big bowl of salad next to an even bigger bowl of spaghetti already mixed with sauce in the middle of the table. Mr. Dwyer set down a dish full of meatballs as big as Bobby's fist. Never in my life have I seen so much food for a regular family dinner.

My stomach rumbled as the garlicky smell hit my nose. "No, thank you for letting us stay the night. Setting the table is nothing. It's the least I can do."

"Oh, pooh. Don't even mention it, dear. Cheryl's talked

you up since you moved here but has been too embarrassed by her dumb old parents to invite you over. I'm glad to finally have a chance to meet you. Besides, we love having a bunch of kids around the house." As she took her seat next to her husband, I noticed how much Cheryl looked like her mother. Same blonde hair, same hazel eyes. The only real difference was the nails. Cheryl's nails were manicured to sharp points and painted hot pink, whereas Mrs. Dwyer's were short and polish-free.

Cheryl shot her mom a look capable of stopping a rabid bull dead in its tracks, but Mrs. Dwyer didn't seem to notice. I looked around at the clean house and the giant table brimming with food. At her mom, sitting up straight and sipping a glass of red wine instead of chugging whisky after whisky. At her dad, who laughed and ruffled Bobby's hair before serving him more pasta than he could possibly eat. How in the world could anyone be embarrassed to have them as parents? If I had Cheryl's parents, I'd legit invite the whole school over every weekend for the sole purpose of showing them off.

"'Scuse me," Bobby said, pointing at a small bowl. "What's this, please?"

While we waited for Mrs. Dwyer to pick us up, I'd told Bobby and Leesh to be on their absolute best behavior and to use manners that would make the Queen of England proud. My heart swelled at his attempt to follow my instructions.

"That's Parmesan cheese, sweetie," Mrs. Dwyer said.

"Stinky feet cheese? Why did you pour it out of the green can?"

"Bobby," Leesh snapped. "Don't call it stinky feet cheese."

"Why not? We always call it that at home because it smells like gross feet."

So much for good manners.

Cheryl and her parents laughed. Mrs. Dwyer wiped her mouth with her napkin—white cloth like at some fancy restaurant. "This isn't quite the same stuff, but it does have the same name. And you're right, sweetheart. It does smell a little like feet. This cheese comes in a big wedge, and we use the cheese grater to grate it ourselves. Would you like to taste it?"

He looked at the bowl suspiciously, but finally nodded. "Yes, please."

"Open your hand, kiddo." Cheryl's dad spooned a small pile of cheese into the middle of Bobby's palm. "I think you're gonna like this, but if you don't, you can put it on the side of your plate, okay? You don't have to eat it." If Cheryl looked exactly like her mom, she was almost the opposite of her dad. Milk-pale skin with a spattering of freckles across his cheeks, black hair, and the bluest eyes I've ever seen.

Bobby brought his hand to his nose and sniffed before licking the cheese right off his palm. Evidently, I needed to have a chat with him about what manners even are.

"Can I have more? For my spaghetti, not my hand, please?"

"You sure can." Mr. Dwyer passed the cheese to Bobby. "Help yourself."

"Thanks!" Bobby dug the spoon down into the bottom of the bowl and came up with a miniature mountain of Parmesan.

"Not too much, Bobby," I scolded. "It's rude to take too much. Nobody else has had any yet."

"Nonsense, Zoe," Mr. Dwyer said. "We have plenty more where that came from. Bobby, you can have all you like."

"Well," Mrs. Dwyer interrupted, "maybe not all you like. If you eat too much, you might get a stomachache, and that wouldn't be much fun, would it?"

"No, ma'am." Bobby dug out another heap of cheese and sprinkled it all over his food before passing the bowl to Leesh. "You should have some, Leesh. It's way better than our stinky feet cheese."

I've never seen my brother enjoy a meal so much. Of

course, Cheryl's parents make way better spaghetti than I do, and real cheese is something we never have at home, so it makes sense he enjoyed dinner. But it was more than good food. I think he was feeling the same thing I was. For the first time since any of us could remember, we felt safe and relaxed at dinner.

Everyone at the table ate and talked and actually laughed together. We went the entire meal without a single meltdown. Nobody threw a glass at a wall or smacked a fork out of someone's hand. Mrs. Dwyer didn't give anyone dirty looks or insult anyone. I let myself pretend Leesh, Bobby, and I were part of the family. Cheryl was our sister, and her parents were our parents.

My eyes burned and something squeezed inside my chest. It's not fair for one person to have so much…everything. Giant house, complete with a decked-out basement bigger than our entire house, more food than you could eat in a whole year, music, laughter, and love. Meanwhile, the three of us are lucky to share two peanut butter sandwiches between us some nights. We have a dad who's gone more than he's home, but even when he's home, it's not like he does us any good. Bobby and Leesh deserve so much more than the life they were given, and I'd do anything in the world to somehow make everything better for them. But what can I do? I'm nothing but a stupid fifteen-year-old kid.

As I stood up to clear the table after dinner, Mrs. Dwyer touched my arm. "Honey, why don't you leave this for Michael and Bobby and come run an errand with me and Cheryl."

"That's awfully nice of you, but Bobby doesn't know how to clean up after dinner, and I don't think he'd like it if I left him here alone with Mr. Dwyer."

"Tonight's as good a night as any for him to learn how to pitch in around the house." Mr. Dwyer folded his napkin in half and set it next to his empty plate.

Leesh picked up the salad bowl. "It's okay, Zoe. You go on. I'll stay here and help."

"You sure?" I didn't like the idea of leaving her in a house with a strange man and nobody to help if things went south.

"Absolutely positive. We'll be fine, I promise."

I looked at Cheryl to see if she had any clue about this sudden errand. She shrugged and rolled her eyes behind her mom's back.

Bobby held the Parmesan cheese bowl close to his chest. "Anyways, I'm not a baby anymore. I'm big enough to do the dishes now."

Bobby certainly looked like he'd be okay, and with Leesh there to step in if something went wrong, I figured it'd be okay to leave for a few minutes. Besides, when your hostess asks you to go somewhere with them, it's rude not to.

On the other hand, going on made up errands is also a solid way to get kidnapped and sold into slavery. I didn't believe Cheryl's parents were that kind of people, though. And besides, what choice did I really have?

REAL 25

I can't believe I was so worried about leaving the house with Cheryl and her mom. Cheryl literally has the best parents on the entire planet, and I feel foolish for even thinking they could do anything to hurt us.

The errand we had to do turned out to be a Target run. We're more Goodwill people, and the bright lights of the department store made me feel somehow naked and invisible at the same time. Part of me worried that Security would come up behind me and kick me out because I so obviously didn't belong in stores that sell new things.

Mrs. Dwyer pulled a cart from one of the rows and pushed it toward the pharmacy aisle.

"Zoe, pick out three toothbrushes, your favorite toothpaste, and whatever else you'll need to get cleaned up."

"Oh, no, Mrs. Dwyer. I can't let you buy us toothbrushes. We have some at home. I could just run in and get them right quick."

"Absolutely not. Your mother is so sick she sent the three of you to total strangers. You are not to step one single foot in your house until she or your daddy tells me otherwise. Until then, I can't let you kids go without basic hygiene, can I? Your mama would never trust me to look after you again."

Did you know they make toothbrushes with every character you can think of on them? They have little toothbrushes for little kids and big toothbrushes for adults, all of them with bristles straight as soldiers' backs. I can't remember the last time we got new toothbrushes. Hell, we only have two of them for all five of us. Gynger and Daddy share one, and the three of us share the other. They're both so old, what bristles are left are smashed down and jutting out in a million directions. Every time I brush my teeth, I spit bristles out along with the toothpaste.

If there ever was a brand name on the handles, it wore off a long, long time ago. The way Cheryl's mom said to get three of them made me realize it's probably not all too common, or hygienic, for five people to share two toothbrushes. Oily shame swirled in my belly as I considered my options. Finally, I picked a Star Wars one for Bobby, a bright blue one for Leesh because it reminded me of the day I painted her nails, and a green one for myself.

"I guess this sounds silly, but I don't remember what kind of toothpaste we have." My voice was barely a squeak, which only embarrassed me more. I was completely overwhelmed by choices. Some of the toothpaste was stupid-expensive, and some of it claimed to be "all-natural". Some even had charcoal in it. Who would brush their teeth with charcoal? How do people pick from so many options? We usually get whatever the dollar store has if the food bank doesn't have any.

"Try this one for Bobby." Cheryl's mom tossed a tube with Spiderman on it into the cart. "And this one for you and your sister."

I thought about asking why Bobby should get his own toothpaste, but she answered before I could open my mouth. "A lot of times, kids complain regular toothpaste is spicy, so children's toothpaste is easier on tender mouths. Plus, kids really like using stuff with cool characters on it."

Now I had guilt to add to the list of crappy emotions I was feeling. Bobby always complains about our toothpaste being spicy, but I figured he was being a brat and made him suck it up. I bit my lower lip and tried to hold myself together when what I really wanted to do was sit on the floor and cry.

Somehow, I managed not to have a breakdown in aisle A3, which was good because we were far from done. After the toothpaste, I had to pick out brushes and hair ties, deodorant, soap, shampoo, and conditioner. Mrs. Dwyer even got me a special face wash and face moisturizer with sunscreen in it. At first, I tried to keep track of how much everything cost so I could pay her back, but after a while, I relaxed and had so much fun I forgot to look at prices.

"We don't know how long you'll be hanging out with us, so let's get you all some jammies and at least a couple of outfits, in case y'all need to stay more than one night."

"Oh, no thanks, Mrs. Dwy—"

"Call me Beth. And don't try and talk me out of it. One of the best things about being an adult is I can do whatever I want. If it's legal and I'm not hurting anyone, nobody can stop me. So," she clapped once and rubbed her hands together. "Do you want me to pick out clothes or do you want to do it yourself?"

Cheryl groaned. "Don't let her choose for you, Zoe. She has *terrible* taste in clothing. Let me help you."

Mrs. Dwyer, I mean, Beth, beamed. "Wonderful. I'm going to leave the cart with you. Pick out two pairs of pajamas, underwear, socks, and enough clothes for three days for each of you. I'm going to the Starbucks at the front of the store, and then I'll head over to the pet aisle to get a bed and some supplies for your sweet little kitty. Come find me when you're done." She kissed Cheryl on the head and left us alone before I could protest.

"Sorry about her," Cheryl said as she shook her head and rolled her eyes at Beth's back. "My mom is so embarrassing."

I wanted to tell her I know what she means, but the truth is, nothing about Beth seemed embarrassing to me. I seriously can't imagine what it would be like to have a mother who obviously cared so much and who would open their home for total strangers. If I was ever stupid enough to bring someone home for a sleepover, I'm a million percent sure Gynger would freak out so hard she'd scare her away.

"Don't apologize. Your mom is nice for buying us the stuff we need. I'm just annoyed with myself because it never even crossed my mind to pack before I left. Your parents must think I'm stupid."

"Nah." She held up a pajama set with little pandas doing yoga before throwing them into the cart. "These are cute. Get them. There's nothing in the world my mom likes more than taking care of kids. She's one of those people who knew she wanted to be a mother since she was like twelve. She told me her dream was to have five or six kids and live in a big house with a staircase banister perfect for sliding down. She said kids should always have access to a good staircase banister."

"But you're an only child, and your stairs don't even have a banister. What happened?"

"She doesn't really talk much about it. When I was little and I asked her for a sister, she said she had 'a hard time with pregnancy,' whatever that means. She seemed so sad, I never asked again. Anyway, I know she's happy to let you stay as long as you want. I bet she'd even let you move in with us if your mom died." She clamped her hand over her mouth and her eyes got wide. "Crap! Not that I hope your mom dies! That's not what I mean."

"It's fine, I knew what you meant." I tried to smile an

understanding smile, even though I really wanted to climb under the clothes rack and hide. I felt like a grade-a jerk for lying to Cheryl and her whole family about Gynger. Here they think she's practically on her deathbed, and all I'm thinking is if the phrase *only the good die young* is true, my mother will live forever.

————

SAFE 12

Dear Diary,

Finally, we're home! I'm thankful to Michael and Beth for taking us in with no notice, but I've been so worried about Mama that every day seemed to drag out forever. It was so hard not knowing if she was okay or if she needed something but was home all alone. I asked Beth if I could come home to check on her, but she wouldn't let me.

"If your mom is so sick, she needed you all out of the house, then you're staying out of there. I know it's difficult, but trust me, she'll be back to her old self in no time if she doesn't have you kids to worry about. She needs to rest up."

Part of me was angry with her for that. I mean, who the heck is she to forbid me from checking on my own mother? But in the end, I stayed away like she told me. The last thing I wanted was to go against her wishes and end up kicked out for not listening.

I was in fourth period, counting down the minutes till lunch, when Mr. Jackson told me I had to go to the office. Even though I don't skip classes or cheat on tests, my heart raced as I tried to figure out what I had done wrong. I guess I wear my emotions on my face, though, because Mr. Jackson smiled.

"You're not in trouble, Zoe. Please gather your things and head on down there."

Even though he said I wasn't in any kind of trouble, my heart still pounded hard enough for me to see it through my shirt. I mean, it's more than a little unnerving to be called out of class to go to the office. Once I got to the office, I thought I'd relax a little, but when I saw Daddy sitting on one of the chairs, my anxiety jumped off the charts. In all my life, Daddy has never picked me up from school, so I couldn't help worrying Mama had taken a turn for the worse.

"Hey-ya, Zuzu." He wrapped me in a bear hug, and his scratchy beard tickled my face. "I'm busting you out of this joint. We have a lot of catching up to do."

I had roughly thirty-eight thousand questions, but I could tell he didn't want to talk about things in the office, so I kept my mouth shut and followed him out to his big blue truck.

REAL 26

The drive home in Daddy's rig felt like it took hours, even though it was only about ten minutes. All the questions I had in the office evaporated as I climbed into the truck. He didn't seem upset, so I assumed Gynger was okay. Or at the very least, not dead. She's never been okay, as far as I can remember. He pulled into the gravel driveway, turned off the truck, and sat there, his arm dangling out the window.

"Why aren't we going in?" I asked.

He closed his eyes and took a long drag from his cigarette, and the smoke burned my nose and eyes.

"I'm sorry you had to see your mama in such a state, Zuzu. That must have been scary for you." He placed his heavy hand on my shoulder and gave it a little squeeze. "I know I don't say it often, but I'm proud of you."

"For what?"

"For your quick thinking. You did the right thing by going to your friend's house. But it's not just that. I'm proud of you because you're smart and tough, and you take such good care of your brother and sister. And your mama."

"I didn't do anything to help her. I ran like a coward." My

voice cracked and I knew I was about to lose complete control and start blubbering like a baby. I stared at the front door and tried to breathe through the smoke.

"I know you don't see it now, but believe me, Zuz. You're no coward. The things you've been through would knock a grown man to his knees." His chuckle turned to a cough. "Believe me, I know a thing or two about falling to my knees over your mama. Sometimes," he took a long drag from his cigarette and blew it out the open widow. "Sometimes, I just don't know. What am I supposed to do? I love her so much, and I want everything to be good."

What was I supposed to say? What even was this whole conversation, anyway? It felt more like my father was talking to me as a friend, and he expected me to somehow reassure him instead of him talking to and comforting his daughter. My stomach growled, and he snapped out of whatever pit he had fallen into.

"Why didn't you call me back? I called you even before I called Cheryl and left you a message. I left you like a hundred messages. I thought you died."

He blew smoke rings and winked at me, just like he used to when I was little. It made me laugh then, but there was nothing to laugh at now.

"I'm sorry, baby. My phone up and quit on me and by the time I got myself a new one and got your message, I was already on my way home. Figured it'd be a nice surprise if I picked you up from school. I'm gonna order us a pizza for lunch. We got a lot of work to do, and I can't expect you to do it on an empty stomach."

Funny how a few minutes can change everything. Before he picked me up, I could have eaten an entire large pizza, but now, the thought of it made me want to barf. *Work to do* sounded suspiciously like code for *we've been evicted again*. If so, we'd need every dollar we had. I took a deep breath of smoky air, held it for a few seconds, and let it out slowly.

"It's okay, Daddy. I'm not hungry." I jumped down from the truck and slammed the door before he could say anything.

Stupid. Stupid, stupid, stupid. I know better than to let myself make friends when we never stay put for a whole year. Why, oh why, did I let Cheryl wear me down? Why did I let Nate talk to me? I should have tried harder to keep them both away.

I opened the front door, expecting to see piles of stuff everywhere, but the living room looked pretty much exactly as I left it. Black spray paint still covered the walls, the couch was still broken, and the blinds were still torn down. Even though I know Gynger had been home the whole time, the living room looked like some sort of twisted museum exhibit.

Daddy's heavy footsteps stopped right behind me. "You sure about not wanting pizza? It'll take us all day to get this place in good enough condition for your brother and sister."

"We're not moving again?"

"Moving? Nah, girl, we're not moving. I promised you I'd keep you here as long as possible, didn't I? You can always count on your ol' dad to keep his promises."

Yeah, well, you make the same promise after every move, I thought. "Where's Mama?"

"She's in bed. I gave her some medicine to knock her out. She should sleep right through our noise, and when she wakes up in a few hours, everything'll be good as new. Like nothing ever happened."

"What about the couch?"

"I guess we'll have to figure something out, won't we?"

I don't know how he expected the two of us to undo all the damage she had done, but we had to try. Paint cans, brushes, and a couple of rollers lined the wall under the living room window.

Talk about Extreme Home makeovers. "I'm going to change out of my school clothes, so I don't ruin them. Will you order the pizza? I think I'm hungry after all."

As soon as I shut the door to my room, I pulled out my phone and texted Cheryl.

My dad picked me up. Mom is feeling better, but the house is a mess. Please thank your mom and let her know we're staying at home tonight. Can she bring Leesh, Bobby and Sammycat home after school?"

After a few seconds, my phone buzzed.

Glad she's feeling better! I'll let my mom know, but your new stuff is still here.

Ugh. I forgot all about my stuff. If Gynger saw new clothes and pajamas, she'd throw an epic tantrum.

Maybe you can keep it there? Just in case she gets sick again and we need to crash with you? She's much better, but the doctors don't know what's wrong with her. It sounded stupid, but it was all I could think of.

No problem! Hey, don't get sick, too, okay? Lunch is lonely without you!

I made one more quick reply and then called Bobby and Leesh's school. Pretending to be their mother, I asked the office to tell them their big sister was already home, but Mrs. Dwyer would bring them home after school. I expected the office lady to laugh at me because I'm so obviously a child, but if she thought I sounded young, she didn't say so.

Business taken care of, I quickly stripped off my school clothes and put on an old tee shirt and a pair of too-short sweatpants. God help us if whatever Daddy gave Gynger wore off before we finished.

SAFE 13

Dear Diary,

Daddy and I worked all afternoon to get the house spic and span for Mama. I guess she really needed a good long break from us, because she slept all the way until dinner. Let me tell you, Diary, it was *so hard* not to wake her up while we were tidying up. I never have sleepovers and I've never been to any kind of camp, so I'm not used to not seeing her every day, and I missed her so much while we were at Cheryl's place. But as much as I wanted to go in and give her a hug, I didn't. Daddy told me she'd feel a lot better if she woke up naturally, so I controlled myself and tried to keep my mind on my work.

After Beth dropped Bobby and Leesh off, their eyes nearly popped out of their heads when they saw how clean we got things. Our house isn't a pigsty or anything, but it's not exactly a museum, either. With three kids, the messes build up fast. But as surprised as they were to see the house, it was nothing compared to Mama's face when she got up.

The second I saw her, my whole body relaxed. It was like someone had wrapped me up like a mummy and I could barely move or take a breath, but when Mama came out of her room, all the wrappings fell away, and I didn't feel smothered anymore. Heck, even Sammycat, who stubbornly refused to come out of the new cat carrier, seemed to be hit with a jolt of energy. As soon as she saw Mama, she bolted out of her carrier and raced around the room.

"Look," Bobby laughed. "Sammy has the zoomies!"

We all laughed, and my heart felt warm for the first time since Mama got sick. I'm so glad we're back home. Everything is going to be okay now that we're back together. I just know it.

REAL 27

Why can't I stop myself from writing in this journal? Every entry brings me closer to discovery. Keeping this journal is a risk I shouldn't be taking, but don't I deserve someone to talk to? Or at least a way to sort through all my shit?

Nate hovered around my locker after third period, like he's been doing for a while now. I usually blow him off, but I didn't try to ignore him today. With everything going on lately, I didn't have the energy to fake being annoyed.

"Hi," I said as I worked the combination on my locker.

"Wait, you're not going to accuse me of stalking you?" I know he was kidding, but for some reason, it made me feel defensive.

Cheryl wiggled her eyebrows and shot me a creepy serial killer smile as she walked by. Real discreet, Cheryl. Thanks.

"Shade, but the truth. I'm sorry for being such a jerk."

"Well, you sort of had a point. I did follow you around an awful lot."

I took a deep breath to settle my belly as I put my books away and slammed my locker. "I don't know how to ask you this without sounding like a complete dork." I tried to swallow the huge pile of sand clogging my throat.

"Just ask." How had I never noticed how kind his voice is? Oh, yeah. Because I never had the guts to talk to him before.

"Do you want to sit with me and Cheryl at lunch?" It was a simple question, but it felt like the most difficult thing I'd ever said.

"Hell, yeah." His smile brought the Sahara back to my throat.

"Seriously? You'll actually sit with us?" I realized right away how pathetic I sounded, but since I'm *Captain Awkward*, I couldn't figure out how to keep my thoughts inside my head.

"I've been *stalking* you for weeks, trying to get you to talk to me. What in the world made you think I'd turn down an invitation to sit with you?" He used air quotes but shot me with the most perfect smile I've ever laid eyes on.

What made me think he'd turn me down? I have absolutely no clue. I guess my self-esteem—or lack thereof, anyway. I might not be able to keep all my thoughts from escaping through my mouth, but at least I had enough sense to keep that bit quiet. Instead of answering, I walked toward the cafeteria. Nate stayed right beside me and chatted away.

I don't even know what he was talking about. I was too busy trying not to notice everyone else notice Nate Evans heading to lunch with ugly Zoe Wilkes. They must have all wondered what the hell he was doing with me, but Nate didn't seem to see their confused glances. Or if he did, he didn't seem to care. I wish I knew how not to give a shit what people think of me, but I might as well wish I were a unicorn or had a billion dollars.

Gynger's stomping around. I need to go check on things, but I'll be back in a bit.

———

SAFE 14

Dear Diary,

So, it turns out, I enjoy the writing prompts in English so much, I wish I had more time to work on them. Ten minutes isn't nearly enough time to say everything the prompts bring up. I suppose it's good it's such a short time, though. Mama has a point. I spend too much time with my head in the clouds and not enough time with my feet on the ground as it is. If Mrs. Thomas didn't stop us after ten minutes, I'd probably waste the whole period writing.

One of Cheryl's friends sat with us at lunch today, which was a little awkward. I've always trusted Mama's advice to keep people at a distance. She says the one thing you can count on is people will hurt you the first chance they get, so it's best not to let anyone get too close. Why are people so awful to each other? Mama seems to have learned this lesson the hard way, and I'm so thankful she cares enough about me to try and protect me from getting hurt like she was.

I can't even tell you how sorry I am for the poor kids whose parents don't offer the same kind of wisdom Mama gives me. They're going to have such a rough time when they leave home because they won't be prepared for how cruel the world is. Not me, though. Or Leesh or Bobby. We may not be rich or have the newest gadgets, but we have something way better. We have real love and support from a mother who doesn't try to shield us from how awful people are.

I want to find a way to thank Mama for all she does for us. Maybe I'll make her cookies or something this weekend.

Gotta run!

REAL 28

I am *so* glad I put away this journal when I did. Seconds after I finished up a B.S. entry in the other journal about how awesome she is, she came into my room without even knocking. I don't know why it still makes me so mad that she doesn't knock. She's made it clear my whole life that I don't deserve privacy and she'll enter my room any old time she wants. I think she was hoping to catch me doing something I shouldn't be doing, but I don't even want to try and guess what she hoped she'd find. Anyway, I don't want to talk about her.

What I really want is to finish talking about lunch.

"Thanks for letting me join you." Nate set his tray across from mine and smiled at me. His green eyes sparkled like jewels and his cheeks were flushed with a hint of pink. "Hopefully, I won't make an ass of myself, and you'll let me sit with you again tomorrow."

"You couldn't make an ass of yourself even if you tried, but you might end up looking like a fool for sitting with me." I don't know why I said that, but I tried to play it cool and act like I didn't just stick my foot in my mouth hard enough to kick my tonsils. Why can't I talk to people like a regular human? What is wrong with me?

Cheryl came into the cafeteria and did her creepy eyebrow wiggle thing again as she passed us.

"I know you probably don't want to talk about your family." He stabbed the little straw into his apple juice box and drank it all at once. "But do you mind if I vent about mine for a few minutes? It's why I waited for you before lunch."

"Go for it." As if I'd tell him I didn't want to hear anything he wanted to tell me.

He smiled his adorable smile and my belly flipped. Even though I was starving, I wasn't so sure I'd be able to eat.

"Thanks. I really don't have anyone to talk to about all the real stuff I'm going through, and I'm too much of a coward to tell anyone the truth."

"Why?"

"I've lived in my house my whole life, so I've never been the new kid. I'm not the most popular dude here, but everyone knows me. I've worked hard to put out this *everything's great, cool guy* vibe because life's way better with lots of friends. But kids talk, you know? If I told anyone about my dad, word could get out and my cool-guy vibe would *poof.*" He made a mushroom cloud out of his hands as he said the last word.

Hold up. The only reason he could talk to me is because I'm not popular enough to gossip? The gentle flips in my belly morphed into a violent roil and I realized I had tightened my grip on the fork. I should have gotten up and walked away right then, but I'm a loser, so I just sat there and kept my mouth shut. He must have realized it was a jerky thing to say because he lowered his eyes and mumbled an apology.

"What I mean," he continued, "is you're the strongest person in this place. You're still basically *The New Girl*, but you've managed to stay away from the new kid trap of either falling into the wrong crowd or changing who you are to try and fit in with the popular kids. You can do your own thing without trying to be cool or whatever. I'm not like that. If I think someone even looked at me funny, I lie awake all night obsessing about it."

"You're kidding, right? Don't sit there and act like you don't know at least half the school has a massive crush on you. And the ones who don't want to be like you. I literally can't think of a single person who doesn't like you."

"That doesn't mean I have anyone to talk to. Sure, everyone seems to like me, but it's not a big deal, since I can't be myself around anyone. They like who I show them, not who I am." Nate pushed his empty tray to the side and leaned across the table. "You walk around being yourself, and I am so jealous of you."

"Don't be. I care so much about what people think that I don't let anyone get close to me because if they did, they'd realize I'm not worth their time. But we both know you didn't want to sit here and talk about me, so what's up?"

He slouched and lowered his head a bit, obviously uncomfortable, which was more than a little bit bizarre. I've never seen Nate look anything but confidant and in control. He took a deep breath like he was about to jump headfirst into the story of his life when Cheryl plopped her lunch next to mine. Takis and a Diet Coke, as usual. I slid over before she could tell me to move.

"Children," Cheryl said in her Principal Williams' voice, "What are we talking about today?" She didn't use that voice often, but when she did, it was hilarious and a bit eerie at the same time. If you blindfolded me, I wouldn't be able to tell Cheryl from Principal Williams.

"Nothing, really," I said.

"It doesn't look like nothing. I could tell from halfway

across the cafeteria you two are elbow deep in an important conversation, and I need to know what it is."

What could I say? *Not much, just boring old abusive parents stuff.* Cheryl's timing sucks. Nate would have to wait to share his secrets with me.

REAL 29

Nate rode the bus home with me today. Even though he doesn't live too far from he school, he never takes the bus because his mom usually picks him up.

"Since Cheryl interrupted us, I thought I'd ride home with you." He slid into the seat and beamed his million-watt smile. "Is that okay?"

"No, sorry. You're gonna have to jump out at the first red light." I pretended not to see everyone staring at us as I made room for him. I felt awkward, but also a little bit special. Okay, maybe more than a little bit. We didn't talk about anything too heavy on the ride, we just chatted about dumb stuff. Who's dating who. The stench of hormones and sweat on the bus. Boring, normal stuff.

The same kind of stuff kids talk about on the way home every single day. The same kind of conversation I've always wanted to have but never did. His leg and shoulder touched mine, even though there was plenty of room in the seat. I spent the whole ride trying to focus on not acting like an idiot instead of on the strange, vibrating heat radiating between us. I've never been as thirsty as I was on the ride home.

Two stops before mine, I stood up.

"This is me." I gestured to the nice, respectable neighborhood that was most definitely not mine. I couldn't stand the thought of him seeing where I live, even if he never found out which house was mine. Better to hoof it home.

"No, it isn't." He stood up to let me out, anyway.

"How would you know? I thought you weren't stalking me."

"It's not like this is actually Dallas. I've ridden my bike past every house in this town at least four hundred times."

"Now you definitely don't sound like a stalker."

He laughed as he fell in step beside me. The smell of bus diesel tickled my nose.

"I have an idea," Nate said after a few seconds.

"Oh, yeah?"

"Okay, this is gonna sound weird but hear me out."

I stopped under a huge oak in a front yard and turned to look at him. "Well, then you better start talking before you scare me away."

"I think we should try to hook up my dad and your mom."

"What are you talking about?"

He ran his fingers through his dark hair. "Your mom sucks. My dad sucks. They could suck together, and we could move in with my mom."

"Hold up. Are you suggesting we arrange a booty call for our parents and then move in with your mother? Talk about messed up. And did you forget about my dad? I know he's never around, but something tells me he wouldn't exactly be thrilled to discover his wife's been cheating on him."

"Look, I'll be the first to admit this plan isn't easy. Or foolproof, but at least it's something."

"And you expect your mom to be okay with it all and take in three extra kids? I know your family is like rich or something, but I highly doubt you can take on me, my sister and my brother."

"My dad makes more than enough to take care of all of us. He might be a dick, but there's no way he's gonna let me and my mom down. If he falls for your mom, he'll make sure you're all right, too. He's too much of a narcissist to give off the impression his life is anything but perfect."

"But he'll get a divorce and shack up with my mother? You were at Ikea and saw for yourself what she's like. I don't think this plan of yours is gonna work."

"You don't know. It might."

"We both know we're not going to do this, so why don't you tell me what's really going on?"

Nate took a deep breath and looked straight into my eyes. "Just because you can't see the bruises my dad leaves doesn't mean they're not there. Like I said, the creep needs everything to look perfect on the outside." He lifted his shirt to reveal a purple-to-green fading bruise on his side.

"Oh, God, Nate. I didn't know. I'm sorry."

"Nobody knows." He adjusted his backpack and shook his head. "Except my mother. She knows better than anyone because she gets the worst of it."

I swear I felt my heart cracking. All those times he wore a hoodie or a flannel when it was hot wasn't because he was trying to be cool, but because his dad hadn't been careful. How could I be so self-absorbed? How did I not pick up on this?

Without even realizing it, we came to the far end of my street. I looked around at the run-down houses with over-grown yards, and shame smothered me like a wet wool blanket on a sweltering night. I stopped walking and turned to look at him.

"I'm so sorry."

"For what?"

"I don't know. For not paying closer attention to you. For

blowing you off. For not wanting you to come any closer to my house. For everything."

"After everything I told you, you're still embarrassed about your house?" He looked hurt, and those cracks in my heart got a little longer.

Stupid tears burned my eyes. "I'm not embarrassed. I'm scared."

"Of what?" He took my hand and squeezed gently.

"I'm late, and the kids got home without me. I know Leesh covered for me because she always has my back, but my mother will be furious. If she's waiting for me in the yard, she'll act all sweet and happy to see me, but as soon as we're alone, her mask will slip, and it'll be hell. Double hell if she sees me with you because she'll think I'm talking crap about her."

"It's not talking crap if it's true. But I get it. This is where we split up."

"Thank you, Nate." I threw my arms around him and gave him a quick hug without even thinking about it. He hugged back tightly. Like someone who needed to be held, and for a moment, I felt our hearts beating together.

"Here." He handed me a folded piece of paper. "My number. Hit me up if you need to talk."

When Cheryl gave me her number at lunch a few weeks ago, I didn't think I could possibly feel any more excited, but I was wrong. It was nothing compared to getting Nate's. My face practically throbbed from smiling so big, and I don't think my feet touched the ground the rest of the way home. I recited his number until I memorized it and then threw the paper away in a neighbor's trash so Gynger wouldn't find it. I was in such a floaty haze, I barely remember getting the rest of the way home.

But you know what they say—what goes up, must come down. The second I opened the door, Gynger flew at me like the Wicked Witch from The Wizard of Oz. You know the saying *three sheets to the wind?* Well, she had to be at least twelve sheets to the wind. She was so wasted when I moved out of her way, she stumbled and fell to the floor.

"Goddamn it, Zoe! Look what you did!"

I did some quick mental calculus to figure out my best options. The first was to blow past her and hope the effort of getting up made her pass out instead. The second was to play the good daughter and help her up. Both carried the risk I'd end up huddled in a corner, but as much as my legs wanted to carry me right down the hall, I couldn't leave her wobbling on all fours like a drugged lion. I forced myself to come closer and clenched my stomach around the disgust swirling in my belly as I squatted down to touch her.

"I'm sorry, Mama." I was happy to hear my voice sounded kind and soft.

"I'm sorry, I'm sorry," she mocked. "You're gonna be sorry if you don't help me up this instant. Why can't you be more like your sister instead of a worthless piece of shit? Thank God I made at least one good daughter."

I don't think I'll ever get used to the way it feels when she says those kinds of things to me, but she can sense weakness, so I made my voice steady and clear.

"You've had such a busy day, Mama." I got her to her feet and guided her to the couch. "Why don't you rest here, and I'll bring you something to drink before I start dinner, okay?"

She fell onto the couch and her legs spread wide. There was no sign of Bobby, but Leesh was curled up in the armchair, sketching and acting like we weren't there. I don't blame her. The only way to survive in this house is to ignore the chaos.

In the kitchen, I considered a problem even trickier than getting her off the floor without getting hurt myself. If I made her a drink, she'd probably pass out for the rest of the night, which would be good for all of us. But she might throw up in her sleep, and I did not want to deal with that again.

If I brought her water, she might accuse me of trying to control her, and that could turn her from drunk-tired to drunk-mean. And to complicate the equation, I didn't know how much she'd had to drink all day, if she'd eaten anything, or if she had taken pills or anything else with her liquor. It was a safe bet she hadn't had much, if any, water all day. I grabbed a glass and tried to find my way out of this mind-maze.

"Zoe! The fuck's taking you so long?" Her thick voice trailed off, which told me she was about to pass out.

"Coming, Mama!" I poured a splash of whisky into the glass and topped it with way more soda than I knew she'd prefer. I filled a second glass with water.

She immediately reached for the mixed drink, but I handed her the water. "Drink this first, so you don't get a sugar headache from the soda."

Apparently, I had solved the equation correctly because she gulped down the water without a fight. I tried to hide my disgust as water trickled out of the corner of her mouth, off her chin, and onto her chest. I took the empty glass and handed her the whisky. Leesh looked at me like I was a special kind of stupid for handing it over, but her opinion was the least of my worries.

"Come help me with dinner," I said to her.

Leesh sighed, dropped her sketchbook to the floor, and pulled herself out of the chair like her body weighed a thousand pounds., She seemed so much older and more tired than any thirteen-year-old should. My heart pinched in my chest a little.

I wonder, do I look older, too? Why is Gynger the only one who doesn't have to grow up?

REAL 30

I've decided I can't keep stressing out about Gynger. She is the way she is and worrying won't change anything. It only puts me in a dark place where all I can think about is dark things. They say you attract what you put out to the universe. I don't believe that's exactly true, but I do think a little positive thinking can help me handle the rough times a little better. Gynger will always be a rotten mother. As long as I live at home, I'll always have to be the responsible one, and I'll always have to tiptoe around her. Since nothing will ever change her, I'll focus on the good things instead of feeling sorry for myself over the bad.

Good things like getting my first phone number from a boy. Nate freaking Evans gave me, Zoe Dawn Wilkes, his phone number. How is something like that within the realm of possibility for someone like me? I'm so overwhelmed right now if I climbed into bed, I bet I could sleep for a solid week. But at the same time, my brain is buzzing like a beehive some kid mistook for a piñata. Even if I had time to take a nap like my body wants, I'm not sure my brain could sleep.

What am I supposed to do with his number? Does he really want me to "hit him up" and what did he mean? Text him? Call? Why is everything so complicated? How do people handle this sort of thing? Is getting a number this difficult for everyone, or just me? I need to talk to Cheryl about this. She'll be able to help. And I'm always going on about how I wish my life were normal. What's more normal than a girl talking to her best friend about a boy?

Wait. Is Cheryl my best friend? What even is my life?

SAFE 15

Dear Diary,

I got distracted on the bus yesterday and missed my stop. Leesh tried to get my attention, but I was so exhausted I didn't even hear her. She ended up getting off without me, and I can't even blame her. She didn't want to get in trouble for being late, too. It wasn't until three stops later and most of the kids were gone that I realized what I had done.

By the time I got home, Mama was understandably upset. Because of me, Bobby could have gotten hurt. Leesh could have been kidnapped and raped. In fact, I could have, too. And on top of everything, dinner was late because it's my responsibility to cook at night. I try so hard to be responsible, but I messed up big time today. To make it up to Mama, I made her a drink and told her I'd cook dinner and clean up afterward.

It was the least I could do. After dinner, Leesh locked herself in her room. She must still be upset with me for being late. Maybe she thinks I ignored her on purpose to get her in trouble. I'd like to believe she knows I'd never get her in trouble on purpose, but nobody can ever truly know what's in someone else's heart. All I can do is give her space and be there for her if she decides she wants to talk to me.

REAL 31

It's not lost on me I do all my best writing at night. I think it's because I can pretend I'm doing homework, but I also think it's because odds are pretty good Gynger won't walk in on me since she's usually out cold by like eight o'clock. Of course, there're no guarantees when it comes to what Gynger will do, but I'll take what I can get. It's normal for all of us to spread out after she's asleep, so it wasn't strange when Leesh went to her room after dinner. Still, I had a nagging feeling something was up.

"Little pig, little pig, let me come in," I growled at her door.

"Go away. I don't want to talk to you right now."

"Too bad, so sad." I came in and plopped next to her. Unlike me, my sister keeps her room super organized. She even made herself a little nightstand by draping a purple sheet from the thrift store over an upside-down cardboard box. Her sketch book and a couple of pencils were the only things on the fake table. "What's going on with you?"

She sat up and hugged her knees but didn't say anything.

She didn't try to kick me out either, though, so I settled myself in and waited.

"I'm happy for you about Nate, but it sucked when you didn't come home with us. She blamed me."

"Blamed you how?"

"I know she's always calling me her perfect little daughter, but when she realized you weren't checking the mail or something, she…it doesn't matter. I don't want to talk about it."

"No, you don't get to bring this up and then drop it."

"You know how she came at you as soon as you walked through the door? It would have been a million times worse if she hadn't vented some of her rage on me." She squeezed her eyes and let out a shuddery breath.

"Oh, God. Did she hit you?" The ramen noodles and peas I made for dinner lurched in my stomach at the thought of Leesh taking my punishment for me.

"It wasn't as bad as what she does to you. Bobby broke a glass a couple of minutes in, and she told me to clean it up before he hurt himself." She smiled and whispered, "I think he did it on purpose."

"I'm so sorry. I swear, I'll never put you in that situation again."

"It's whatever. You didn't even do anything wrong. I'm way too used to you being my shield. I don't know how you do it all day, every day. I don't have it half as bad as you, and I hate living here."

"Me, too. We'll be out of here soon enough, though." I put my arms around her and hugged her hard.

"No. You'll be out of here soon enough, but I won't. And when you're gone, who's going to keep her from coming after me? Or, God forbid, Bobby?"

REAL 32

I've been so worried about my own problems. I never stopped to consider what things are like for my sister. That's not really true, though, is it? No. The truth is, I assumed I knew what things are like for her, but I never took the time to find out for myself. When she said Gynger will probably target her after I leave, my heart about died. It seems like forever before I graduate, but it's not too far off. What will happen in the years Leesh has left? And after she's gone? Who will Gynger hate when we're both gone? Bobby?

If we still had grandparents, I'd pack us all up in the middle of the night and find a way to their house. Bone tired, I'd knock on their door as Leesh and Bobby nestle into my side for comfort. We blink as the porch light turns night into day. The quietly creaking chains of the old, green porch swing sing my brother and sister closer to sleep as we wait for someone to answer. After what feels like a week, Grandpa finally opens the door, just a crack, because nothing good ever knocks in the middle of the night. Grandma, in her pink, quilty robe, peeks over his shoulder. Little wisps of hair snake out of her long gray braid, and I feel a little sorry for waking them both up so late, but happy to be somewhere warm and safe.

At first, they blink, not quite understanding what we're doing on their porch in the middle of the night. They look around for Gynger or Daddy, but when they see we're alone, they open the door wide, hug and kiss us on the head and cheeks, and whisk us inside. The house, always so clean and warm, smells like cinnamon and apples.

Without even asking why we're alone, Grandma sits us around her big yellow table and sings quietly as she whips up a batch of chocolate chip pancakes and bacon. Even though it's three in the morning, Grandpa whistles like a morning bird and makes a pot of coffee. The smell of food and coffee makes our stomachs rumble, and Grandpa sends us to wash our hands for the earliest breakfast in the world.

What is my problem? What's the point of this stupid fantasy? We don't have grandparents or aunties or uncles. Nobody will ever rescue us from our life, and if anyone makes us pancakes, it has to be me. If anyone will keep us safe, it has to be me, too. No more being careless or coming home late so I can hang out with a boy. No selfishness. From now on, my brother and sister come first.

———

SAFE 16

Dear Diary,

When I sit back and think about how far I've come since we moved here, I'm amazed at myself. Not three months ago, I was scarfing my food down alone and then hiding out in the bathroom for the rest of lunch so I wouldn't have to sit by myself and look like a loser. And now, look at me. I have Cheryl. And one of her friends started sitting with us, too. He seems nice, and if he didn't obviously have a thing for her, I'd probably have a thing for him. He's one of those rare guys who's cute and smart and nice and I totally get why Cheryl gets flustered whenever he's around. Not me, though. I have way too much on my plate as it is, and I don't need any more distractions. Especially of the male variety.

REAL 33

Today, Nate sat with us at lunch like he's never sat anywhere else. He pretended not to notice his arm brushing against mine, but there's no way he missed the ten-thousand volts of electricity that jumped from me to him. It's so easy for me to sit in my bedroom and tell myself I can never fall for anyone, but when I see him, I forget everything I promised myself.

I can't help but dream what it would be like to walk home with him every day. What it'd be like for him to come over and watch TV with me or to walk to McDonald's together to share a twenty-piece McNuggets. When he looks at me, I can almost pretend I'm a normal girl and we're both going through normal, awkward stuff. Pretend we can figure out how to be friends and then we can morph our friendship into something deeper.

When it comes right down to it, I'm pretty sure he's interested in me, even though I have no earthly idea why. Maybe he sees I'm broken because he's broken, too. He hides his cracks better than I do, but he has his fair share of them after what he's told me about his dad. They say opposites attract, but they also say all the best relationships are based on something common. Does having shitty parents count?

My brain is like two warriors battling it out. One part tells me I'm a mess and don't deserve love, friendship, or hell, even respect. The other part tells me I *do* deserve those things and so much more. I deserve happiness, peace, and adventure. I deserve a best friend and a first kiss. How is it possible to believe two opposite things about yourself? Either I'm a regular kid in a shitty situation, or I'm an emotional black hole and will ruin anyone who gets too close.

GOD! Why does everything have to be so confusing?

REAL 34

It's been two weeks since Nate moved to our lunch table, but he hasn't taken the bus with me again. He tried to last week, but I asked him not to.

"Why not?" he asked. "I don't mind walking home from your stop, and trust me, my mom is happy not to have to pick me up."

"I ended up in a world of trouble for coming home late the last time. I can't risk it happening again." It wasn't a complete lie, but not the total truth, either. I would happily get in trouble every day for the rest of my life if it were just me, but now that I know Gynger will turn on Leesh, it's not worth the risk—no matter how badly I want to spend time with Nate.

"What if I promise not to let you miss your stop?"

"I don't think so. I don't like depending on anyone else. If something goes wrong, I prefer to have only myself to blame."

"I gave you my number two weeks ago. Why haven't you texted?"

The question took my breath away, and I tried to find something not stupid to say. In the end, I settled on the truth.

"My phone's only for my mother to reach me in an emergency. I'm not allowed to text or call anyone." God, how humiliating.

"And you go along with that dumb rule? Do you think she'd actually find out if you used it?"

"It's never been worth it to find out. You barely know the half of what she's capable of."

He ran his hands through his shaggy brown hair and shook his head. "I would if you told me more, but I'm sorry."

I dug my left thumbnail into the palm of my right hand to keep myself under control. "I don't need your sympathy, or your stupid apology. Your family is every bit as effed up as mine, so it's not like you're all superior or whatever. Get over yourself."

He took my left hand and gently moved it away from my right. That damned electricity tingled from my hand, up my arm all the way to my throat. I wanted to stay quietly angry with him, but instead, I felt both electrified and safe. How annoying.

"I just mean the way your mom controls everything about your life sucks. You should be allowed to chat with your friends after school."

I pulled my hand out of his and rubbed it on my pants, trying to wipe away the sweat and the tingle. "It's fine. You didn't do anything wrong, I'm feeling off today. Please don't ride the bus with me anymore, okay?"

All the rest of the day, I couldn't stop thinking about what he said. I should be allowed to do all the same things other kids get to do. Why can't I text my friends? Why aren't I allowed to hang out at the mall? I don't go to games or dances. I don't go to the parties even though there's one practically every week-end. I don't go anywhere or do anything, ever. I think Gynger's trying to control me because she can't handle that I'm growing up. I have a life and all she has is a crumbled down house and three kids who are terrified of her. I think she's jealous of me. Screw her.

After I fixed Bobby his snack, I turned the sound off on my phone and texted Nate.

Hey, it's Zoe 😊

What Gynger doesn't know can't hurt me.

REAL 35

Today's writing prompt in English, "Write about a delicate or fragile object."

I was so proud of my entry, I asked Mrs. Thomas if I could come in at lunch to copy it so I could add it to my journal at home. She surprised me by offering to make a copy for me if I wanted to follow her to the teacher's lounge.

Handle With Care

You push past her in the halls, not even noticing
The books you knocked out of her hands.
Why should you?
Unimportant
Worthless
Invisible
Maybe you have a class with her, but you don't know her name.
What's it matter?
Loser
Trash
Parasite

She picks up her books and doesn't bother yelling at you.
Why should she? You can't hear
Her shouts
Her cries
Her despair
But if you could see the invisible girl in the hall, you'd see
Her glass-egg heart, cracked but beating strong
Her wild, untamed-horse spirit running on a mountain
She is stronger than you could ever dream, and you don't need
to handle her with care
Because she's made of stone.

Is this a poem? I've never written a poem before, and I'm sure it's way too whiny to be any good. I don't know why I wrote it, where it came from, or even what it means. When I saw the prompt, the words bled out of me, and I couldn't stop them. By the time I finished, my nose was stuffy, and tears blurred my words. After Mrs. Thomas gave me my copy, I texted Nate and Cheryl to tell them I'd be in the library. I spent the rest of lunch looking through the poetry section, and I came home with three books.

———

SAFE 17

Dear Diary,

I think I wrote a poem in English today. It was so much fun that I went to the library at lunch and checked out a few poetry books. There are probably all sorts of rules for how to write real poetry, and I don't know any of them, but I thought it might be fun to learn.

Mama picked up one of the books while I made Bobby an after-school snack.

"Is this for some English project?" She set her drink next to the pile of library books and flipped through the one in her hand.

"No, ma'am. I just thought it might be fun to learn how to write a real poem."

"Ain't nothing in the world ever been made better by a poem, girlie. Poetry is for the liberal elites who live off their daddy's trust funds and drink fancy wine when it tastes the exact same as the three-buck bottle." She tossed the book back on the table and it slid to the floor, like the trash it is.

Sure, it was fun to write a poem in class, but Mama's right. What good is poetry when there are hungry children in the world? What good does a poem do when there are kids who are abused every single day? What good are words when there are bills to pay and mouths to feed?

I'll return the books first thing in the morning.

REAL 36

I've got to find a way to get us out of here. She's gone too far this time. Too. Far. She can target me all she wants. I can take being kicked and having my hair yanked out by the fistful. I can handle her silent treatment and her words that squeeze my heart like barbed wire. I cannot—will not—sit by and let her hurt Bobby.

BOBBY! He's still a baby. What kind of monster beats up a six-year-old? And Joel—I refuse to call him *Daddy* ever again—JOEL was right there when it happened, and he didn't even try to stop her. He just sat at the table, staring at his sweating beer can and pretending everything was fine. Another normal day in the Wilkes house.

What was Bobby's great offense? He brought home a note from his teacher saying he was too talkative in class. It's not a big deal. He gets those notes all the time, and sometimes she even sees them. Hell, sometimes she jokes about them. Says things like *I guess your stupid ass teacher expects a classroom full of robots instead of little kids.* Rich, coming from the woman who expects her own kids not to speak unless spoken to. Most of the time, I take the notes and sign them for Bobby, so I don't have to bother her with them.

She was already hopping mad when we got home. Before we even reached the yard, we heard her screaming at Joel. Hell, I'd be surprised if the whole town and the next one over didn't hear her. I'll never forgive myself for not making us all come in through the back door like we usually do when they're fighting, but I didn't because all the rain flooded both yards and I decided I was too precious to walk through a little mud. I wish I could go back and do it differently, but there's no such thing as a Time Turner, and I'm not God.

As soon as we walked into the house, I sent Bobby and Leesh to their rooms. Bobby stopped at the bathroom on the way and forgot his backpack in there. Why didn't I notice it? I'm usually so careful, but right off the bat I made two horrible mistakes. Not long after Bobby came out, *she* stomped down the hall and slammed the bathroom door. The picture frames in the hallway rattled, and the picture of little Leesh holding baby Bobby fell to the floor.

A minute later, she let out a monster roar. Bobby, always so secure in his safety, peeked his head out of his room and she ran toward him, the note crumpled in her hand. She grabbed him by the arm and yanked him out of his room. He was so shocked, he didn't even scream. He wiggled around until he broke her grip. He ran down the hallway into the living room, but she was right on his heels.

"Mama," I yelled. "Mama, STOP!"

I stood in front of her, hoping to slow her down, ready to take her fury for Bobby, but she pushed me into the wall. It took a couple of seconds to catch my breath enough to get back up. By the time I got to the living room, she had him cornered. He was curled into a tight ball, exactly the way I curl up.

"You like talking? Talk now! What do you have to say for yourself?" Her voice bounced off the walls and I prayed the neighbors wouldn't hear us. "How dare you embarrass me like this?"

She pulled her leg back and kicked him in the head. She kicked her baby. IN THE HEAD! Thank God she wasn't wearing shoes. His head must be hard as concrete because she roared again, but this time she roared in pain.

"Look what you made me do!" she screamed.

Bobby didn't move, so she grabbed him by the hair and pulled him up, exactly like she pulls me around by my hair.

I thought I was going to be sick right there on the floor.

"I said, look at me!" She dragged him to his room and slammed the door behind them.

God. My hands are shaking. My whole body is shivering like I'm naked in a blizzard. I can barely see through my tears. When I was little, I used to think tears were magical. I believed a purely cried tear could change the world. Now I know better. Bobby's tears only fed her rage. Joel just sat there, acting like nothing was happening, and me? I wanted to jump in. I wanted to do something to distract her, but I'm as bad as Joel. I didn't do a damn thing to help my baby brother.

I could say I was in shock, or afraid I'd make it worse for him, but that would be a lie. The truth is, I was too afraid to move. I know the pain. I know the kicks and the punches. I've experienced them more than anyone, so I should be used to them. I should have done something really, really bad to distract her from him, but I'm a stupid, selfish coward. I hate myself.

I'm so sorry, Bobby. I let you down, and I will never forgive myself.

I have more to say.

She's locked herself in her room. The bottle of whisky is missing, so I assume she took it with her. Priorities, yo. Joel took off after she went to her room. He didn't say a single word. He just got up and walked right out the front door. A second later, the truck rumbled, and he drove off. He acted like nobody else even existed. What the hell is wrong with him? I don't know where he went, but my guess is the liquor store. I wish he'd stay gone forever. What good is he? He doesn't make enough money, and he doesn't keep her from hurting us, so why is he even here?

I still wanted to throw up, but I kept myself together and went to Bobby's room. I found him lying on the floor, curled into a corner.

"I'm so sorry, sweetie." I squatted down next to him and my heart shattered like thin ice when he looked up at me. His eyes were swollen from crying and he winced as he sat up. I put my arms around him and helped him to his bed to lie down. Something about sleep and head trauma bit at the back of my brain, but I couldn't remember exactly what. Are you supposed to let someone sleep after they get hit in the head, or keep them awake? I almost always sleep after Gynger hurts me, but is it because it's what you're supposed to do, or is it more because I want to escape the pain?

"Do you want some water?" I asked.

"No, thanks. It hurts too much." His voice was small, broken. Tears burned my eyes to hear him be so quietly polite, but I blinked them back. Crying in front of him would only make him feel worse.

"Well, I'm going to bring you some anyway, and you have to have at least two sips for me, okay?"

I about lost it when I heard his reply, "Nokay."

When I came back with the water and a cold, wet washcloth for his head, he was on his side, facing the wall. I rubbed his back, and his face went all squishy as he turned to sit up.

"It wasn't your fault, Bub. Do you understand you didn't do anything to deserve what she did to you?"

Instead of answering, he took the cup from my hand and sipped. "Why is she like this, Zoe?" His chin trembled and he blinked hard as he tried not to cry.

"I don't know. Maybe she was born this way. I don't remember her being different, anyway."

He handed me the water and laid back down. When I brought my hand to his head, he flinched, and my heart broke into about a million more pieces than it already was. Did he think I was going to hit him, too? I'd never hurt him. Never.

The entry I made a while back about what will happen to my sister and brother when I move out? I've been thinking a lot about it. Gynger usually craps on me and not the others. Sure, sometimes she'll go after Leesh a little, or maybe yell at Bobby, but not often. Since he's her baby, the physical stuff has always been off limits. At worst, she'd maybe throw something toward him without hitting him. So why now? Why, after all this time, did she decide it's okay to attack him? Is it because he's not a baby anymore? That makes sense, I think. She can't stand to talk about any of us growing up. Like, if I tell Leesh she's getting tall, Gynger gets all weird and reminds her she's still her baby girl.

Sometimes, when she gets drunk, she pulls Bobby into her lap. "Promise you'll never grow up and leave your Mama, baby. Promise you'll always love me. You'll always stay with me."

And he does. He says all the things she tells him to, because what little kid wouldn't? But she's like a lion in the wild. She's tasted his blood, and he'll never be her safe little baby again.

Why didn't I stop her? It's my job to keep them all safe, and I was too scared to do the one thing I'm supposed to do. I failed him. His pain, his *blood* is on my hands, and I hate myself.

We have clothes and toiletries at Cheryl's house. Would her mom put us up again? I'm sure she would, but I can't. Lying about Gynger being deathly ill worked one time, but no way will it fly again. But telling her the truth about what it's like here is out of the question. I'm not sure about anything except the fact that I absolutely cannot talk. If I talk, we get separated. Leesh is on a shaky bridge as it is.

If we get separated, her bridge might collapse, and she'd fall right off the edge. And Bobby? He'd probably be okay after a while, but he's still so young. He wouldn't understand why we're not together, and he'd be heartbroken. He's a cute kid, so I'm sure eventually someone would adopt him, but... Hell, let's be honest. I can't handle the idea of my brother and sister not being my brother and sister anymore.

I don't know how to keep Gynger from hurting them, but I

do know we have no choice but to ride the storm out together, in our own home.

———

SAFE 18

Dear Diary,

Daddy had to leave again. The morning after Bobby got in trouble for being too talkative at school, he had already left without even telling us goodbye. When he comes home, he usually stays all weekend, but there must have been some emergency to call him away on a Saturday. I guess dealing with Bobby really took it out of Mama. She went to her room after he got into trouble and said she didn't feel good. She's been so sick. She can't even get out of bed by herself.

Since he wasn't around to take care of Mama, it fell to me to do it, which, of course, I'm happy to do. It breaks my heart to see her so weak. When she needs to go to the bathroom, she hammers on the wall with one of her boots and I run to help her. She needs to lean on me all the way down the hall. When she's done, I help her back to her room and tuck her back into bed, making sure her boot is close enough to the bed so she can reach it the next time she needs me.

She isn't eating, either. When I bring her a new bowl of soup, the old bowl is always sitting right where I left it. I don't know what to do. I'm trying my best to keep the kids quiet so she can get all the rest she needs. I stay close by so I can help her if she bangs on the wall to get my attention because poor Mama is so weak, she can't even talk.

I try to get her to drink water, but she can't sit up long enough to drink, and she won't let me help her sit because she doesn't want to make me sick. I wish I knew how to help her. She's starting to worry Bobby. I asked her if she wanted me to stay home from school to take care of her, but she said the quiet would be good for her and she didn't want me missing school on account of her. Typical Mama. Even when she's practically on her deathbed, she worries about our education.

I hope she feels better soon.

REAL 38

Gynger's been weird since she hurt Bobby on Friday. When she goes off on me, she'll go to her room for an hour or two, and when she comes out, she acts like I don't exist. She still has a meanness to her, but it's quieter. Like, she'll make sure to cuddle Bobby or tell Leesh she's her favorite daughter right in front of me. The second half of my punishment is for her to pretend I was never born. That hurts almost as much as the hitting, but in an entirely different way.

Once, I read an article about a religious group in Pennsylvania or something. They isolate themselves and live like it's the eighteen-hundreds. If one of the members of the community does something exceptionally bad, the whole village acts like they don't exist. Even the person's own parents do it. They're not even allowed to sit at the same table as their family. They call it *shunning*, and it's so painful that shunned people frequently pack up and leave everything and everyone they've ever known. I can't imagine leaving my brother and sister behind. Not in a million years.

It's hard enough to keep myself together when Gynger shuns me for a few hours or a day. I can't imagine how painful it would be if it lasted months or years and it was everyone I love. When she finally stops ignoring me, which is usually as soon as Bobby gets a splinter or there's a gross smell coming from the fridge someone needs to deal with, everything goes back to normal.

What she's doing is new. It's as if she's shunning herself, and I don't understand it. I try to get her to eat, but she leaves the soup I bring her on the nightstand, which seriously pisses me off. It's not like I can magically make food appear from nothing, and here she is, wasting it like we have a magical soup fountain. When I pick up the old soup, there's always at least one roach in it, but sometimes more. They climb up the bowl and fall in. Death by chicken noodle.

Can you believe I'm actually worried about her? Her room is so dark, and it stinks. I know she's not showering, but is she not even wiping herself after she uses the bathroom? Earlier, I tried to open her window, and she yelled at me and threw the stupid boot she bangs on the wall at my head. Fine. Rot away in your own filth and stink, see if I care. Maybe if I stop bringing her food, she'll get her ass up and find something to eat.

REAL 39

My safe journal hasn't moved since my last entry, so I know Gynger hasn't been reading it. Has she decided my life is so dull there's no point in spying on me anymore? I hope so. She's not wrong, though. Other than whatever drama she causes, my life is ridiculously basic and not much fun.

Sometimes I have a strange, restless feeling. Like I'm going to scream or cry if I don't do something to break up the routine of my life. Like on Friday nights, I think about the parties I don't get invited to, the dates I don't get asked on, the mall hangouts nobody includes me in, and I feel like if I don't scream or cry or throw something, I'll fall down dead. The thing is, Cheryl *has* invited me to hang out, and I always turn her down because Gynger wouldn't let me go anywhere, anyway. I'm so lonely and I don't want to be anymore, but I'm every bit as trapped as Rapunzel ever was up in her tower. And funny not funny, it also occurred to me *my* mother pulls on my hair just like Rapunzel's mother.

I imagine my soul is a dragon trapped inside my chest. It doesn't want to be there, so it claws at my heart, bangs on my ribs, and threatens to tear me open from the inside so it can fly away. But no matter how much it beats on my chest or squeezes my heart, I know it'll never get out. Even if I ever got invited to a party, I know I'd never get to go. My heart dragon understands exactly how I feel and knowing I'm not the only one who's trapped and restless makes me feel better.

Speaking of feeling better, Leesh is still not okay. Every day this week, she's gone straight to her room and shut the door. She tries to be quiet, but I can hear her muffled crying—like she's burying her face in her pillow. When she comes out for dinner, her eyes are puffy. A little bit ago, she came out to use the bathroom, and I stopped her in the hall.

"Hey, I don't know what's up with you but—"

"Don't. Just back off, okay?" She pushed into the bathroom and shut the door.

A second later, I heard the small click of the lock. "There's no need to lock me out, you know. I have zero desire to watch you pee." After a couple of minutes, I sat down next to the door to wait for her. Even though I knew she couldn't stay in there forever, it sure seemed like she was trying.

Finally, she flushed the toilet. I stood up as she opened the door.

"Leave me alone." She tried to push past me, but I stepped in front of her.

"Please talk to me. I'm worried about you."

"Well, don't be. I'd be fine if everyone gave me some fucking space."

Her voice sounded hard and angry in a way I've never heard before. I was so shocked by her anger, I moved aside and watched her trudge to her room. She moved like she was trying to walk through molasses. Her door clicked as she closed it softly. That small click was a thousand times worse than a slam. It reminded me of a cocking gun.

I don't know how to help her. I don't know how to help any of us. I thought my sister was on a shaky bridge alone, but she's not. If her bridge falls, it's taking down all of us.

REAL 40

I told Gynger I had to stay after school today to work on a history group project.

"No way." She belched and leaned back into the couch with her fingers laced behind her head. "I expect you to get your ass home at the same time you always do. Not one minute later, you hear me?"

I was prepared for her to say something like that. "Please, Mama. This is really important. If—"

"More important than your brother and sister? More important than your own mother? I carried you in my body for nine months. Pushed you out and gave you a damn good life. You're saying a history project is more important than me? I knew having you was the biggest mistake of my life. I wish we had had enough money for an abortion like your father wanted."

Even though I've heard different versions of those words as far back as I can remember, they never lose their sting. This time, though, they didn't sting quite as bad. Maybe because I figured she'd come at me with something like that, so I was prepared. When she catches me off guard, those words hit like a gut punch, so I took the light sting as proof that I'm getting better at predicting her.

"But Mama, this is a double-major grade. If I bomb it, I'll fail history and I'll have to take summer school. And you know what everyone thinks of the kids who go to summer school."

She squinted before slowly nodding. "It's disgusting how mothers let their kids run around failing classes. Those kids have zero respect for their mothers, and why should they? They can't even do their job right. They should have done those kids—and the world—a favor and sterilized themselves before spreading their legs around town."

I don't understand her fascination with abortion and pregnancy, but at least I had something to work with.

"Those mothers should be so embarrassed. I mean, they're ruining their kids' lives. I'm so lucky to have you for my mama. You understand how important it is for me to pass all my classes."

"You know I need you here after school. Can't you do the whole project yourself?"

I couldn't have wished for her to play into my plan any better.

"I wish. But half the grade is for teamwork, and one of the kids in my group is a little snitch who's always trying to get on the teacher's good side by ratting on the other kids. Mr. Jones will fail me for cheating, and then I'll end up in summer school, anyway. Believe me, if I could skip out on this, I would. I'm sorry, Mama."

God, do other kids have to apologize for doing their assignments? Never mind, this assignment isn't real. The point is the same.

She reached toward the coffee table trunk and grabbed her drink. "Snitches are bitches and get stitches," she chuckled as she took a long drink. "I can't have the world thinking I can't control my own daughter, but you better get your ass home in time to feed the kids their supper. You know I don't have time to deal with dinner."

"Of course, Mama. Thank you."

"And don't make a habit of this, either."

As if it's my fault a teacher assigns a group project and someone else is a tattletale.

"I won't, Mama. Thank you."

Freedom! I conned my way into an hour of freedom! Why didn't I try this sooner?

REAL 41

"So," I set my tray down across from Nate. "Do you guys want to hang out for a bit after school?"

Nate and Cheryl exchanged a look, and Cheryl placed the back of her hand on my forehead. "No. No fever. Did you get knocked upside the head or something?"

Girl, you have no idea.

"I'm fine. I just need to get out of the house for a bit and I thought it'd be nice to hang out with my friends. Is that so weird?"

"For most people, no. For you, yes. I've been begging you to hang out since the first day you got here, and you've never taken me up on it. Why now?" She set her Diet Coke down and studied me.

"I have something I want to talk to you guys about." I tried to sound casual, but my voice trembled. "It's important, and I don't want anyone to hear us."

After school, they met me at my locker, and we walked out the huge double doors together. All around us, kids shouted and shoved each other. Some ran, some stood around in groups, chatting and laughing. A symphony of adolescence.

"Where to?" Nate asked.

"I don't know. Somewhere quiet where we won't be bothered." *Someplace Gynger won't be able to see me if hell freezes over and she decides to take the van for a joyride.*

"It's quiet out behind the auditorium. I hang out back there sometimes when my mom can't pick me up and I'm not ready to go home."

We sat against the wall, Nate on one side and Cheryl on the other. The warm bricks felt so good on my back, I wished I could take a nap right there.

Instead, I steeled my nerves and started. "Something's wrong with my mother."

SAFE 19

Dear Diary,

Even though it put her out and she had to watch the kids after school for me, Mama was so nice to let me stay after school to work on my group history project. Unfortunately, Evan didn't do his share and now we have to meet at least one more time to get it all finished, or we'll all fail. If Kara weren't such a teacher's pet, I'd do Evan's part for him so we could all move on, and I could focus on the kids after school. But Kara the Snitch would definitely run off and tell Mr. Jones. Then I'd get in trouble for cheating, and I'd still fail, anyway.

I hope Mama will understand and let me take one more afternoon. I know it's a big sacrifice for her, especially after she's been so sick. I feel so bad I have to ask, but if I fail, everyone will think she's a bad mother who can't control her daughter. People shouldn't be so judgmental because they never know what someone's life is really like, but I guess they are the way they are, and all anyone can do is try to deal with it. Still, Mama doesn't deserve to have people thinking bad things about her parenting.

Group projects are so unfair. Not everyone has all the time in the world to meet after school. Some of us have actual lives to live.

REAL 43

Sitting against the warm brick wall behind the auditorium, I wondered how much of the truth I'd have the nerve to share with Cheryl and Nate. I figured I'd tell them Gynger drinks too much and even when she's not drinking, she's still more terrifying than any horror movie monster. I didn't expect to spill my guts to them, but once the words started coming out of my mouth, I couldn't stop them.

My teeth chattered, and I shivered uncontrollably as I told them about her "joke" with Sammycat. It was a borderline hot day, and I sat there shivering as if the bricks were made of ice in an igloo. By the time I got to how she hurt Bobby, my heart had stopped pumping blood and pumped ice water instead.

Cheryl put her arms around me, and I snuggled into her side, even though I wanted to run away. Her soft floral warmth comforted me, and I didn't even try to stop the tears from running down my cheeks.

"When we stayed with you for a few days, it's not because my mother was sick," I confessed. "She had some sort of breakdown and kicked us out of the house. She was seeing things that weren't there, and she completely destroyed the house. I was afraid to leave her alone, but I was more afraid to stay. I'm so sorry I lied to you."

"Don't even worry about it, Zoe. You did what you had to do to keep you and your brother and sister safe. I'd have to be a real asshole to be mad about that."

Somehow, her understanding didn't make me feel better. It made me feel even more like a pathetic loser. What in the world does she get out of being friends with me? I'm nobody. Nothing. Why should she even care?

"But," she continued, "I understand why my mom said what she did now."

Here it comes. "What'd she say?" I didn't really want to know, but I had to know all the same.

"Nothing bad. I overheard her telling my dad there's more going on than you wanted to share. She also told me to make sure you know you guys are welcome to stay with us any time. I thought she was just being polite, but I get it now. Her foster mom spidey senses must have been tingling. But I also think she sorta fell in love with Sammycat, too."

The more I tried to hold myself together, the less I could. I opened my mouth to say something funny, but all I managed was a choked sob. God, how embarrassing.

"Here." Nate handed me a small package of tissues from his backpack.

"Of course, you're the kind of guy who keeps tissues handy." It was a stupid attempt at a joke to lighten the mood.

"My mom makes me keep them. She says it's better to have them and not need them than..." he trailed off and looked down. "I'm sorry."

"What for?"

"I don't know. I guess talking about my mom."

For a moment, I hated him. I didn't need his pity or his stupid apology, and it's not like he had a fairy tale perfect family either, but life with Gynger has taught me to keep my mouth shut and my true thoughts to myself.

"Jeez, you're such a Boy Scout." I took the tissues and blotted my nose.

I once read when people learn something bad about you, they can't see you for yourself anymore. No matter what you say or do from then on, all they see is the trauma you lived through. You become a walking, breathing version of your trauma, and it changes the way they act with you. So, what about someone who lives with bad shit every day? Someone whose mother is an abusive asshole? Someone who is always one meal away from starving and always in fear of not paying the rent? How can anyone ever see me as something other than those things?

REAL 44

Epiphany: A moment of sudden insight or understanding.

We had that word on our spelling test a couple weeks ago, but as I read through my last few journal entries, I actually understood what an epiphany feels like because I had one.

My whole life, I've been convinced I'm not good enough. Not good enough for my mother's love. Not good enough for friends. Not good enough to even take up space. In one of my entries, I wrote *how can I be worth loving when my own mother doesn't even love me?* When she says having me was a mistake and she wishes I was never born, it feels like death by sharp words. It hurts, but my epiphany is, just because Gynger doesn't love me doesn't mean I don't deserve to be loved. In fact, how she feels about me says everything about what kind of person she is, not me. I have Bobby to thank for that.

She beat the crap out of Bobby. She kicked him in the head. Called him the same terrible names she calls me. Doing and saying those things to him doesn't make them true. Whatever she feels about him, I know Bobby's a great kid who one hundred percent doesn't deserve what she did. If she can be so wrong about Bobby, maybe she's wrong about me, too. Cheryl and Nate certainly seem to think I have worth, anyway.

This is huge, and it makes my head swim. She always says trusting people is how you end up hurt and it's better not to trust anyone than to get stabbed in the back by someone you trusted. How can she not realize she stabs me in the back every time she insults or hurts me? She's my mother. Our mother.

And we can't trust a single thing she says. More evidence she's wrong about me now and has probably been wrong my whole life. Nobody else is out to stab me in the back or take advantage of me. It's just her. I don't know what made her this way, but I hope I can remember she's the problem, not me.

MAYBE

The world is Black and White
Made of ice and fear and cold
No room for Blue or Green or Gold
Only Yes or No
Jump-and-Run or Die
There is no room for I Don't Know
The world is All or Nothing
My way or the highway
No room for options
But…
Maybe that's this world, not MY WORLD.
Maybe I'm on the wrong planet
An ice planet ruled by an Ice Queen
I don't belong here
Maybe there's a better place
A safe place
Maybe I can build a rocket and blast off
Leave this ice planet and its Ice Queen far behind
Maybe then, I'll finally be warm.

———

SAFE 20

Dear Diary,

I know Mama's right. I really should give up on writing poems. I'm not smart enough to even kind of understand what they mean, forget about trying to write them. It's a waste of time and energy. It should be as easy as simply not thinking about them, but it isn't. Something is pulling inside of me, always tugging on my brain. I can be doing the most boring things, and I suddenly hear myself singing a made-up song.

Or I'll look at a pair of scissors and I'll challenge myself to find a word that rhymes with *scissors*. If I can't find a rhyme, I'll make up a story that involves scissors. Well, no. They're not stories, but they're not poems, either. Poems have structure and I don't know enough about that stuff to write a real poem. My things are just words that sound good to me.

Sometimes, I think I should write them down, but it's not worth the effort. It's fine enough for me to make up words while I'm vacuuming or working on dinner, but it's something else entirely for me to waste my time by writing them down when I could be doing useful things. I think I like it better this way, anyway. I can play with the words in my head, but I never have to face how embarrassing and bad they are if I don't write them down.

REAL 46

Oh, God. I made a mistake.

Today's writing prompt might get me killed. *Describe your last birthday*. I hate these personal prompts, but I've gotten good at making shit up for them. I don't know why, but today, I wrote the truth about my last birthday. I don't know what came over me. I didn't even stop to think about the prompt. I just opened my journal and my pencil scribbled across the page like someone else controlled it.

I disappeared into myself, and everything and everyone around me blurred out of existence. My hand wrote. And wrote. If I believed in possession, I'd think that's what happened to me. I was aware my hand was moving, and I knew I was sitting in class, but everything except the journal faded so far into the background I didn't even hear the timer beep.

Mrs. Thomas walked up and said something to me, but I couldn't make out what. She didn't even sound real. It sounded like when you're underwater at the pool and someone above water is trying to talk to you. She put her hand on my shoulder and I slammed back into awareness as I whimpered "no" and flinched.

She moved her hand and squatted next to me. I blinked. I tried to focus in on her eyes, her dark skin, but the world and everyone in it blurred like a painting left in the rain. My cheeks were wet, and I couldn't breathe through my nose. I looked down. Fat drops warped the words on my page. I had been crying.

"Zoe, honey." She was close, but she didn't touch me again. "Would you like to go to the restroom?"

Uh, how about NO. I didn't want to sit there all snotty and upset, but I'd rather cover myself in beef broth and run naked through a pride of lions than get up in the middle of class. All those eyes staring at me. Judging me. No way.

"I'm fine. Sorry." I shut my journal, hiding the truth away from both of us.

If she goes against her word and reads that entry, I don't know what will happen, but I know it won't be good. If she reads it, she'll know everything. How we don't have enough to eat most of the time. How my own mother forgets my birthday more often than she remembers it. And worst of all, she'll know what Gynger did to me that day.

I hadn't meant to, but I lost control and wet myself while Gynger beat the actual piss out of me on my birthday morning. After I peed myself, everything got a hundred times worse. If she reads that entry, Mrs. Thomas will know I had to clean up my own piss and blood before going to school. On my birthday.

Please, God. If you're real, if you're listening, don't let Mrs. Thomas read it. Please make her keep her word. I promise I'll never doubt you again if you just keep her from seeing that entry. I'm so stupid!

REAL 47

They say the apple doesn't fall far from the tree. Is it true?

"I see you," she slurred from the couch a couple of nights ago. "I see you studying them books and losing your head in them. I see you walking around all high and mighty. Let me tell you something, girl." She leaned forward and squinted at me like I was a dead rat. "The apple doesn't fall far from the tree. Oh, it can fall off, but it ain't going nowhere. That apple will always be right there, under the tree that made it, until it rots." She paused for a long drink. The ice clinked softly against the glass.

"And once it's rotted down to mush, it feeds the tree that bore it to begin with." She leaned back and smiled stupidly at me. "Now, ain't that some beautiful shit right there?"

"I guess so." What could I possibly say?

"From now on, I'm calling you Apple, so you don't forget where you come from." She laughed like she made the funniest joke ever told. My stomach tightened and my mouth opened to release a scream, but I shrugged instead. She'll call me whatever she wants to call me, no matter what I think.

She's wrong. Apples are round. As soon as I fall off the

tree, I'm going to roll down the hill as far away as I can. Every day, I wake up and do a million things to be as different from Gynger as I can. I never yell at anyone. I don't complain about doing chores. I make sure my clothes are clean, even if they are old. When she changes her clothes in front of me, I see her stomach, huge and flabby for someone so skinny, and I promise myself I'll never let my body get like hers. I go to my room and do sit-ups until my stomach burns and I can't even move.

She can call me whatever she wants, but she can't turn me into her, and she can't keep me here.

REAL 48

Cheryl, Nate, and I have taken to hanging out behind the auditorium during lunch. I don't know why nobody else has claimed it since it's perfect for private conversations.

"We have to get you out of there," Nate said. "I think she could literally kill you. I'm afraid for you."

"That makes two of us," I replied.

"Three," Cheryl chimed in. "I know my mom would let you move in if you wanted."

"What? Don't be ridiculous. I'm not leaving Leesh and Bobby, and I'm sure your mom would get sick of us after a week."

"My mom? The lady who let all of you stay with us after exactly one second of deliberation? The lady who took you out and got all of you new clothes and deodorant? The woman who made a point to kiss all three of you before bed and hugged you before school? The woman who always wanted a huge family? Good Lord, Zoe. Why is it so hard for you to trust me and my family?" Sadness danced in her green eyes.

Way to go, Zoe. You finally make a couple of friends, and you blow it in like fifteen seconds. "I'm sorry, I just—"

"No, I'm sorry." She snuggled her head into my shoulder and a strange, hidden piece of my heart came to life. "It just hurts how guarded you are when I've never given you any reason not to trust me."

"I don't want you to think I'm not grateful for everything you guys did for us before, but I've heard houseguests are like fish. They only last three days before they go bad and start smelling up your house." A fire truck wailed past the school, and I squeezed my eyes against the noise.

"Last time, you stayed in my room, and Leesh and Bobby shared the guest room. But I bet if you wanted, I could convince my mom to let all of you have the basement, which is practically a full guesthouse. Then, you'd still have your privacy, but you'd have us right there if you needed anything." She nudged me with her shoulder. "We could be neighbors. Think about it, okay?"

"I don't think it's a good idea. Don't be mad, but please don't say anything to your parents, Cheryl. I mean it."

She smiled and gave me another nudge. "It's not as big a deal as you think it is, but I won't ask them if you don't want me to."

"I definitely don't want you to, but thanks."

Nate unscrewed the cap of his water bottle. "I wish I could offer to let your brother stay with us, but there's no way my dad would allow it." He took a long drink of his water. When he looked back at me, his cheeks and ears were pink.

"Don't even stress it. Thank you."

I know he hides bruises, but I wonder if things are as messed up at his place as they are at mine. Maybe Cheryl's parents would let him stay, too?

———

SAFE 21

Dear Diary,

Cheryl invited me for a sleepover. Aside from when we stayed with her when Mama was sick, I've never been to one before. In fact, I pretty much thought sleepovers were something invented by writers to give kids an excuse to get into trouble. No way could slumber parties or sleepovers be a real thing.

I thanked her but told her no. Mama's still not feeling so hot. Even if I thought she'd allow me to go, I could never abandon her. Besides, I'm pretty sure I know what her answer would be if I asked her. There's no way she'd let me run wild and unsupervised at all hours of the night. Who knows what could happen to me? I could be kidnapped and taken to another country. I could be raped or murdered. A million terrible things could happen, and Mama loves me too much to let me take such a stupid risk.

I hope she feels better soon so I can thank her for watching out for me the way she does. What did I do to deserve a mama like her?

REAL 49

"Zoe," Mrs. Thomas said as the bell rang. "Can I talk to you for a moment?"

My stomach jumped to my throat and my heart dropped to my toes as I approached her desk.

She smiled softly and touched her twisted-out black hair. "I've noticed you've been upset the last few days. Is there anything I can help you with?"

"No, ma'am. I'm fine." *Liar, liar.*

"Sweetie, fine doesn't look the way you've looked lately. It seems like you have some big things happening in your life. Being a teenager is hard. The emotions are so big and so much happens all at once. I remember feeling half-crazy all the time when I was your age."

"Really, everything's fine. I'm just tired. My mother and little brother are both sick and I think I'm fighting off the same bug." *Pants on fire.*

She pursed her lips and raised her eyebrows. She obviously didn't believe me. "Well, I hope everyone feels better soon. And you take care of yourself, so you don't get sick, too."

"Yes, ma'am."

"If you ever need someone to talk to, or if you need a bit of a break, I'm here."

"Thank you." I felt like a worm under a magnifying glass.

My cheeks burned and my throat felt like a boa constrictor was squeezing it as I rushed through the halls. I couldn't breathe. The hall went tilty, and my lips and fingers went numb and tingly at the same time. I moved to the wall and sat next to the water fountain. If I didn't, I knew I'd pass out in the middle of the hallway.

My heart sounded like a thousand soldiers marching in my ears. I tried taking deep, slow breaths to slow my heart down, but I couldn't get enough air. The invisible snake moved from my throat to my chest. Was I having a heart attack? Was I going to die next to the fountain? I leaned the back of my head against the wall and closed my eyes. Far away, the warning bell rang.

REAL 50

It's been two weeks since she hurt Bobby, and she's still hardly coming out of her room. Maybe she comes out when we're at school, but I don't think so. If she did, there'd be signs. A dirty plate on a counter, or the blanket on the couch, moved to a different spot. But nothing ever changes. At first, we were all as quiet as possible. It was like someone covered the whole house with a heavy blanket to absorb every sound. After about a week, things got back to normal, or as normal as anything ever is in this house.

When I couldn't stand it another minute, I hauled out the vacuum and sucked up a week's worth of dirt and cat fur. The whole time, I wobbled between terror about her coming out to scream at me and hoping she would. This thing she's doing now is way scarier than how she usually is, and she's the scariest person I know. At first the break was kind of nice, but now it's sorta pissing me off. Why can't she put on her big girl panties and take care of her family? Why do I have to be the adult?

Leesh is still in a weird place, too. She comes home from school and shuts herself in her room like Gynger. After she opened up to me about her guilt that one time, she never mentioned it again. In fact, I feel like she's going out of her way to avoid me. I think she feels bad for being honest with me, like how I feel like garbage about being honest in my school journal. I wish she'd let me tell her I'm not mad and I don't blame her.

Even though Bobby's the one Gynger hurt this time, he's being his regular six-year-old self. He's quieter, but only because he doesn't want to wake up Gynger, not because he's broken like Leesh seems to be.

I'm so tired. I feel like I'm trying to fly a kite that's not really a kite—It's a tornado, and if I lose control for even a second, the tornado will destroy everything.

REAL 51

"Hey," Cheryl jogged to catch up with me on my way to my locker before lunch. "Good news! My mom said you can stay with us."

"What?" I felt like someone yanked the whole Earth out from under my feet. "Why would you do that? I specifically asked you not to say anything to her. You promised you wouldn't."

Gynger is right. You can't trust anyone. You can't trust them to keep a secret and you sure as hell can't trust them to look out for you. The only person you can ever count on is yourself.

"I know, but I shouldn't have made that kind of promise. You're in a dangerous situation, and if I can help, I will."

I grabbed her arm and pulled her into the empty art room for privacy. I could not have this conversation in the middle of a crowded hallway. "So, what? You expect me to bail on my brother and sister so I can save my own ass? I already told you, I am *not* leaving them there with her. Not even overnight."

"Of course not. My parents said you can all stay until things settle down."

"Until things settle down? What even does that mean? Things will never settle down as long as my mother's alive." Clay vases lined the shelves along the wall, and it took everything I had not to smash every one of them on the floor. I inhaled deeply and tried like hell not to scream at Cheryl. "I can't believe you told them. I asked you to keep your mouth shut. I never trust anybody, but I trusted you."

"Don't be mad at me. I didn't tell them the whole thing. I told them your dad is out of town and your mom got sick again and can't take care of you right now. This isn't a forever thing. Think of it as a little vacation."

"You don't understand. She's never going to get better. If I packed us all up and moved them into your house, even for a weekend, my mother would come completely undone." I heard my voice raising, but I couldn't do anything to stop it.

"Well, she didn't knock down our door last time, did she?"

"That was different. She kicked me out. It was her idea, so I had to do it. If I left on my own, she'd see it as a betrayal. It's all or nothing with her."

"I don't know what *all or nothing* means."

How could I even begin to tell her? It's too fucked up to explain right, but I had to try.

"It's like everything is black and white. She doesn't see shades of gray or green or purple. You're either on her side, or you're her sworn enemy. She either adores you or she hates you. Life is either magical and beautiful, or it's a death swamp. For some reason, her brain can't process that, sometimes, things can be medium. She doesn't know you don't have to hate a person because they think your favorite show is boring. She can't understand that because someone chooses to spend time doing other things doesn't mean they hate you and never want to see you again. If we left her alone, she'd see it as abandonment and who knows what she'd do?"

Cheryl pulled her lipstick from her purse and reapplied it

slowly, probably trying to stall long enough to understand what I meant. "Well, what could she do?"

"It's impossible to know. She could call the cops and try to get your parents arrested for kidnapping."

"No way would she do that." She studied my face. "You're not exaggerating?"

"I'm not exaggerating, I'm just getting started." I inhaled, and my breath sounded shuddery. "She could show up at your house and start shit. Banging on the doors and windows. Screaming. Crying. Making a scene. Ask Nate. He's seen what kind of scene she can make if she's in the wrong headspace. She might throw rocks through your windows or set your house on fire. Who knows? Literally everything is on the table with her."

Cheryl blinked quickly and shook her head. I've heard the phrase *shellshocked* before, but I never really understood what it meant until then. She looked terrified and confused all at once. Like she didn't know what was true and what wasn't.

Good. Welcome to my life.

"And even if she didn't do anything to your family or house, she *will* go off the rails somewhere. Sometimes, she goes through my room like a tornado. She tears the bed apart, dumps all my clothes out of the dresser, and pulls my posters off the wall. She destroys everything. *Everything.* Then, she screams that I made her do it and tells me I have like twenty minutes to clean it all up. If I don't do it in time, she starts all over again."

"Are you serious?"

"That's her reaction to small things, like if I clink the plates too loudly when I'm putting the dishes away, or if I'm trying to hold back a sneeze and make a funny face. She thinks I'm making a face at her and goes ape-shit. If we moved out, she might blow holes in the roof. Literal holes. Or she could set her own house on fire and tell the cops I did it. She could check

Bobby out of school and disappear with him forever. Or," I was crying, and I didn't even care. Thank God I had the fore-sight to drag us into the art room. "Or she could sink even deeper into her depression and kill herself. Either on purpose or by starving herself or getting so drunk she passes out and chokes to death on her own puke."

Cheryl put her arm around me and pulled me into her.

"I'm sorry. I had no idea how bad it is. I mean, from what you've said, I knew it was bad, but I didn't really get it."

I pushed her off me and wiped my eyes. "It's still just the tip of the iceberg."

"Tell me what to do to help."

The snakes living in my belly woke up and slithered, oily and cold. "Nothing. There's nothing you can do except back off. Tell your parents never mind and leave me alone."

I imagined building a giant wall around myself. I opened up to her and Nate, and she came this close to ruining every-thing. I cannot let anyone close enough to do that kind of damage, no matter how lonely I am.

"Don't start this again, Zoe. I'm not going to let you push me away."

"Look," I snapped. "I don't like you, okay? I don't like Nate, either. You're both pathetic fucking losers and I'm embarrassed to be seen with you." I forced myself to laugh and hoped it sounded more convincing than it felt. "I can't believe how stupid you both are. And you actually believed that stuff about my mother? I knew you were dumb, but I had no idea you were that dumb."

I doubt she believed me, but she gave me a sad smile and walked through the classroom door without another word.

Brick by brick, I built my wall higher. So high it blotted out the sun.

SAFE 22

Dear Diary,

I got into a fight with Nate and Cheryl, and I'm not speaking to them anymore. It's for the best. I don't have time for their petty dramas. I have enough on my plate without them, anyway.

Mama's still under the weather, but when I came home from school yesterday, she was cuddled on the couch with a blanket. I asked if she felt well enough to eat. When she said yes, I was so relieved, I ran to the kitchen and made her the last can of *Spaghetti-O's*—the kind with the hot dog chunks in it. She always says they look like turds, so I picked every single hotdog chunk out and put them in a bowl for Bobby's snack. When I brought the food to Mama, she smiled and thanked me for taking such good care of her. I can't even explain how happy it made my heart to see her eat a couple of bites. Funny how something so small can make me feel so good.

Hopefully, she'll be back to herself soon.

REAL 52

Joel still hasn't come back since she hurt Bobby. Where in the world is he, and why did he take off and leave me here to pick up the pieces? He's never gone this long, and I keep moving back and forth between worrying about him and hating him. How nice it would be not to have to come home to her every night. How nice to forget you have kids who need you, and to pretend everything's okay when it's all going down the sewer.

It's not like he does much for us anyway, so maybe he should stay gone for good. He doesn't protect us from her when he is here, and when he's gone, he hardly sends home enough money to squeak by. We barely make rent most months. Hell, I just fed Gynger the last can of *Spaghetti-O's*. Actually, it was the last can of anything in the house, and I was trying to save it until we really needed it.

Last year, I learned about Civil War hardtack. It was a gross biscuit type thing made with flour, water, and some salt. It wasn't exactly a buttery Ritz cracker, but it did the trick for filling stomachs. At lunch, I used the library computer to find out what else I could make with flour, water, and maybe a bit of oil, sugar, and salt. I copied down recipes for pasta, crepes, crackers, and even flatbread. I studied those recipes the way smart kids study the periodic table. It doesn't matter how many things you can make with flour and water if the electricity is turned off, though. And that's what I was saving the *Spaghetti-O's* for. A day when there were no other options.

I suppose, in a way, that is what happened, though. There was nothing else to eat and Gynger had come out of her cave looking for food. What choice did I have but to give them to her? And somebody, please tell me what good is a dad who lets things even get to that point to begin with? No food, no money, no protection. Yeah, he can stay gone for all I care.

Maybe he has another family somewhere. A normal family. A wife who isn't a volcano. Maybe he spends every night with them. Maybe he's giving all his money to his real family instead of to us because they deserve it more than we do. Or they deserve it more than Gynger and I do, anyway. If he really thinks Leesh and Bobby don't deserve every good thing the world has to offer—which his behavior seems to prove—then he's crappier than I thought. Just thinking about it makes me hate him, and I've never hated him before.

It doesn't matter why he's gone. Whether he has another family or is avoiding this one, the result is still the same. I'm left here to hold down the fort and protect everyone from Gynger. There's not even a bag of beans in the pantry, and we're out of money. I can't get a job because Gynger would accuse me of trying to avoid her. It would also put Leesh in charge, and I can't do that to her. Especially now, as depressed as she is. I refuse to do to her what Joel does to me.

I think it's about time for me to go to the food bank again. I've avoided it until now because Gynger doesn't like to accept charity, but we've run out of options. She says begging for handouts makes her look like an unfit mother. I don't know how she doesn't understand that beating us and not providing for us also makes her an unfit mother. I will never understand the way she looks at the world. How can she be so convinced she's doing the right thing when she clearly doesn't give a damn about our health and wellbeing?

Maybe she doesn't need to know I went to the food bank. I'll tell her I found twenty bucks in the bathroom at school, and I used it to buy a few extras. And if she finds out I picked up a box of cheap, free food and freaks out on me, it'll still be worth it. She might be fine starving herself, but no way am I gonna let my brother and sister go to bed hungry again.

REAL 53

I failed my algebra test, and I have no idea where I went wrong. I swear I know this stuff. And if that's not bad enough, I tanked my history test, too. What's going on? It's like my brain decided to pack up and move to New Zealand. I can't think straight. I can't concentrate on whatever happens to be in front of me. Like, with my history test, the words all blurred together. Kinda like trying to read through glasses smeared with oil.

When they swam back into focus, I couldn't stop staring at the word *military*. It looked all wrong. Should there be an E in there somewhere? Am I sure it's not spelled "milatary"? And what the hell did that word mean? I knew I knew its definition, but all I could think of was how wrong it looked. It was scary, getting sucked into a word like that, but not being able to comprehend it.

Maybe I'm going crazy. Maybe this is exactly how it started for Gynger. It's possible she wasn't always the way she is now. If this is the beginning of the end for me, I can tell you one thing for damn sure. I will not go off the deep end without a fight. I refuse to let myself off the hook so easily. I cannot—

WILL NOT—let my grades fall and my mind slip. It simply can't happen. If I don't get scholarships, I won't go to college. If I don't go to college, I'll never get out of here. I'll never break free, and I'll never be able to help Leesh and Bobby.

It's time to put childish things, like this journal, away, and focus on the things that matter. My grades. My brother and sister. Staying alive.

———

SAFE 23

Dear Diary,

I'm not feeling myself these days. I haven't been sleeping very well, and I'm having a hard time concentrating. My brain doesn't know which things to focus on and which things don't matter so much, so it feels like someone is changing the channel in my brain every three seconds. It's exhausting.

Cheryl keeps pestering me to hang out with her at lunch, but I told her I have to make up a couple of tests I didn't do so well on. I was so afraid when I asked the teachers if I could retake the tests, but they were both cool with it. It was embarrassing, though, because I told them how worried I've been about Mama being so sick, and I almost started crying. I told them I know it's not a good excuse, but I promise not to let myself get distracted again. Thank God, they both agreed to give me a second shot. I definitely won't blow it.

Daddy hasn't even called. I hope he's okay.

There's a dance next weekend, but I'm not going. I want to stay home to rest and study. I've been exhausted lately, and the idea of going to a loud dance filled with a bunch of stupid boys wearing too much dollar store body spray sounds like torture.

REAL 54

I should have known telling Cheryl off wouldn't do any good. All I wanted was for her to back off and leave me alone, but she hasn't left me alone since the day she introduced herself, so why would she start now? It doesn't matter what I say or do, she's always right there. I don't know why she's so obsessed with me, but it's hard to avoid someone who goes out of her way to run into you every three minutes.

Nate texted me earlier. He said Cheryl told him I need some space, but he wanted to let me know he's there if I need him. Then, get this, he asked me if I wanted to go to the dance with him. How tone deaf can he be? I need space, so he asks me to a dance. And even if it weren't completely tone deaf, it's not like going is even remotely a possibility. Gynger would never allow it, but even if she did, I can't trust her alone with the kids. Besides, I don't have anything to wear. At least it's not a formal dance, but I don't even have a sort of cute dress.

Holy crap. I just realized I was asked on my first date by the hottest boy in school, and I didn't even get all stupid-girl excited. I'm not sure what my feelings are for him anymore. Three months ago, I would have peed my pants if he so much as smiled at me. Now, he asks me out and I feel a bunch of bundled up things all at once. Embarrassment, shame, panic, dread, annoyed. I mean, yeah. Maybe I'm a bit happy, too. But it's weird.

Now that Nate and I are friends, the stupid crush I had on him has changed. I love being with him, but I've also been so happy being his friend, I don't even want to risk ruining what we have by trying to turn our friendship into something deeper. Well, that and I don't have the time or the luxury to let myself get all gushy about anyone. No way. My life is too complicated for friends, forget about dating. Jesus, Zoe. Do you even hear yourself? Here I am, saying I don't want to ruin our friendship by letting myself think about being his girlfriend, but I'm pushing him away and trying to get him to turn his back on me? I'm doing a pretty good job of ruining our friendship all on my own, aren't I?

Why can't I have the things other kids have? Why do I have to be the only adult in a two-parent family? Why can't I be selfish and live my own life? I should be joining clubs, going on dates and to parties. I should be counting down the days until I can drive. I should be letting myself develop crushes and letting myself make a whole crew of friends. But no. Instead, I'm stuck in this crumbling house, doing my best to pretend everything is normal while my father is off doing who knows what and my mother slips further and further into…what, exactly? Depression? Madness? Psychosis?

And then there's Leesh. She still won't talk to me, but she's so far down a deep hole, I don't think she could hear me even if I shouted. Every day, I worry more about her.

REAL 55

Enough is enough. I can't stand watching Leesh wither away like a sunflower in the winter. I think she might be hurting herself. She's taken to wearing long sleeves, even though it's too hot for them. I'm not an idiot. I know what that means. Or what it could mean, anyway. I hoped I was wrong.

"Here's the thing." I plopped onto her bed, and she rolled her eyes at me.

"Leave me alone."

"Why? Does lying here doing nothing take all your concentration?" I hoped she'd at least smile, but she just sighed and stared at something nobody else could see.

"You're not still feeling guilty about the way Mama treats me, are you? Because it's not your fault, and I'm not mad at you."

Leesh rolled onto her side, turning her back toward me. "I don't understand why you can't stay out of her way."

"Even if I could magically stay out of her line of fire, I wouldn't. It's not like I'm looking to piss her off, but if she's coming after me, she's not gunning for you or Bobby. I'd throw myself into a pit of sharp knives if I thought it'd keep you guys safe."

"Nobody is asking you to protect us, Zoe. I can handle myself just fine. I don't need your help. Why can't you stop hovering over me?"

"I get you want me to give you space—" She flinched when I put my hand on her shoulder, but I continued. "But I'm worried about you and until you give me a reason not to be, I'm keeping a close eye on you."

"I don't know what you're talking about."

"Come on. Do you think I don't know why you're wearing long sleeves when it's practically a hundred degrees outside?

"You know Mama doesn't really hit me. I'm not covering up bruises if that's what you're thinking."

"Actually, I'm not worried about bruises. I'm worried about cuts." I let my statement hang in the air like humidity in August.

Leesh covered her head with her pillow. "Please, go away." Her voice was muffled and far. Like she was in the bottom of the knife pit I said I'd throw myself into.

I didn't know how to help her, so I curled up next to her and hugged her tight, like when we were little. And like when we were little, she spooned right back into me.

"Are you cutting yourself? Can I see?"

I pushed myself up on my elbow and gently lifted the sleeve of her green flannel. I expected her to yank away, but she didn't. At the sight of her unmarked wrist, a tiny bubble of relief swelled in my chest. Maybe I had been wrong after all. But as the sleeve neared her elbow, the angry red lines I knew she was hiding showed themselves.

"Oh, honey, thank you for trusting me." I planted a kiss on her arms and fought to control my voice. "I'm so sorry you're going through this, but I promise you're not alone."

I'm not sure if she heard me over her sobbing, so I rolled her sleeve back down and held her tight as she cried herself to sleep.

SHE DESERVES

Red lines cross her arms like dusty desert roads in summer
Dry
Angry
Leading to a distant land that knows no pain
It shouldn't be like this for her.
She deserves
Playing in the woods
Warm cookies on a cold day
Comfort when she's sad
She deserves
Safety
Sleepovers
Popcorn and pajamas
Staying up all night—
Afraid only of the monsters in whispered ghost stories.
But the one-way red lines she tries so hard to hide
Remind her

Monsters are real
And there is no escape.

THE KINGDOM

This is my kingdom
This is my domain
A place full of madness
A home for the insane.

All boxed in, no way out
And you can't win unless
You know what it's all about.

Served on a plastic platter
Red Queen calls for more
The cook wants to hide
And runs for the door.

The jesters all are crying
The king has no control
Good guys wear black
And you fall into the hole.

Deeper and deeper
There is no end
You think you're going to die
But you're already dead.

You tell yourself it's only a dream
But the pain is too real
All you can do is scream
To hide what you feel.

Nothing makes sense
Chaos in control
There is no way out
Of this deep, dark hole.

This is your kingdom
This is your domain
A place made of your madness
For you are insane.

REAL 58

No matter how hard I try to give up poetry, I keep coming back to it. I don't know anything about the stuff, and I know I'm not any good at it, but what does it matter? It's not like I'm ever going to be a poet. Anyway, do poets still even exist?

What I love about the so-called poems I write is that it's a hell of a lot easier to express what I'm feeling in an abstract way than it is to be blunt. It's also a little extra insurance. If Gynger ever saw one of my poems, she might not think it's about her. I could tell her it came from a mysterious voice in my head. She's so desperate to believe she's the perfect mother she imagines she is, she'd probably let it go. In a strange way, writing in poems gives me more freedom to say what I'm really thinking.

I wonder if I could ask Mrs. Thomas for poetry tips. She hasn't said anything since I broke down in class the other day. In fact, she's acting like I never freaked out at all. And if that wasn't strange enough, none of the kids in English has mentioned it, either. If there's one thing teenagers are good it, it's treating their classmates like shark bait at the first sign of weakness. Is it possible I didn't freak out? Maybe I imagined the whole thing. Maybe everything I think is real is actually in my head.

No. That can't be. Those lines on Leesh's arm are as real as my nose. I know for a fact I didn't make those up.

Why is everything so complicated? Do other people question reality like this? Why can't I be a normal kid with a normal family, living a normal, boring life? It's exhausting to always wonder if I'm making up everything I know is real.

Will I be this tired forever?

———

SAFE 24

Dear Diary,

I haven't written much lately because there isn't much to write about. In fact, I've been thinking about giving up on writing entirely. This has to be the most boring diary ever written in the entire history of diary-keeping. I don't see the point in even trying, you know.

Sometimes I wish something exciting would happen, but my life is so dull I can't even think of anything interesting to write about in here. It's tricky, though. As much as I wish something interesting would happen, I absolutely do not want the kind of drama famous diaries are known for. I don't want to find out Daddy has a secret family or anything like that.

But since nothing ever happens, I wonder what the point is of keeping up a diary at all. Mostly it's because I think I might enjoy reading it years from now when I'm grown and living on my own. I think it'll be nice to come back home through these pages. I know how silly and sentimental I sound, but hey. Whatever keeps me writing—even if it is only now and then.

Do other people run out of things to write about in their diaries, or do they really have so much going on they can write every day and still have more to talk about the next day? I think half of what other people write is probably made up. I mean, how can you keep your priorities straight when your life is so hectic you have to write about it every single day?

Mama has a saying that reminds me of this. *A snake never shows its true colors.* I think she might be mixing up a couple of other sayings, but her version is so much better. It means you can't believe what people say, because basically people are lying snakes in the grass. You can't trust a venomous snake to tell you it's venomous. I wonder why Mama never tried to be a writer. She's smart enough, and her ideas are definitely interesting enough to read about.

But in my case, I think it's a blessing in disguise I don't have a lot to write about. I have all the time I need to focus on the things that really matter. Family, helping around the house, my grades. I bet the kids who have interesting lives are self-absorbed jerks. I bet they don't spend time helping their little brothers with math. They don't cook or do laundry. They just walk around, oblivious to everything but themselves. The joke will be on them, though.

One day, they'll be on their own and they won't know how to function without their mamas to take care of their every need. They'll live like pigs, letting empty pizza boxes pile up because they can't figure out how to boil spaghetti. They'll be stuck wearing dirty clothes because they won't know how to run a washer. And when they do figure it out, they won't know to separate out their whites and all their underclothes will come out pink.

Did I mention there's a dance this Friday? It's all everyone is talking about. It seems so strange to me. I mean, don't they have other things to think about? Are their lives really so luxurious they can all walk away from their responsibilities whenever they want?

I feel sorry for them. Oh, sure, they're living it up now.

"Go on to the dance, honey, and let me take care of your laundry!"

If you ask me, that's some crappy parenting right there. I'm so glad Mama instilled a good work ethic in me when I was little. I learned how to do laundry by the time I was in like first grade!

Whoa. Can that be right? Was I really Bobby's age when I learned how to do the wash? I think so, because I have the clearest memory of dragging a chair all the way over to the washer so I could open the lid and reach the knobs. I remember putting the clothes in and not being able to see inside the drum. I remember how heavy the box of detergent was and how hard it was not to spill it everywhere. It's hard to believe I've been in charge of laundry for so long. I guess time really does fly when you're having fun—haha!

It may not be the most exciting life, but at least my clothes will always be clean, and I'll never have to rely on frozen pizza for dinner when I'm on my own.

Wow! It turns out I had a lot more to talk about than I thought. Okay, so it's mostly about boring old laundry, but I still filled up a couple of pages. Maybe I will try to keep writing.

TTFN!

REAL 59

Break's over. Gynger is clearly feeling back to herself, if her current nastiness is any indication.

"Cinderella, get your princess ass in here," she yelled from the couch.

She's never called me Cinderella before, so that already set my nerves on edge. I took a deep breath and went to see what she wanted.

"Isn't a dance coming up? I saw it on the sign out front of the school."

Well, that's a plain lie. I know for a fact the sign in front of the school doesn't say anything about the dance because the bus drives past it twice a day. This is one of the stupid games I have to play. She says whatever stupid thing she wants, and I have to act like it's true as rain. But I have to be careful, because sometimes she says things that aren't true just to trap me into a lie, which she'll accuse me of making up to begin with. She's been reading the diary again.

Who needs high school dances with living room dances like this?

"Yes, ma'am. It's next weekend." Best not to deny there's a dance since I wrote about it.

"And you want to go, don't you?"

I looked down at the stained, brown carpet, trying to figure out the best way to keep this dance from going up in flames. "Not really. I'm curious about it since I've never gone to one, but not so curious I actually thought about going. It seems like a giant waste of money. I wasn't even going to mention it to you."

My stomach spun harder than our washer's spin cycle, and I thought I might throw up. I'm used to this stupid dance, but for some reason, my Spidey senses screamed extra loud.

"Well, I think you should go."

Wait, what? Did I misunderstand her, or was this part of her trap? I commanded my eyes to look up from the floor and I forced a soft smile to my lips. My best impersonation of a grateful teenage daughter.

"Oh, Mama! You're so nice, but I don't really want to go, you know?"

"No, I don't know. What else do you have going on?" She set her sweating glass on the wobbly coffee table trunk.

"Nothing. It just seems so frivolous. Anyway, even if I wanted to go, I don't have money for a ticket, and that seems like the kind of thing I should pay for myself." I scratched the back of my head and swallowed my fear. Was this what a deer feels when it sees a mountain lion deciding whether to attack?

Her eyes darkened as she glared at me. "What, do you think I can't provide for you?"

Ding! Ding! Ding!

"Of course not, Mama, but there are so many better things to spend money on."

Like food. And rent.

"Have you kids ever wanted for anything? Ever needed

something and haven't gotten it? Haven't you always had a roof over your head and food in your belly?"

And the dance shifts into high gear. She can't possibly believe we've never gone to bed hungry or woke up shivering because the heat had been turned off, but once the dance has started, there's no way out. You have to dance your way through to the final song and pray you don't slip and break your neck along the way.

"That's not what I mean at all. You already do so much for me. It seems ungrateful to ask you for money for something so silly.

I don't know how I managed to say exactly the right thing to make her pick up her drink and settle back into the couch. She just as easily could have picked up her glass and thrown it at me. Or pushed me into a wall. Or-or-or a thousand other things mothers shouldn't do to their kids. I was obviously getting better at dancing with her.

"Well," she brought the tumbler to her lips and sipped. "Thank you for noticing. You don't need to worry about asking for money as long as you don't make a habit of it. Your father finally pulled through, and we have a bit of cushion right now. I think you should go. It'll do you good to get out of the house for a bit."

I still feel like it's some sort of trap or test I failed, but what could I do except hug her and thank her a thousand times? When she's in a good mood, it's best to do whatever you can to keep her there, because when she comes down, she comes crashing like a meteor.

———

SAFE 25

Dear Diary,

Good news! Mama said I can go to the dance. I didn't even have to ask her, either. A few minutes ago, she called me into the living room and told me she knew it was coming up and said I should go. I tried to tell her I wasn't sure I even want to go, but she reminded me a girl's gotta get out of the house every now and then. And she said she'd give me money for the ticket.

What will I wear? Will anyone want to dance with me? Will there be an actual punch bowl, like in movies? Will some kid try to spike it? I better stick with the water fountain, just in case. It would be an absolute disaster if I didn't know the punch was spiked, and I came home drunk. Mama would never trust me again, and I wouldn't blame her because I wouldn't trust myself anymore, either.

I cannot believe I'm going! I'm so excited, I know I won't be able to sleep a minute. Come on, Saturday! Hurry up and get here.

REAL 60

Do not get your hopes up, Zoe Wilkes. Do not. You know how she is. One day she promises the moon, and by dinner she denies the moon even exists.

I know my odds of actually going are only slightly better than winning the lottery, but both are so damned unlikely it's best not to count on either. What's that ridiculous saying she always messes up? *Don't count your horses before the chickens hatch.* I hate how we have to act like every ridiculous thing she says is gospel. Even though she messes up those phrases all the time, I'm going to take it to heart. I didn't realize how badly I wanted to go until she mentioned it, which is where the danger lies.

If I'm not extremely careful, she'll see how much I want this and she'll change her mind, just because she can. *The Lord giveth and the Lord taketh away.* In The Church of Gynger, you always have to be prepared to lose what she generously gave to you. And even if you don't lose it, you can be damn sure it was given with extremely long and tangled strings attached. If I do get to go, I know that's likely not the end of it.

I don't know what it will be, but there will be a cost. There always is.

Why the hell can't I have a mother who doesn't get off on playing God all the time? Is it too much to ask to be excited about a dumb dance without also having to worry about all the ways the universe will explode if I go?

REAL 61

When Cheryl first started talking to me, I was so annoyed with her for not taking the hint and leaving me alone. Well, for once, I'm glad she can't take a hint any better than I can catch a ball. I don't know why she forgave me after the way I treated her last week—God knows I wouldn't have forgiven me for being such an ass. I still can't shake the feeling Gynger's using the dance to set a trap for me, but I'm glad I have Cheryl and Nate to help me untangle this mess.

We decided if I do get to go, we'll go as a group. Cheryl invited me to sleep over afterwards, but I nixed it real quick. I don't want to push my luck. Besides, if I'm not there to make sure the kids get to bed at a decent hour, I'm like ninety-nine percent sure they'll stay up all night.

Cheryl thinks she has something I can wear, but I'm not so sure. She's way taller than me, and I'm so skinny, I imagine anything of hers will hang on me *like a cheap curtain,* to steal another phrase from Gynger. I tried to tell Cheryl I can come up with something at home, but she insisted on bringing a sack of stuff for me to try on tomorrow. Part of me is worried Gynger will get upset if I bring someone else's clothes home, which is why I left all the stuff Cheryl's mom, Beth, bought us at her house when we came home.

I think there's a high likelihood Gynger will accuse me of accepting charity and telling the whole world she can't keep her own kids properly clothed—even though she can't. If she asks, I think I can get around it by telling her Cheryl's parents bought the clothes for her, but she doesn't like them so she's giving them to me. And if I don't like them, we can yard sale them for a bit of extra cash. The extra cash angle is sure to smooth over any hard feelings, but I need to be careful not to let her sell what I want to wear—if I find anything good to wear, that is.

It surprises me how excited I am to try on what Cheryl brings me. She has incredible fashion sense. If a miracle happens and I find something good to wear, I bet I'll feel just like Cinderella at the ball. I can't believe I'm going to my first dance with my gorgeous friends, one of whom is Nate Evans. What even is my life? How can things be so magical on one hand and so nightmarish on the other? Sometimes I get dizzy trying to sort it all out.

I have to play it cool. I will not let myself get carried away. I have to remember this can all crumble away at any moment. Gynger makes and breaks promises as often as some mothers make chocolate chip cookies, so it's best to keep my expectations low. What if she told me I can't go, and I went anyway? A little teenage rebellion is a good thing now and then, right? She can't control me forever, can she?

For every action, there is an equal and opposite reaction. If I went against her orders, what would the opposite reaction be, and who would it impact? While I'm out dancing and drinking punch and pretending my life is fabulous, she'll be here, furious I disobeyed her. She always needs a target for her anger, so who would she punish in my place? Leesh, the Good Daughter? If Gynger comes after her, I'm afraid it'll push

Leesh deeper into depression and those little cuts on her arm will start going a lot deeper and she'll really hurt herself. That leaves Bobby.

Gynger's been hugging and cuddling him a lot lately, and he's soaking it up. They say a kid will go through all kinds of mental gymnastics to convince himself his parents will always protect and love him, even when experience has proven his parents are a danger to him. If Bobby is any indication, I'd say there's something to that theory. The problem is, she's like a mountain lion that's had its first taste of human blood. Now that she's crossed the line and hurt Bobby, he'll never be off limits to her again.

The stakes are too high. If she changes her mind, I can't rebel. I have to be a good little girl and do what my stupid mother tells me, so nobody gets hurt. If I don't, I'm basically playing the most messed up version of Duck, Duck, Goose ever.

I hate my life.

REAL 63

I heard part of an old reggae sounding song the other day while I was waiting to cross the street. A white convertible stopped at the light.

Nobody move, nobody get hurt. Nobody move, nobody get hurt

The light changed, and the car took off. I don't know what the song was about, but I felt it all the way to my soul. It made my bones hurt.

THE RULES

Don't walk too loud
Don't turn up the TV
Don't clink your spoon
Don't crunch your cereal
Don't gulp your drink
Don't burp.
For the love of all that is good, don't let the cupboard door
slam.
Don't let the floor get dirty—but
Don't run the vacuum.
Entertain your siblings—but
Don't laugh.
Laughter can only mean we're making fun of her.
Stay out of her sight
But run to her the moment she calls.
Feed the kids
But don't make a mess in the kitchen
Do the dishes

But do them silently.
Do your homework
But don't brag about good grades.
Never, ever be smarter than her.
Do the laundry.
If the washer is broken, use the tub. Use shampoo or soap if
you have to.
Don't breathe too loud
Don't get sick
Don't have a headache
Don't cry
Don't be afraid
If you are afraid
Do not let it show.
Never hit back
Never scream back
Cover your head
Curl into a ball
Disappear
That's how you survive

REAL 64

I found a CD called *In the Heat of the Night* by Pat Benatar at the library. I kinda recognized the name of the singer, but I picked up the CD because of the cover. It wasn't even that great of a cover, especially by today's standards. Kind of cheesy, actually, but it still called to me. I turned the CD over to read the songs. I was pretty sure I recognized one of them, but one I'd never heard of, *Don't Let it Show*, caught my attention. For some reason I can't even begin to understand, I had to listen to it. As soon as I got home, I dug out the old CD player from my closet, put on my headphones, and skipped right to that song.

Oh. My. God!

I know I said I felt like the reggae song was singing to my soul, but this one…it's like she made the song just for me. The whole point of the song is if you want to survive, you have to keep your true thoughts and feelings to yourself.

Even if it's taking the easy way out, keep it inside of you. Don't give in. Don't tell them anything. Don't let it show.

I mean, wow. It makes me feel hurt, but strong at the same time. I don't know if that even makes sense. Like in a movie, where a person is learning how to fight, and they keep getting knocked down. There's usually a point where they fall and think they can't keep going. Then, right when their opponent thinks they'll give up, they pull themselves up and fight with strength they didn't even know they had. They're hurt, but powerful.

I think this is my theme song.

I've been exploring poetry, but now I wonder if music is something I might want to do. I listened to it at least fifty times, and every time it punched me in the stomach hard enough to take my breath away. Music has the power to help people feel less alone. If I could write a song that helps a teenager in the future get through their shitty life, then that's something important and worth working for. The problem is, I don't know anything about writing music. Is writing songs a job? Can you just write words and let someone else come up with the music? Is it too late for me to learn how to read and write music?

What are the words to songs called again? Lyrics. Is there such a thing as a lyric writer? Lyrics and poems are pretty much the same thing, and lots of songs need words, so it's a real job, right? Or maybe not. Maybe the only way to be a lyric writer (I have to find out what that job is called, if it even exists) is to be in a band and write your own words. I can't play any instruments, and we don't have the money for me to take classes even if I knew which one I'd want to learn. Let's face it. I'll never be in a band. Like all my other dreams, this one evaporates before I even get a chance to get excited about it.

———

SAFE 26

Dear Diary,

A few days ago, Cheryl invited me over to try on clothes for the dance, but I told her I had to get home to help with dinner. Then yesterday, she surprised me with two bags of clothes to try on. I can't even believe the things she put in the bags. It's all so nice. Designer jeans, nice tops, even some cute little purses. She said I can keep all of it if I want. The stuff she likes, she outgrew. The things she doesn't like were mostly gifts from her grandparents. To be honest, I can't tell why she wouldn't absolutely adore everything she brought me. Her grandparents have such good taste in clothes, I never would have guessed old people bought them.

The only problem is, I'm the least fashionable person I've ever met. Maybe I can convince Leesh to help me figure it out. She's actually really good at putting cool outfits together.

I can't believe this is really happening! I'm so excited! But I have to remember to keep the clothes locked in my closet, so Sammycat doesn't crawl in them and leave fur all over them.

REAL 65

Leesh is slipping further and further away from me, and I don't know how to bring her back. I don't know how to help her through this because *I'm* the cause of it. I'm both afraid and angry. I'm not mad at Leesh, I'm mad at Gynger and Joel for putting us in this terrible situation to begin with. Angry my sister feels so much guilt for not being the target of Gynger's irrational rage that she can't even begin to believe me when I tell her I don't blame her. And I'm angry with myself, too, for all the times I've been snippy or short with her. It just made her feel I really did blame her, even though nothing could be further from the truth.

I said she's slipping further away, but that's not right. It's more like she's getting smaller. She's dropping weight like crazy, and since food is already scarce, it's not like she has room to lose much. I think she's stopped eating lunch, which is so hard for me to understand. I mean, I hate school lunches, but when times are bad, they're the only real meals we get. But it's not just the losing weight thing.

It's like she's taking up less space. When she sits on the couch, she doesn't spread out anymore. She folds into herself, wraps her arms around herself like she's trying to make herself tiny. She's fading, and I'm afraid she'll never come all the way back. I imagine her as the girl from my school journal entry *What if I fall?* In my mind, just as she's about to step off the ledge, I grab her from behind, pull her to the safety of the roof, and hold on to her for dear life. I can never let her fall. Never.

God, why the hell are my priorities so messed up? Here I am, giddy over some stupid dance when my sister is vanishing in front of me. I hate myself for being so selfish, but a piece of my brain whispers it's okay for me to be excited. Shouldn't I be allowed to look forward to regular teenager things? Shouldn't I be looking forward to my future, thinking about what I want to do with my life? Logically, I understand it's not selfish or unreasonable for other kids to feel these things, so why is it so wrong when I do? The smart part of my brain is barely a whisper, though, and I can only hear it when I'm alone at night.

If anyone should feel guilt, it's Gynger. She's the one to blame for this whole messed up family. She's the one who refuses to get a job. She drinks and screams and beats the snot out of me if the TV is too loud. She's the one who makes Bobby and Leesh witness all her meltdowns. She's the one who put me in charge of raising two kids and somehow, I'm also responsible for taking care of her, too, basically making me my own mother's mother.

Who does that? Why the hell is it my job to raise this family? To keep the house clean when she's home all day? To decide which bills to pay and which to ignore? And while we're at it, somebody please tell me why I should have to listen to her complain about her sex life? Why do I have to solve her problems for her? I'm a kid! The only thing I'm supposed to be in charge of is turning in my homework and reasonable chores.

Here's a secret I've never even given myself permission to

think. As much as I hate the pressure of having to make financial decisions or listening to her personal problems, part of me kind of likes it. At least when she's talking to me like an adult, I'm getting halfway positive attention instead of painful attention. When she says I'm smart and thanks me for my advice, I get all warm and puffy inside. It makes me feel smart and helpful instead of stupid and worthless. Maybe it's not the kind of love and attention mothers should give their kids, but it's all she seems to be able to give me, and it's better than nothing, isn't it?

I'm so tired. I worry about everyone all the time. I worry Joel will get in an accident and die. Or Gynger will choke to death on her own puke while I'm at school. I'm terrified Leesh will disappear so far into herself, she'll never find her way back. I worry her cutting will go deeper, and she'll decide life isn't worth the pain anymore. I know Leesh and Bobby aren't getting their needs met. They don't have enough to eat, they aren't in soccer or karate or any other kind of lessons. They don't even have many toys.

I know it sounds like a cliché, but the worry is like a constant weight on my shoulders. Can we pay the rent this month? A heat wave is coming. Did we pay the electricity so we can at least run fans if we can't run the AC? The food bank is closed, and I forgot to go the other day. How will we make it through the weekend? If I get food, how can I spin it so Gynger doesn't think I'm saying she's a shit mom? How can I make her understand we need to eat without causing her to freak out?

Are my grades good enough for me to get a scholarship so I can get out of here after I graduate? Should I get a job? If I do, will the kids be safe here alone with her? Will Gynger even let me get a job when, according to her, I should keep my ass at home to watch the kids? Will Cheryl and Nate realize what a loser I am and stop hanging out with me?

Am I sharing too much in the safe journal? Is Mrs. Thomas keeping her promise not to read our class journals? Have I exposed us all for the freaks we are? Sometimes, I think I see her looking at me like she wants to say something, but she never does. Maybe she wants to move me to the remedial class. Maybe I'm not smart enough for on-level. Or maybe she's reading all of our journals and she's not sure if she should tell me she knows about my family.

I can't even begin to imagine what it's like to be a normal fifteen-year-old. Would I get bored if all I had to worry about was my nail polish matching my lipstick? But even if I were bored, it would be absolutely magical not to feel the weight of the world on my shoulders every minute of every day. Sometimes, I'm so exhausted I can barely keep my eyes open at school. Sometimes, my head hurts for days and nothing makes it feel better. Sometimes my neck feels like a toothpick and my head like a watermelon. On those days, I put my head on my desk and do my best not to fall asleep as I take notes.

I feel like I'm being crushed under a mountain of stress, and sometimes I think the only thing I'll ever feel is crushed. I do feel a little better when I write, though. Crappy as my poems are, and dangerous as it is to make real journal entries, at least writing gives me some relief.

———

SAFE 27

Dear Diary,

Tonight's the night! It's dance night. Leesh and I were able to put together an outfit and it looks AMAZING. The jeans fit me perfectly. They hug me in the right places and relax out in the right places. I topped the jeans off with a long, flowy white shirt that's kind of cut at an angle. The left side hangs down almost to my knee and stops in a little V. The right side stops just below my waist. When I first saw the shirt, I thought it would look stupid on me, but Leesh made me try it on, and she was so right. It feels weird to admit it, but I actually think I look cute!

I'm meeting Cheryl at the school about half an hour early. She's bringing some makeup and jewelry to pull everything together. I've never been much of a makeup person, but I'm glad she offered. It's nice to get dressed up now and then. I do wish I had a cute pair of shoes, but it's not a huge deal. I cleaned my shoes the best I could, and since it won't be bright, nobody will get a good look at them, anyway. I'm not going to let old shoes bring me down. Plus, I don't want to look like I'm trying too hard.

Okay, there are still a few chores I need to finish up before I can get ready.

TTFN!

REAL 66

Oh, shit. Tonight's the night, and I just realized I don't have anywhere to put this journal. None of the purses Cheryl gave me are big enough for it, and there's no way I can leave it here. What am I going to do? Maybe I can hide it in my waistband. My shirt is long and flowy enough. Or maybe I could beg Leesh to keep it? I know she'd never go snooping around trying to find my personal stuff, but who could blame her for reading a journal I put directly into her hands?

Speaking of my sister, when Leesh helped me put my outfit together, she seemed to come to life. It's the first time I've seen even a hint of her old self in ages. It's like a light flicked on and lit up her whole face when she saw Cheryl's—my—clothes. Honestly, I had no idea she has such a good sense of fashion, probably because she can't do much with the random charity box clothes we get. I know she's only in seventh grade, but I bet she could make a ton of money being a fashion designer someday.

She studied and discarded pieces faster than I could even tell what they were, and Sammycat didn't waste any time building herself a designer nest.

"Nope, this will make you look lumpy. Not this—the color's all wrong for you. Yes. Yes. Maybe. No."

It was like watching Van Gogh paint. If she had been born into a different family, she'd definitely rule the school. I hate the way her talents are wasted in this sorry excuse for a family. Even though I had a solid idea of what I wanted to wear in the first fifteen minutes, I also knew her happiness wouldn't last, so I dawdled as long as possible, pretending I couldn't make up my mind, just to let her be happy a little bit longer.

I tried on the same clothes a hundred times, making up reasons I didn't like them. Leesh patiently explained the pros and cons of every possible combination, and I swear she glowed as she talked about cut and texture. I would gladly try on a whole warehouse full of clothes to see her sparkle with excitement. Under all her sadness, Leesh is still in there somewhere, and maybe she can find her way back from the darkness.

I still can't believe Gynger hasn't changed her mind yet. I'm not sure why she wants me to go, but as long as I keep this journal out of her hands, it doesn't matter. She could turn my room inside out and upside down, and I wouldn't even blink. There will be nothing in here for her to find, anyway, so she can go ahead and do her worst. I decided to bring my backpack to the school with me. I'll put a couple of Cheryl's old purses in it and tell Gynger Cheryl changed her mind and wants them back. It's the best plan I could come up with on short notice, and I think it'll work fine.

I feel guilty about leaving the kids alone with her, but Jesus, she's their mother. She should be able to handle them for the evening. I mean, history has proven she's not even capable of handling a runny nose, but Leesh is, and she promises she'll be on high alert the whole time.

I warned Bobby to be on better than his best behavior, and to stay as quiet and as far away from Gynger as possible. He and Leesh can have apples and PB&J sandwiches, so dinner is taken care of. As long as they don't get into a knife fight, everything should be okay. I deserve this, right? To be a kid for just a few hours? Everyone deserves a break now and then. I keep trying to convince myself I'm not abandoning my brother and sister, but as soon as I start to get excited, I think about all the catastrophes waiting to happen.

It's better not to even think about what could go wrong, because there are at least a million things. Instead, I should focus on friends and fun. Let my imagination run wild. What if I get my first kiss tonight? I mean, I don't even really want it to be like that with me and Nate, but it's not like I suddenly see him as a brother, either. He's still the same gorgeous guy he's always been, but our friendship is way more important than a stupid crush I used to have. But thinking about being there with him tonight makes my stomach spin like one of those teacup rides at the fair.

Wobbly stomach aside, who knows if Gynger will ever let me out to play again? I have to let go of all the negativity I'm feeling and enjoy myself. Hell, not even enjoy. I want to memorize every single second because if I never get another chance like this, at least I'll have my memories.

———

SAFE 28

Dear Diary,

Oh, my God, the dance was fantastic.

"Zoe," Cheryl squealed when I met her in front of the school. "You look perfect."

How embarrassing and totally untrue. She slayed in her

green, strapless dress and matching heels and everyone spent the night staring at her as if she were a movie star. I always knew she was gorgeous, but I felt like Quasimodo compared to her.

"Thanks, but my sister basically told me what to wear. If I had to pick out my own outfit, I'm sure you wouldn't be as impressed. But you! Holy wow, you look like a model."

"Stop it. You're gorgeous, girl. You need to own it."

Part of me wanted to hide under a bush, but I ignored that part and smiled instead. "Thank you."

"That's more like it." She hooked her arm through mine, planted a kiss on my cheek, and we followed the crowd into the gym.

I've heard the cafeteria get loud, but lunch-loud is nothing compared to dance-loud. We practically had to shout to hear each other over the thumping music. My throat feels like ten angry kittens attacked it from all the yell-talking but it was totally worth it. A blue cloth covered a long table near the wall, and there were so many bags of chips and trays of cookies, I bet everyone could have had ten of each and there would still be leftovers. I wish I had thought to bring some home for Mama, Leesh, and Bobby, though. It would have been a fun treat for them.

Half-sized bottles of water were piled into big tubs, taking the place of the punch bowl from my imagination. I guess the teachers finally figured out punch bowls and teenagers don't mix. What a relief! Girls are hit over the head with warnings never to drink anything we don't open ourselves basically since we're two years old, so I had already decided to avoid the punch. Safety first! I knew I'd eventually get thirsty, and I was glad for all the water bottles so I wouldn't have to gulp from a water fountain like a camel in the desert.

I don't know where TV shows and movies get the idea kids dress up for every little dance. The girls plan their outfits, but they plan them for school, too. It's not like they're in four-inch heels and sexy dresses. Well, except for Cheryl and a few other popular girls. The boys mostly wore jeans and either button-down shirts or nice tee-shirts. Shows and movies would be way better if the people who wrote them actually spent time with teenagers. It's kind of embarrassing how out of touch with us they are. A few minutes after Cheryl and I walked into the cafeteria, Nate showed up, looking incredible but still casual.

He floated from group to group, hugging some people and fist-bumping others, but eventually he wandered over to me and Cheryl and spent most of the night with us. When a dance circle formed, he was the first to jump in. Not only is he fear-less, but the boy's got some serious moves, too. I'll never understand why he's so nice to me all the time. Maybe it's some kind of trick. I don't want to be negative, but Mama's right, you can never truly trust anybody. Sooner or later, Nate will disappoint me. The best thing I can do is be prepared so it doesn't hurt so much when it happens. Until then, I'm going to enjoy myself.

REAL 67

Somebody call the Pope because there's been a real-life miracle. I spent the whole dance trying not to think about all the horrible things I could come home to, and I mostly succeeded. The worries never left my head completely, but I did a pretty good job of shoving them into a dark corner of my brain. After all, if I was so worried about things blowing up at home, maybe I shouldn't have been selfish and left Leesh and Bobby. Since I was out, I might as well try and enjoy myself. Thank God Nate and Cheryl never left me alone to fend for myself.

"Zoe," Cheryl squealed as she ran up to me in front of the school. "You look perfect."

How embarrassing and totally untrue. Her blond, wavy hair flowed over her bare shoulders and her tight, silky green dress looked more like the sexiest prom dress in existence than something you'd wear to a dance in a cafeteria. I always knew she was gorgeous, but for the first time since I met her, I felt the same flutters in my heart and belly I used to feel before Nate and I got close. I shoved the butterflies all the way down my body and imagined them flying out of my feet. Cheryl is my best friend, and that's it.

"Thanks, but my sister basically told me what to wear. If I had to pick out my own outfit, I'm sure you wouldn't be as impressed. But you! Holy wow, you look like a model."

"Stop it. You're gorgeous, girl. You need to own it."

Part of me wanted to hide under a bush, but I ignored it and smiled instead. "Thank you."

"That's more like it." She hooked her arm through mine, planted a kiss on my cheek, and we followed the crowd toward the gym. My face tingled where she kissed me, and I thanked every god I could think of the hall lights were too dim for her to notice my blushing cheeks.

What is wrong with you, Zoe Wilkes? Stop this nonsense this moment.

"I want to drop my backpack off at my locker," I said as we approached my locker hall.

"Sure. Why'd you bring it, anyway? Don't tell me. You finished all your homework early and figured you'd bring it back to school tonight, so you don't forget it on Monday."

What a ridiculous theory. I've never been the kind of person to get homework done early. "Yeah, something like that."

Looking back on the night, I can't believe how perfect it was. They played all my favorite songs and Cheryl, Nate and I danced to almost every one. When the first slow song of the night came on, Nate shocked the hell out of me by asking me to dance, and once again, I thanked the universe or whatever for hiding my blushing face under dim lights.

I never learned how to dance, but he didn't seem to mind. He hugged me close as we spun in slow circles and didn't even complain when I stepped on his toes. The butterflies came back, and I let myself float in the cloud of his herby cologne—like a mix of rosemary and mint.

"All right, you two, break it up." Cheryl stepped between us and took Nate's place. "It's my turn."

"Fine," Nate said as he stepped away, "But the next slow one's all mine." He winked at me and flashed his swoony smile. "As long as you agree, anyway."

I can't believe I spent the whole night dancing with both of them. I don't know what the hell was going on with me, but I felt like I imagine being drunk feels like. Giddy and dizzy and, can you even believe it? Pretty. In all my wildest dreams, I couldn't have asked for a more perfect night. I'm going to assume the way Cheryl made me feel was nothing more than excitement at being out of the house. I mean, what else could it be?

Even after I floated through the front door and expected to find a war zone, the night continued to be perfect. Nothing was smashed. Nobody was hiding or crying. It was…normal. Leesh and Bobby were curled up, sleeping on the couch. The TV was on, but the sound was low, so it wouldn't disturb Gynger, who was nowhere in sight. I crept toward her room and sighed with relief at the closed door. Either she got herself to bed, or Leesh had to herd her. Whatever. At least she was out for the night, and nothing too awful seemed to have gone down.

I'm annoyed with myself for worrying so much but can't even tell you how relieved I am I didn't come home to World War Three. Maybe Gynger's getting better. Maybe there's still hope for me to be a normal teenager who does normal teenager stuff. Maybe we've finally come to the end of this lifelong horror movie.

Maybe, maybe, maybe
Don't be such a big, stupid baby.

God, I'm embarrassed by how dumb I sound. I may not be an adult, but experience has taught me people don't change, especially people like my mother. Still, it can't be all bad to hold out a little hope, right? A tiny little pearl of hope I keep tucked away deep in the most private part of my soul. Maybe holding on to the pearl makes me stupid or naïve, but I can't let it go entirely. People who've given up all hope of a better life end up like...well, like Gynger, and there's nobody else in the entire world I want to end up like less than her. Just like I made myself enjoy the dance despite all my worries, I'm making the choice to hold on to a little bit of hope. From now on, I'm going to grab on to all the little bits of good and sunshine that come my way.

REAL 68

Well, guess who finally showed up last night after being gone for two weeks? I stared at the shadows on my ceiling, trying to fall asleep, but my brain flat refused to shut down. As I finally drifted off, his big blue rig rumbled out front. The headlights made the shadows creep like monsters across my wall and ceiling. Those shadows used to scare me, and I'd hide under the covers until they disappeared. Then, I got a little older, and I realized the shadow monsters weren't what I needed to be afraid of.

It's hard to believe only a couple of months ago, I would have jumped out of bed and run to the porch to greet Daddy if I heard him come home, but last night, I didn't. Why bother running to meet a father who's just going to leave again in a day or two, anyway? A father who can't protect us when he's gone and won't protect us when he's here. He's not even really a father. He's nothing but another body to clean up after. A person who comes around occasionally and throws everything out of balance until he disappears without so much as a pat on the head.

And don't even get me started on Gynger after he leaves again. That's a whole 'nother mess for me to clean up. Jesus, lady. He's been coming and going like this for years. And before that, he left the house for whatever jobsite before the sun came up and didn't get home until after dark. You'd think she'd be used to it by now.

It's not like he's heading off to war, but every time he leaves, she spirals down into this deep pit. It's not quite like how she got after she hurt Bobby, but it's still bad. The first few days after he leaves, she's more dangerous than a long-forgotten land mine. At least with an abandoned land mine, nobody knows danger is buried underground, and it might never even blow up. She's more like a mine everyone sees and knows goes off again and again, but nobody can disarm it or predict what will make it blow. Each time, you're left wondering what you could have done to prevent it.

After she explodes and your guts are dripping off the walls like a botched paint job, you're grateful you're still alive, but terrified to move because you know it'll happen again. What's even worse is, after she blows up, she acts as helpless as a toddler. She gets to freak out, explode, bruise me, make me bleed, and then, when she's done, I have to get up and bring her a drink. Get up and bring her food. Do the dishes. Fold her laundry. I have to lower my eyes and tell her *I'm* the one who's sorry.

I'm sorry, Mama. I hope you can find it in your heart to forgive me, even though I don't deserve your forgiveness. I'll do better. I promise.

I could take lessons and learn every dance ever invented, but this is the dance I will always know best. Taking on her crap and making it my own so she doesn't feel bad. Why do I do that? Why does she expect me to? What would happen if I stopped?

So yeah. Forgive me, *Daddy*, if I don't jump out of bed and come running to hug you. She'd probably accuse me of trying to seduce you if I did, anyway.

REAL 69

I know Nate's told me his dad is awful before, but I've been so caught up in my own problems, I never even bothered to ask him about it. What kind of shitty friend am I? I'm here in my own world worried about my brother and sister, worried about what to wear to a stupid dance, and the whole time, I never even thought to ask him if he's okay. He's worked so hard to be my friend, but I never ever spared two minutes to be his.

He showed up with a black eye today. When I asked him what happened, he sorta shrugged me off. Like an inconsiderate jerk, I pressed the issue.

"Come on," I snapped. "You're always trying to get me to open up to you, but now you don't want to tell me what happened to your face?"

"It's not a big deal. I fell, okay?"

"You fell? Onto your eye? That's not how falling works."

For the first time since I've known him, anger flashed in his eyes. Rage, hot and heavy as a cast-iron skillet, practically radiated from him. I swear, if I put my hand on his arm, it would have come away blistered.

"If you really cared what goes on with me, you'd—I don't know—ask me now and then."

"You're right, and I'm sorry. I'm an ass with zero social skills, which is why I don't have friends." I hoped my stupid attempt at humor would diffuse him a little.

"True." His voice was quiet, and I had to lean in close to hear him over the kids shouting in the hall. "But you also push everyone away, partly by not talking about your life, but partly by not asking anyone else about theirs. It's not healthy."

I wanted to defend myself, but this was about Nate, not me. I owed it to him to at least attempt to be a halfway decent friend. "You're right again. I want to do better, but if you don't want to talk about what happened, I understand."

He was quiet for so long, I thought for sure he didn't want to talk to me. Finally, he broke his silence.

"My dad," he said through a clenched jaw. "He got wasted and went after my mom. When I tried to come between them, he punched me."

"Shit, Nate. I'm so sorry." I put my hand on his shoulder, half expecting him to jerk away, but he didn't. "It was a nice thing to do for your mom, though."

"No. It was pointless and stupid. I only pissed him off even more and made things worse for her. I know better than to get involved."

I thought about Joel and how he just sits there and doesn't protect us, and how that makes me feel like I'm not worth saving. Like, if he doesn't stop it, it has to mean I really deserve it.

"I'm sure your mom appreciates what you did. You stuck your neck out for her. She knows you love her and have her back."

"You'd think so, wouldn't you? But nope. After he took off, she totally freaked out on me. She said if I had minded my own fucking business, he would have run out of steam a lot sooner. She stopped short of saying it was my fault, but I could tell she was thinking it."

"Have I ever told you how much I hate my father?" I don't know why I said that, but it was a relief to say it out loud. "He knows what my mother does, but he never gets involved. He never even gets mad at her for hurting me. He just sits there and pretends it's not happening, watching the ashes on his cigarette turn into snakes and fall onto the floor. I wish he'd try to help me the way you did."

He shrugged but didn't say anything.

"At the same time," I continued, "I think I get where your mom is coming from. It's my job to protect the kids from my mother, and if Bobby jumped in the middle of things and got hurt, I'd never forgive myself. My dad should protect me the way I protect Bobby. The way you protected your mom."

"He should protect you. When my dad comes at me, my mother always jumps in for me. It's not like he gets violent often, anyway. He has a lot of stress at work right now. It's nothing like what you go through every day. I just hate that my mom is so mad at me right now."

I didn't know how to respond. We both have an awful parent, but it's not a shitty parent competition. The warning bell rang, and we split up. As I sat down at my desk, I had an epiphany. It isn't Nate's job to come to his mother's rescue any more than it's Bobby's job to come to mine. In the end, we're all nothing but kids who have to grow up too fast in messed up families.

REAL 70

Please secure your own oxygen mask before assisting those around you.

That's what they say you should do on airplanes. If you help others before you can even breathe, death could come for all of you. I secure my mask. Breathe deep. Let the oxygen hit my lungs. My brain. I look under my seat for strength.

Some people don't follow instructions. They take a deep breath and hold it as they secure their own mask to someone else's face, refusing to let a little thing—like the lack of air—stop them from helping.

Some people, brave and intense, create their own atmosphere. The yellow mask dangles uselessly from the ceiling as their power and rage creates a personalized air only they can inhale.

And isn't that better, anyway?

Oxygen masks can fail, but rage will never let you down. The air can stop blowing, or the hose can spring a leak. But if you learn to hold your breath until you manufacture your own air, nothing, not even lack of oxygen, can take you down.

REAL 71

I used to be Daddy's Little Girl
Standing on his dirty boots as he danced me across the floor.
When I got hurt, he'd swoop me up and hug me to his chest,
His strong heartbeat chasing the fear
And the pain
Away.
He used to hold me in his lap
Tell me I could do anything
Be anyone
Go anywhere.
"Little Darlin'" His beer breath a sour cloud of comfort
"Don't you think for a minute you ain't good enough. No rich
little girl with fancy shoes and an ugly purse will ever be better
than you. Stay away from the bullshit, baby girl, and you'll be
just fine."
His words confused me and kept me warm at the same time. I
believed him.
I used to be Daddy's Little Girl.
Riding shotgun on his liquor store runs

My wind-wild hair whipping through the open windows
The songs on the radio lost under the rumble of the engine and
the roar of our laughter.
I used to be Daddy's Little Girl,
But along the way, something changed.
I stopped being little
He stopped loving me.
I grew up. Grew angry
He stopped being my hero.
Heroes never let the bad guy win.
Heroes fight for those smaller, weaker than them
And Daddy?
Well, the only thing he fought for was the chance to disappear.
I used to be Daddy's Little Girl.
Not anymore.
No more waiting to be rescued
To be wrapped in a blanket and whisked away from danger.
No more counting on someone who will only let me down.
Daddy's Little Girl had to grow up
And she will save herself.

———

SAFE 29

Dear Diary,

I have so much to do. I can't keep track of it all. Mrs. Thomas says when you feel overwhelmed, it helps to write everything down so you can see exactly what's on your plate so you can prioritize. I guess that makes sense, but what if everything feels like a priority and not all that important at the exact same time? Okay, some of it is important, like that Midsummer's Night Dream essay and studying for *another* algebra test. But do I even need to write those things down since I already know I have to do them? Making lists seems like a waste of time to me, but like they say, "Don't knock it till you try it."

Zoe's To-Do List for Today

1. Finish Midsummer's essay
2. Study for algebra
3. Make dinner
4. Tidy up the house
5. Laundry! (I almost forgot!)
6. Ask Leesh to take out Sam's litter
7. Take out the litter myself when she never gets to it

I know there are a lot of other things I need to do, but now that I'm trying to get them all down, my brain completely shut off. I wish I had a normal attention span. When we have time to work on homework in class, everyone else can keep their heads down and work until the bell. Not me. Instead, my brain gets heavy, and my eyes feel like they're coated in hot sand. Or I'll know what I need to do, but I end up sitting there, zoning out. Sometimes, I get carried away by stories I make up about the other kids, but other times I go completely blank.

My teachers probably think I'm a complete idiot. I don't know why my brain doesn't work the way it should. It used to. I used to be able to keep everything in neat little boxes in my head and only pay attention to the most important box at the moment. Now, it's like there are still boxes for all my thoughts, but they've been dumped into a big pile, and I end up sifting through the rubble, trying to find the things I need.

Seriously. Do you even hear yourself, Zoe Wilkes? You

sound absolutely bananas. Something is wrong with you. How about instead of spending so much energy putting thoughts into imaginary boxes, you keep focused on the everyday stuff? Dinner. Laundry. Homework. My sister and brother. Nothing else really matters.

REAL 72

How do I get myself into situations like this? Well, I know how. The question is why do I keep getting myself into situations like this? I guess I know that, too. I have to keep writing in my other diary, because if I don't, Gynger's going to wonder what I'm trying to hide and we all know what she'll do if she thinks she'll find something I'm hiding. And if she doesn't find what she's looking for, things will go from bad to kill-me-already faster than I can duck. This is an impossible situation, and I hate it so, so much.

"Oh, look at you, you poor, poor little slave girl." She came into the kitchen, all sharp words, and dirty looks as I filled the big pot with water. "It must be so hard for you to balance everything you need to do, you poor thing. Cooking dinner, doing homework. It's all so much." She wiped imaginary sweat off her forehead with the back of her hand.

Gray squeezed at the edges of my vision, and my lips and fingers went numb. I pulled myself out of the creeping dark, turned the water off, and faced her.

"What do you mean, Mama?"

She spouted more garbage about how hard my life is and what an unfit mother she is for not making homemade pizza every night. My heart stuck in my throat. I tried to swallow around it and sound casual as I carried the pot to the stove.

"That's so silly, Mama. You know how much I love cooking dinner. I'm so thankful to you for teaching me all the skills I'll need when I'm on my own." Here we go, dancing again.

"So, you don't think I'm a shitty mother?"

"What? Absolutely not." *Liar.* "I've said it before, but I really do mean it. I feel sorry for girls whose moms baby them and make them every single meal. Those girls will never learn how to cook for themselves, much less their families. You're smart for thinking ahead." I put the lid on the full pot to get the water to boil faster. "I'm just sorry I'm not a better cook yet. You're probably so sick of spaghetti."

I took the empty glass out of her hand and made another drink—more ice and soda than whiskey. "You go put your feet up and I'll call you when dinner's ready, okay? It won't be long."

"You sure do take good care of your old mama. You don't have to be in a rush to move out, you know. You could stay and help me with the kids. Get a job. Save money."

I'd rather move in with a pack of wild boars. "Thank you, but there's no point in even thinking about it yet. I'm years away from graduation. Go on ahead and enjoy your drink in peace before dinner. It'll be ready soon." I don't know who or what was watching over me, but she actually walked away without yelling or dumping the pot of water all over the floor.

I hate dancing with her, but I'm good at it. What I'm not so good at is figuring out who I am. I feel myself cracking. Who's the real me? Am I the big-eyed girl in my Diary? The girl who works hard and is confused by everything around her? Or am I the me I feel like right now? The one who's furious. The one who's sick with rage? But what good is rage when I still bend over backward to protect my mother instead of trying to find help for her? Or for us? How is it possible to love someone you don't like? How can you be so protective of someone you wish would disappear forever?

REAL 73

"Don't be mad at me," Cheryl huffed as she jogged to catch up to me before school.

"Why?" I tried to give her a disapproving look in advance of whatever she was about to tell me, but she didn't even register it.

"I know you told me not to, but I talked to my parents again, and they said all of you can stay with us!" She smiled so big you'd think her parents had given her a brand-new Corvette.

I definitely didn't share her enthusiasm. All the butterflies I felt at the dance turned into lead weights.

"Oh, my God, Cheryl, again? Why? I thought I could trust you! Now your parents know about my family. Why would you do this to me after I distinctly told you not to?" I couldn't breathe, and familiar numbness crept into my lips and fingers.

"Calm down." She rubbed large circles on my back. I could easily imagine Beth doing the same thing to her to help her calm down, and I had to fight the urge to shove her away from me.

It's not fair how some people have parents who actually

love and want them, and other people are dog shit on the bottom of their parents' shoes. I didn't want to calm down. I wanted to run away. I wanted to climb into a locker and hide until I died, and my skeleton turned to dust and crumbled away.

"Get away from me." I stopped fighting the urge and pulled myself away from her. I felt like I was being pulled up and out of my body, floating above it and watching this conversation happen below me.

"Will you listen to me? I didn't tell them the truth. You asked me not to, and I would never betray you. I swear."

That brought me down a little.

"It was actually a brilliant lie, if I do say so myself. I told them your parents' anniversary is coming up and your mom wants to go on a trip with your dad because they never got a honeymoon. Since your dad travels for work all the time, they barely get to spend any time together. My parents always make a huge deal about how important it is to nurture their relationship since I'll move away eventually, and it'll just be the two of them. Ew. Anyway, I knew my mother would want to help. She offered to let all of you stay the whole time your parents are on vacation, even if it's weeks."

Cheryl beamed and it would have been easy to let myself get excited with her, but as much as I wanted to, I knew we couldn't run away to her house. It would put her family in danger, and Gynger wrecked our family more than enough. I refused to let her destroy Cheryl's.

"Look," I said. "I'm touched by how much you want to help, and it means everything to me that you're not saying empty words because you think you should. It means more than you know. But," I took a deep breath and held it as I tried to figure out how to continue without sounding like a jerk or an alarmist.

"If I ever run away, I'll definitely have to bring Leesh and

Bobby with me, especially since she's already hurt Bobby once. But we couldn't stop running when we reached your house. We'd have to run far and fast. Out of this stupid town, out of this county, out of the state. Hell, maybe even out of the country. We'd have to run so far, we all forget where we came from, and there would never be any chance of her finding us. She'd kill us if she ever did. No question about it."

"I think you're being a little extreme, Zoe. If you stayed with us, my parents could protect you. I know it."

"I can't take the risk. And if you care about me like you say you do, keep your mouth shut. You can't tell your parents *anything* about my life. If they called the cops, we could be taken away and separated, and then I wouldn't be able to protect my sister or brother at all."

"No, my parents would protect you. I know they'd move you all in before they'd let you go with random strangers." She smiled at me, and I wanted to slap that smile right off her face.

"You can't tell the future. And even if they did want to take us in, would they be allowed to? Aren't there rules for who can take kids in if they're removed from their home?"

"I don't know how it works, but my parents probably do. If you would let me ask them instead of making me tell them stupid stories about why you need to stay with us, we could find out."

"You don't know the rules, because you've never had to think about this kind of thing. Anyway, odds are the state wouldn't take us away. We have a roof over our heads and Leesh and Bobby had it hammered into them their whole lives that if we get taken away, we'll get split up and it would upset our mother so much, she'd die. I'm the one who gets the worst of her anger, so there's no reason for them to tell anyone about our situation. If things ever got bad enough for me to talk—to a teacher, to your parents, to anyone—and we didn't end up being taken away, guess whose life would be a living hell afterwards? She'd know I told someone about our *private family stuff."* I air quoted the words I'd heard a hundred million times. "She'd freak out so much, she'd literally murder me." My teeth chattered, and I shivered uncontrollably.

Cheryl put her arms around me and hugged me tighter than I could remember being hugged since I was a little girl and Joel gave me bear hugs. I wanted to melt into her and let her warmth pass to my body, but I stiffened up and pulled away.

"I feel so helpless, Zoe. You're my best friend, and I want to keep you safe. I love you."

"I—" the words I wanted to say caught in my throat, so I said different ones instead. "I know. Just please let me handle this, okay?"

REAL 74

I've been thinking a lot about how I told Nate I can't stand my dad, and I can't shake the stomach-spinning shame. No matter how hard I try, I can't figure out why I feel so badly for telling him. Maybe it's because you're not supposed to feel angry with both of your parents if only one of them treats you like garbage. Maybe if he and Gynger took turns whaling on me, it'd be understandable, but he doesn't. All I can figure is I'm a horrible person. Nate and his mom are close, and he doesn't hate her for what his father does to him. No, he keeps his anger on his dad, where it belongs.

Why should I be so mad at someone who never lays a finger on me? Isn't it like hating all dogs because your neighbor's aggressive, neglected dog bit you? It's immature and irrational. If there are two things I refuse to be, it's immature and irrational. Gynger lives her whole life based on the Holy Scripture of Immaturity and Irrationality, and I want no part of that religion. Plus, it could be worse. I know Joel will never hit me. He never even yells at me. Nate doesn't have the same luxury. His mom was furious when he stepped between her and his dad, so now he probably feels like he can't really trust her not to hurt him, but he still loves her, anyway.

Sometimes, I'm afraid Gynger is right. Maybe the apple doesn't fall far from the tree. Maybe whatever is wrong with her was passed down to me; I just don't have symptoms yet. Like when someone has the flu, they can be contagious before they even know they're sick. I know things like depression can run in families, so why not whatever Gynger has? There's so much I don't know, but one thing I do know is I have to be so, so careful. If I'm really a ticking time bomb, I don't want to ever explode on Leesh or Bobby. I don't want to go off on Nate or Cheryl. They're the only people besides Leesh and Bobby who care about me, and I can't afford to go ape shit on them.

The way Gynger bases her whole life on the Scripture of Immaturity and Irrationality, I base mine on the fear of turning out exactly like her. You know those rubber WWJD bracelets people wear? I think they're supposed to remind you to be a good person. Like, if you're in a situation where you can act like a huge jerk, you're supposed to look down and think, *is this what Jesus would do?* I feel like my whole body is a giant WWJD bracelet, but swap the J for a G, and instead of doing the same thing as Jesus, I try to do the exact opposite of Gynger. My plan is to live the most opposite life from her I possibly can. I'm never going to drink. Never going to do drugs, not even something like cold medication. And never, never, will I *ever* have kids. It's too dangerous.

———

SAFE 30

Dear Diary,

Oh my gosh, guess what? Mrs. Thomas asked me to stay after class a minute. Naturally, I was worried I was in trouble for failing a test or something. I told her I had to get to algebra, but she said she'd write me a note.

"Don't worry, you're not in trouble." I guess she sensed my fear.

I wanted to tell her I've never heard of anyone being asked to stay after class for a good reason, but I kept my fool mouth shut for once and followed her to her desk while everyone left the room.

"I won't keep you long." She sat on the edge of her desk and crossed her legs like she planned to keep me there all day. "How do you think you're doing in my class?"

Um, what in the world was she talking about? My brain keeps shutting down. I keep forgetting what I'm saying and doing. More and more, I feel like I'm floating outside of my body, not even connected to it at all, but looking down and trying to force it to do the things it should be doing. I feel it a lot when I'm working on our class journals. The weird tingly feeling in my hands and lips work together to make me feel like I'm floating or falling, or maybe a little of both. If she calls on me, my vision turns gray and hazy before everything is blotted out by blackness. Most of the time, I feel like a stupid failure, so how in the world can I be doing well in anything?

She said the last few essays I've written have been "insightful" and "thought-provoking" and she thinks I'm capable of so much more. I told her I didn't feel like I was doing so hot in her class, and I was really stressed out about failing it. Then, get this. She told me she thinks I should move into Honors English. But wait, there's more. She said the Honors class would benefit from having me. Can you even imagine? Zoe Wilkes in an honors class? A class for the smart people of the world?

I don't know what Mrs. Thomas sees in me, but she promises there's something special about me. I'd never go so far as to call myself special, but it feels good to hear. She said I could take a little time to think about it, but I should let her know if I want to transfer ASAP. Usually, the policy is to wait until the new semester, but sometimes, for a special circumstance, they allow a mid-semester transfer, and she definitely considers me a special circumstance. If I do this, it's possible my whole schedule could change. Luckily, Mrs. Thomas teaches Honors English, too, so at least I'd still be with her and not a new teacher.

I'll never forget, even in a thousand years, her words.

"Zoe, you have a gift. Your mind is sharp, and you see the world differently. You have a way with words I haven't seen once in the fifteen years I've been a teacher. You're a natural born writer, and your talents are squandered in this class. The world needs to know who Zoe Wilkes is, and that starts with living up to your potential."

Don't worry. I'm not gonna get a big head from all those nice things. If even half of what she said is true, I owe it all to Mama. She's the one who taught me to put everything into my education. She's the one who brought me up to believe in the power of hard work. Heck, I barely deserve any credit at all. I am who I am because I have such a good mother.

REAL 75

So yeah, all of that really happened. I still don't know what to make of any of it, and I'm considering tearing those pages out of the safe diary. I know Gynger will take issue with someone telling me I have potential and I'm smarter than I give myself credit for, but you know what? I don't really care. I know I'm late to the party, but I'm finally starting to realize she'll feel and react the way she feels and reacts, and ninety-nine percent of the time, it has nothing to do with me.

Maybe sometimes I push back a little too hard, or I'm more disrespectful than I ought to be, but I think most of the time, she's completely irrational and she'll either tolerate me or hate me on any given day for her own mysterious reasons. I'm getting so tired of walking on eggshells and broken glass all the time. Still, it's best not to let her see those pages. Her jealousy makes her do awful things sometimes, and the last thing I need is to have Gynger rolling up to my school and causing a scene.

Mrs. Thomas told me to talk to my parents about transferring, but I'm not going to. If they need a parent's signature on the transfer paperwork, I'll forge it like I do for Bobby's notes.

I want to do this. Even if it means my schedule changes. Even if it means I'll have more reading and homework. I know it doesn't make sense, especially since I already don't have enough time to do everything I have to do. I'm already cutting corners on cooking and cleaning up. How many nights in a row can you really have pancakes for dinner? As of now, the answer is three. Who knows, maybe after tonight, it'll be four. Luckily, Gynger can't remember one night from the next, so if she bitches about pancakes again, I'll tell her we had grilled cheese last night and she'll believe me.

As long as Bobby doesn't contradict me, she'll buy it because it's easier than trying to remember for herself. Besides, she avoids reality so hard she can't let herself hear there's nothing else in the house to eat. She keeps her dumb head in the sand when it comes to how broke we are. I could probably tell her I made steak and baked potatoes for dinner last night and she'd believe me just so she doesn't have to face the reality of our empty cupboards.

Holy tangent, Batman! Where did *that* come from?

Back to the subject. If I don't transfer, everything stays exactly the way it is now. And the way it is, is...well, it's comfortable. I know what to expect and I don't have to put much effort into thinking, which is definitely a good thing. My brain isn't always so good at thinking, so it makes sense to stay put.

But at the same time, I'm flattered, and I feel somehow obligated. Not only to Mrs. Thomas, but to myself. For the first time in my life, someone sees something in me other than a poor, stupid, trashy girl, and I feel like I owe it to myself to see if Mrs. Thomas is right. Maybe there really is more to me than what I've always been told there is.

REAL 76

It's been two days and I haven't mentioned transferring to anyone. Also, I hate myself for being so weak, but I tore those pages out of the diary. I was careful not to leave torn edges in the binding, and I don't think she'll be able to tell. I thought long and hard about whether or not to tear them out, but in the end, there was no debate. When I come home with an A on a hard test, she either mocks me or screams at me for thinking I'm better than her. I mean, yeah, I'm better than her for a lot of reasons, but getting a good grade on a test isn't one of them. If she knew a teacher thinks I'm actually smart, Gynger would blow a damn fuse.

She's so confusing. She insists I be perfect, so everyone thinks she's the best mother in the world, but when I do well, she's so threatened by me she has to knock me down. I don't know where her insecurity comes from, I just know I need to do everything I can to keep it at bay. I wonder what it would feel like to come home and share exciting news with my mother and have her hug me and tell me she's proud of me? What could I do with my life if she were supportive instead of jealous? I bet I could be in all honors classes if I wanted. I bet I could even be a cheerleader if I wanted. I don't, but I could. I don't think there's anything I couldn't do if I had a real mom.

Annnndd—this kind of thinking is dangerous. When I go down the path of what it would be like to have a normal family, I always end up angry. Then I start to think I can prove myself and Gynger and the rest of the world wrong. Prove I can be something more than what I was born to be. Sure, this way of thinking makes me feel strong, but feeling strong makes you cocky, and when you're cocky, you mess up and the world laughs at you. Not *with* you. At you. There's no point in dreaming about how my life could be different. Things are the way they are, and I can't change them.

It doesn't matter how badly I want to transfer, I can't do it. I'll only make a fool of myself and disappoint Mrs. T. Hell, she'd probably walk me down to the remedial class herself and pretend she never even met me after she discovers her mistake. I'm staying put, end of discussion.

So much for making a firm decision and sticking with it. I was all set to tell Mrs. T I wanted to stay in on-level, and I even planned a whole speech. Something along these lines:

Oh, Mrs. Thomas! I'm so flattered you want me to transfer to Honors English. I'm beyond flattered you think I'm smart enough for it, but my life is already so busy, and I don't have the time to put in all the work an honors class needs. And, if I can be honest with you, even if I had all the time in the world, I don't have the brain an honors class takes. As much as my heart wants to move, I know I'd end up holding the class back, and that wouldn't be right. I think it's best if I stay put.

Instead of dawdling in the hallway or in the bathroom between classes, I rushed to English so I could tell her before I lost my nerve. I figured it'd be better to do it before class so I wouldn't have to sit with a nervous stomachache for an hour.

"Zoe!" Her smile spread across her face and her eyes sparkled like she was actually glad to see me. "I was just thinking about you. How're you?"

"I'm fine, ma'am." My voice was shaky and hot tears burned my eyes. "Allergies," I lied.

"I've been a teacher for a long time. I know what allergies look like and what they don't." She passed me a box of tissues and didn't say anything else until I got myself under control.

"I take it you're not going to transfer, then?" Her voice was gentle but rimmed with disappointment.

"How'd you know?"

"People don't usually cry when they're about to share positive news. I know you were excited about the idea, but I also know how much the idea scared you. Two plus two always equals four."

She would have made an excellent shrink if she hadn't become a teacher. I guess, in a way, they're kind of similar.

"I'm so busy," I mumbled at my shoes to avoid her eyes. "I have so much happening at home right now, and I don't have enough time. I'm sorry." Tears burned my eyes, but I'd rather run naked through the halls than let them fall. "Thank you so much, but I'm sorry."

"Can I trust you with a secret?" I looked up, and she smiled at me again. "Maybe I should have told you sooner, but I didn't want you to make your decision based solely on this information. If you transfer, you'll actually have less homework than you do now."

"What? How? Isn't it a harder class?"

"I suppose it's harder for some people, which is why it's not available to everyone. There is more reading, but not actual homework. You read the pages on your time, and we have discussions in class. We do essays now and then, but there's always ample time to get them done in class if you work diligently, which I believe you would."

"I don't understand. The workload is lighter for a harder class. How?"

"Oh, no. The workload isn't lighter, the homework is. In class, you'll be expected to dive deep into the things we read. Homework is easy, absorbing and interpreting work is a lot harder. You'll work so hard in class that I don't want you to work outside of it. I want your brain to have a break every night so it can process all the hard work from the day. Something tells me you understand a little about hard work going unseen."

Talk about an understatement. All I do is work my ass off for nobody to see it.

Other students drifted into the room, and I felt exposed standing at her desk as everyone sat down around me.

"Are you sure about your decision? I can give you more time to think about it."

"I don't need more time," I said. "When will my new schedule start?"

Not the answer I set out to give, but I'm one-hundred percent certain it was the right answer.

———

SAFE 31

Dear Diary,

The school made some weird changes to my schedule and now two classes have switched places. I have no clue why they switched things around, but what are you gonna do? It doesn't really matter since only the time of the classes has changed. I even have all the same teachers. It would have been nice to get some sort of notice this was going to happen so I could prepare my brain for it, but everyone knows students are expected to go along with whatever the Almighty Administration says. We're not allowed to have any kind of opinion about our own education.

It was a little strange being the new kid in classes I've been taking since we moved, but it's way better than being the new kid in an entirely new school. Anyway, it's not like I left friends behind in my old classes or am planning on making friends in my new ones. It's business as usual. Do my group assignments, answer questions when I'm called on, and keep up with my homework. I am glad I got to keep Mrs. Thomas, though. She's my favorite teacher this year, even though a lot of students don't like her because she pushes us to do our best.

One of my favorite things about her is how she encourages us to talk about the books we're reading. In my old class, the kids didn't like to participate in those discussions, which sucked because it made it so I couldn't share my thoughts, either. Not that I have many interesting thoughts worth sharing, but still. When nobody wants to talk, it's annoying to have that one person who does. I hope this new class is more talkative, so if I do have something I want to say, I won't annoy everyone else.

REAL 78

ALERT! ALERT! ALERT!

Nate is in my new English class! This is not a drill and it's *not* a joke.

We've been friends for a while now, so I'm not sure why I'm so weirded out by having a class with him. I should be glad he's there. He's a safe person. A bridge from one world into another. A few months ago, I'd have been completely over the moon to have a class with him, but things were different then. He was the guy of my dreams and completely out of my reach. It would have been exciting to have a class with him so I could be near him.

Now? Well, I still like him, but my feelings are complicated and we're just friends. Like me and Cheryl. I get those same electric tingles when she touches me as when Nate does, but it doesn't mean anything. I bet butterflies and electricity are a normal part of friendship, only I never learned that because I've never had friends before.

This is going to sound ridiculous, but now that we're friends, I see Nate less as the drop-dead gorgeous boy of my dreams and more like a real person. I used to have an idea what

Fantasy Nate would be like, but Real Nate, my friend Nate, is so much better than the fantasy guy. I don't even miss Fantasy Nate because I care so much about the real person he is.

I think the reason I'm flipping out about this is because he still doesn't *really* know me. Yeah, I've shared some dark shit with him and Cheryl, but I've also kept my guard up the best I can. He seems to think I'm smart and interesting, but I'm afraid he'll see how wrong he is about me.

My stomach wobbled walking into class today because I felt like the new kid again, but I'm used to it. I've been the new kid so many times, I could write a book about overcoming *new-kid* nerves. At first, I didn't see him. His desk is near the back corner, and he was turned around in his chair, talking to the person kitty-corner from him, turned away from me. I didn't know where to sit, so I went up to Mrs. T's desk to ask her. She pointed to a desk and finally I noticed him. She put me right next to Nate.

I didn't tell anyone I was changing classes. Not Leesh, not Cheryl, and definitely not Nate. He turned around and did a double take when he saw me coming toward him.

"Hey," he said. "What's wrong? Is everything okay?"

I guess he thought I was crashing his class to bring him some sort of bad news. Goes to show how much he knows me. I'd never crash someone's class. I nodded and slumped into the desk next to his.

"Wait, you're in this class now? Why? How?"

"I think Mrs. Thomas made a terrible mistake. Or I did. I'm not sure. A few days ago, she asked me if I was interested in transferring, and yesterday, I told her yes."

"She invited you to transfer into Honors?"

As much as I adore Nate, the shock in his eyes made me want to punch him in his face. It doesn't happen often, but every now and then, I get this overwhelming desire to hit something. Or someone. I never do, though. The whole

WWGD philosophy of living my life strictly forbids punching people—especially people you care about.

"Wow, I'm feeling the love. Thanks for the vote of confidence." I turned away, dug through my backpack and scolded myself for overreacting.

"I'm an ass. I didn't mean it the way it sounded." His voice tickled my ear. I looked up and saw he had come to my desk. "It's just weird. I've never heard of someone being asked to transfer in here mid-semester." He winked and smiled. "I told you you're smart. This'll be so good for you. Maybe not so good for me, though."

I waited for him to explain.

"You're going to make me look bad, and I'll have to work extra hard to keep up with you. You're gonna stomp the grading curve for all of us."

The bell rang, and he smiled again as Mrs. Thomas shut the door and took her spot at the front of the room.

"Class," she called us to attention. "I'm sure you all noticed we have a new student joining us."

Oh, God. Please don't do this to me. Please no, please no, please, please, please no.

"Zoe, why don't you stand up and introduce yourself to us?"

Shit.

————

SAFE 32

Dear Diary,

Leesh was pretty down in the dumps for a little while. Every time I tried to ask her if she wanted to talk about it, she completely shut me out. I hate to butt my nose into business that's not mine, but as her big sister, I'm morally obligated to help her through whatever's eating at her. Over the last two weeks or so, I've noticed small changes in her, and she seems more like her old self than she has in a long time.

Maybe it was hormones getting the better of her. I know sometimes I feel like emotional dog crap because my hormones make everything feel bigger than it is. I'm going to back off a little, but I need her to know I'm still here if she needs me. I hope she doesn't feel like I'm all up in her business, but as long as she knows she can always count on me, I guess I'm doing my job right.

———

SAFE 33

Dear Diary,

I can't believe how well school is going! It seems like just a few days ago everything felt so overwhelming and complicated, but now it feels like everything is simple. Well, maybe simple isn't the right word, but the fog around my brain is finally clearing and I'm able to focus again. I'm especially enjoying English these days. Even though it's the same class, the vibe is totally different because of the kids. I feel like I can participate and not be an annoying jerk because other kids are participating, too.

We aren't doing writing prompts anymore, which is a little disappointing. I didn't think I'd like them, but in the end, they were one of my favorite parts of the day. It wasn't always easy to write about the prompt, though. Some days, my brain would spin and spin and never come up with anything to write about.

Some days, I'd read a prompt and think, "What in the world am I supposed to do with this?" Then I'd pick up my pencil and write some random word, and before I knew it, my hand cramped from all the writing.

And there were lots of times when the timer beeped and we had to stop. I'd look down and see I'd written three whole pages. I know three pages doesn't sound like a lot, but it is. When I'd look around the room, I'd see other kids were lucky to get even one page. I guess there's something inside of me that opens when I write.

A diary is a lot harder than a journal you keep for class, though. For one thing, I don't have a whiteboard with a writing prompt for my diary. Whatever I write about in here is entirely from my own head, and sometimes, I can't think of a single thing to write about. My life is dull, and I can't bring myself to write the same things over and over again. If I did, I'd end up as depressed as Leesh.

Okay, I shouldn't joke about that kind of thing because depression is no laughing matter. Maybe I should start writing in pencil so I can erase the stupid things I say, but I don't want to. There's something I love about writing in pen. It's so permanent. I wonder what I'll think if I read through this when I'm thirty? Will I be embarrassed by the misspelled words? Will I be able to read the handwriting from my past? Will I cringe at all the stupid things I say?

I wonder who I'll be when I'm thirty. I know Sammycat won't still be alive, but will I have another cat? Or a dog? Or maybe a boa constrictor? Will I have kids? Right now, I hope the answer is no. I want to live my life for myself, and when you have kids, nothing is about you anymore. Maybe I sound selfish, but I think it's responsible. I don't think women should have kids if they don't want to. Every kid should be born to parents who love and want them, like me and Bobby and Leesh. But who knows?

Maybe I'll change my mind and decide the only thing that will make my life better is having a kid. The future is far away, and anything can happen between now and then. Maybe I'll be a famous lyric writer. Or maybe I'll own a small bookstore with a coffee shop attached like the kind you see in movies. Maybe I'll go to cooking school and become a chef. I don't love cooking, but I'm okay at it, so maybe someday it could become my passion.

I just had an idea. I'm going to make a writing prompt for my next entry.

Where do you see yourself in fifteen years?

REAL 79

Where do you see yourself in fifteen years?

That was meant to be a prompt for my safe diary, but I think it deserves more honesty than I can give it there. Not everything in the other diary is a total lie, but I never tell the whole truth, either. Gynger has a way of spinning things, so they seem way worse than they are. I think this prompt has major spin-potential.

I usually don't think too much about my future. Not the far-off future, anyway. I spend a ridiculous amount of time thinking about the near future. About how I'll wash the clothes since we're out of soap, how I can help Leesh come back to herself, how to help Bobby with his homework without also making Gynger fly into a jealous rage. I dream about how things will be better when ~~Daddy~~ Joel comes home.

Hang on, I'm gonna pause my prompt for a sec. I need to talk about how I wrote *daddy* a second ago, even though I said I don't want to call him that anymore. The thing is, mad as I am, I still love him, and I miss him when he's gone. Yeah, I'm furious that he abandons us constantly and doesn't even try to keep us safe from her, but at the same time, I don't completely hate him.

Sometimes, I remember what it was like when I was a little girl. I'd stand on his feet, facing out toward the world. He'd make fists with his thumbs straight out, like a hitchhiker. I'd grip each thumb, and he'd pretend to be a robot and move in the same direction I pushed his thumbs. If I wanted him to stop, I'd gently pull back on his thumbs and he's stop right in his tracks, sometimes even with one foot in the air. My favorite was when I'd push both thumbs in opposite directions and he'd shimmy side to side and make "beep-boop-boop-buzzz" noises like he was shorting out.

I don't have any fun memories with Gynger. I do remember her trying to play with me when I was really little, but only for a few minutes. She'd get bored and wander off, or she'd get mad at me for something and the whole game would be ruined. Once, we were playing hide-and-seek in the house. I counted to twenty and shouted, *Ready or not, here I come.*

She almost always hid behind the couch, so I looked for her there first. Sure enough, there she was. When I found her, she didn't laugh and go count so I could hide. She told me she dropped an earring and was looking for it. When I insisted she was It and it was my turn to hide, she accused me of not counting all the way to twenty and said she didn't play with cheaters. I cried which only made her angrier.

"Oh, wahh-wahh! You poor whiny-crybaby-cheater. Nobody wants to listen to a little baby cry. Go outside and cry to the ants. Maybe they'll care."

So, I did. I cried so hard, I thought I'd never stop. I picked up a stick and dug a hole in the ground. I imagined my tears watering the hole and a giant plant, like Jack's beanstalk, grew up-up-up out of the ground and into the sky. I saw myself climbing to the top where I'd live in a castle with the giants and the golden goose.

I knew the giants would love me and keep me safe and never, ever dream of eating me. They'd make me a soft bed out of the fluffiest feathers the goose saved just for me. Since I was living with giants, everything, even the food, would be huge. Apples the size of a school bus. Cookies as big as my living room. I was so little, I could eat and eat until I thought I'd explode, and there would still be enough food for the giants to feast.

Eventually, my belly rumbled, and I realized it was getting dark, so I went back inside. Gynger sat on the couch, staring at the TV. No delicious smells came from the kitchen, so I went to my room and hoped dinner would be soon.

Whoa. I wrote like four pages, and I didn't even answer my own prompt. What the hell is wrong with me? I must have some sort of attention span problem. Something really is wrong with my brain. I knew transferring to honors was a mistake. How can I ever keep up with a class full of smart kids when I can't even follow my own prompt?

Whatever. This was a more interesting entry, anyway. I don't know where I'll be in fifteen years, so that's probably why I got so far off track. It's hard to think about next month, forget about next year. And fifteen years from now?

I'm afraid I won't be alive.

———

SAFE 34

Dear Diary,

It's a good thing Daddy got paid when he did because the electricity went out in the neighborhood last weekend, and by the time it came back on, the food in the fridge had spoiled. All of it. If there's a silver lining to the power going out, it's that it had been a while since our last shopping trip, so we were almost out of food, anyway. Still, it hurt to throw out what was left. Wasting food seriously upsets me, and I tried to salvage the eggs, but Mama reminded me we can get food poisoning from spoiled eggs. Even though it hurt my stomach to throw them out, I knew Mama was right. I'm glad she was there to keep us all from getting sick. Or maybe even dying.

Mama put me in charge of grocery shopping to replace what we lost. She dropped us off at the store and said she'd be back in about an hour, after she ran some errands. I asked what she wanted me to buy, and she said she trusts me to make good decisions and not spend too much money. It's a huge responsibility to shop for the whole family, and I can't even tell you how good it feels that she trusts me so much. I'll bet you a hundred dollars not one other kid in my school is trusted with such an important thing.

Since I didn't have a dollar amount to spend, I did my best to stick to the staples. I loaded us up on pasta and hot dogs—store brand because they're the same as the expensive kind, but a lot cheaper. Two big bags of frozen veggies, and even cans of tomatoes. I could have bought pasta sauce but decided not to. What's pasta sauce anyway, but tomatoes, garlic and some spices? I bet I could make four jars of sauce for the less than what one pre-made jar would cost. I also got some eggs, more flour, and even though it's not a necessity, a small jar of cinnamon because what we had was expired. I think I did a good job with the shopping, and I didn't even cave when Bobby picked up a candy bar.

"Wouldn't this hit the spot, Zoe?" he asked.

My heart about melted, and I was this close to buying it for him, but I didn't. I just agreed it really would hit the spot and asked him to put it back. He's too young to be getting cavities, anyway.

REAL 80

When I write something truthful in my safe diary, I get scared and walk away from it to make sure everything's okay. I make sure she's calm and the kids aren't being too noisy. That she's not hovering right outside my bedroom waiting for me to write something a little too unflattering, no matter how much I sugarcoat things. Then I think about what would happen if she found this journal, where I don't even try to hide what life is really like.

Last week, I discovered a loose floorboard under my desk, so I've been keeping this journal there at night. I like to think some kid from fifty years ago used to hide their treasures or maybe even their diary there, too. It's a shame I didn't know about it when I first started the other diary. I could have hidden it there instead of the closet this whole time and she would have never found it and I would have never had to start this journal. Even though she has no idea about the floorboard, I'm still terrified she'll somehow find this journal.

I imagine I tuck it behind my waistband and pull my shirt over it so I can get a glass of water without pulling up the floorboard, but she's in the kitchen and in one of her moods.

Before I know it, I'm on the ground, curled up to protect my head from her kicks, and she notices the journal. She yanks it out of my pants and flips through it. Once she realizes it's not for English, she'll take a closer look, and I'd be dead meat for sure. And I don't say *dead meat* to be hyperbolic (we learned that word in English recently, and I want to use it as often as I can). I honestly believe she's so unstable she might literally beat me to death if she read this journal.

My last entry in here gave me so much anxiety, I gave some serious thought about ripping those pages out and burning them in the backyard. But stupid as it sounds, I didn't want to lose the things I wrote about Joel pretending to be a robot or about my beanstalk daydream. Life is so stressful and terrifying most of the time, it's easy for me to forget I used to be a little girl who had fun. Joel wasn't just Joel back then. He was Daddy.

I think it's probably important for me to hold on to as many good memories as I can because they remind me I wasn't a rotten kid. It wasn't my fault she always hid in the same place. What was I supposed to do, pretend I didn't know where she was? I need to remember things weren't the way she tried to convince me they were. I didn't change the rules of the game, she did. And when six-year-old Zoe didn't want to play her game by saying I cheated, she threw a tantrum like a child.

I feel crazy more often than I don't, and I have a hard time trusting what I know. That doesn't make sense, but most things in my life don't, either. There are so many times, every day, when I doubt reality because Gynger keeps changing the rules of the game. Or she takes my words and twists them around until it's not even remotely what I said. Future Zoe, if you're reading this, please don't let yourself forget what it's like. Here's an example.

Last weekend, the kids and I were watching TV when a commercial for Reese's Peanut Butter Cups came on. Being a commercial, they made it look like the most delicious thing ever invented.

"That would really hit the spot right about now." If I had known Gynger had come out of her room, I wouldn't have said anything.

"What's that supposed to mean?" she demanded.

"I didn't mean anything. It's just been a long time since I had one and it looked good."

The couch creaked as she plopped onto it. "So Little Queenie wants chocolate. Shall I drive to the store for you, Your Highness? Bring back a whole bag of chocolate just for you? Or would that not be enough for you? How about an entire goddamn cart full of chocolate?"

The more I tried to tell her I hadn't meant anything by it, the louder she got.

"What did I do to God to deserve such an ungrateful shit for a daughter? I work my fingers to the bone for this family and still, it's not enough for her. Tell me, Jesus, what did I do?" She got up from the couch faster than I've seen her move in a long time and stomped to the kitchen.

Leesh gave me a sad look and bustled Bobby outside.

"Let's see if there's any chocolate in here." Gynger opened the spice cupboard so hard it hit the wall. She stuck her whole hand in and swiped everything out in long heaves. The cinnamon lid popped open and brown powder made a mushroom cloud at her feet.

When she didn't find the chocolate she knew we didn't have, she did the same thing to the next cupboard. And the next. Thank God most of our plates and cups are plastic because she wouldn't have been any gentler with glass. Actually, it looked like she got extra satisfaction from the sound of coffee mugs and glass bowls shattering. I didn't know what to do except stand there, still as a wax girl statue, and watch while she ruined the entire kitchen.

Satisfied there was no hidden stash of candy in the cupboards, she moved on to the refrigerator. I mean, what the actual fuck? We never have enough food, as it is, and she gets it in her head to tornado through the fridge and throw what we did have on the floor? Rage coursed through my veins like lava and I knew I'd have to go back to the food bank to replace what she ruined if I couldn't calm her down.

The wax melted, and I stepped toward her. "Mama, stop!" Cinnamon tickled my nose and burned my eyes. I'm usually so good about not letting her see me cry, but when she started on the fridge, I completely lost it. I can't remember exactly what I said, only that I was hysterical. I remember apologizing to her and telling her she was right, and I'm spoiled and ungrateful.

None of it mattered. Nothing could stop her from her mission of turning the kitchen into a disaster zone. When she finally tired out, she stood there for a minute, hunched, and panting like she'd just run a marathon. Egg yolks mixed with milk in a slimy puddle. Nearby, flour and cinnamon mixed into a dirty sand. Deconstructed pancakes all over the floor. I swallowed back barf as I looked at all our wasted food.

She looked up at me and shook her head slowly. She squinted and squeezed her lips into a tight circle.

"Look what you made me do. Are you happy now, Your Highness?"

The quiet of the storm overwhelmed me, but it held long enough for me to hope maybe the storm had passed. She shook her head at me again and then spit on the floor. She. Spit. On. The. Floor. Like she was some kind of cowboy in an old west saloon. Who does that?

I tried to pull myself together. Tried to stop my tears and get myself under control, but a dam broke behind my eyes. Even though tears always have a hefty price tag, the dam flooded. Her tantrum must have sucked everything out of her, though, because she barely looked at me.

"You have thirty minutes to clean this shit up before I make you start all over again." She shuffled out of the kitchen and slammed her bedroom door.

And if all of that isn't messed up enough, wrap your head around this, Future Zoe. That happened last weekend, but I didn't bother writing about it until now. I don't know if I didn't think it was worth writing about or if I wanted to block it out of my memory, but I've decided I can't bury all this stuff anymore, even if writing about it could get me hurt.

I was lucky that day. She didn't touch me, and the worst that happened was the kitchen got a good scrubbing and we went to bed without dinner since we didn't have any food to eat.

So why am I crying right now?

REAL 81

I still can't figure out why Mrs. Thomas wanted me to move, but I'm glad she did. Even though I still feel like a major fraud who'll be discovered any second, I'm glad I let myself do what I wanted for once. The homework really is a lot lighter, which still seems so strange to me, but Mrs. T. was right, the in-class work does take quite a bit more effort. But I'm loving it, and honestly, it's kind of easy for me. In fact, I finish earlier than almost everyone else. It's been two weeks, and, and I'm pleased to announce I got one-hundreds on both of the quizzes we had. Both!

What I don't understand is why my brain seems to be working in this class but not in all my others. I still space out and have a hard time focusing, even when I'm trying to force myself to stay alert and in my body instead of floating outside of it. I wonder what would happen if I moved to all honors classes? Is my brain working better in English because I'm not bored? I didn't know I was bored before, but now that I look back, it's crystal clear I was.

Would the homework be lighter in the other honors classes, too? Is that like some great secret only rich people know? It seems like the Venn diagram of rich kids and kids in accelerated and honors classes is a perfect circle. Maybe rich parents know their kids will have more time for things like dances, sports, volunteering, and student council if they're in the honors classes. And because the kids have more time for extra stuff, they're more well-rounded, which makes them more attractive to good colleges. Since they get into better colleges, they get better jobs and make more money, and they continue this cycle by making sure their kids are in honors classes. It keeps the rich, rich and the poor, poor.

Maybe this is some next level conspiracy theory stuff, but it does seem to make sense. Is there any chance I could pass myself off as someone who belongs here? Is it possible for someone on the poor-kid track to switch lanes to the rich-kid track? If my crazy conspiracy theory is true and I can jump tracks, so many more opportunities will open up for me. Think of what I can do for my brother and sister if I can make my way up this invisible ladder.

It wouldn't be easy, and I'd have to find a way to fool everyone into believing I belong, but if this new English class is any indication, I might be able to pull it off. I thought I'd be an outcast in this class, but everyone took to me like it was nothing. Nobody even seemed to question why I was there. Maybe college isn't as far out of my reach as I always thought. Maybe I can create a better life than the universe or God or whatever expects me to live. Even better than Gynger expects for me—if she expects anything for me at all. Sometimes I wonder if she realizes I'll eventually grow up and move out. I think she thinks I'll always be here for her to kick around.

Screw that and screw her. I'm the one in charge of my life, not her. Not some unseen force. Not a system that rewards the rich and punishes the poor. I'm going to do *everything* I can to get out of this mess, starting with working harder in all my classes. No more letting myself off the hook by saying I'm too tired to focus. No more putting my work on the back burner because my brain doesn't work the way it should. No. More. Excuses.

———

SAFE 35

Dear Diary,

Cheryl invited me to her sleepover birthday party. Her parents will order pizza and have all kinds of junk food. They'll light the fire pit in the back yard and set out a smore's bar. Cheryl hates cake, so instead, she'll blow out a candle on a toasted marshmallow. First of all, how freaking cool. Second, who in their right mind hates cake? I've never met a cake I haven't fallen deeply in love with, anyway. Maybe they have it every week, so it's not special to her anymore.

Diary, I'm terrified to go. She has so much money and never has to worry about where her shoes or winter coat will come from. All she has to do is tell her parents what she needs, and they take her shopping for stuff. She doesn't brag but mentions things in an offhand way. Like she'll grumble at her phone and then say it's old and she needs to upgrade it, or how her laptop is slow, and she hopes she gets a new one for her birthday. I can't even fathom what that feels like.

Our family doesn't even have one computer, and I had to talk to my teachers to let them know. Luckily, they all worked with me, so I don't get in trouble for not turning in things that are due at midnight on Sunday or whatever. Mrs. Thomas even gave me permission to handwrite my papers and turn them in the old-fashioned way, if that's easier than carving out time to go to the computer lab.

Wouldn't it be amazing if Cheryl got a new computer and gave me her old one? I'd never ask, but it sure would make my life a lot easier to have even a slow computer. I don't need it to edit videos or play games. I'd just like to be able to turn in my assignments like everyone else.

Another reason I don't want to go is because it's on Saturday, and Saturday is laundry day. It would be totally unfair of me to leave it all for Mama. When I told Cheryl I didn't know if I could make it, she begged me to do whatever it takes to come. Maybe I could do laundry after school on Friday? Or on Sunday? The part of me that doesn't want to go is a tiny sliver compared to the part that does, so I have to find a way to make it work. I've never been to a birthday party or a sleepover, and those things seem like important experiences to have. I'm also afraid to go because I don't have money to get her anything. She told me she's telling everyone not to bring gifts, but who shows up to a birthday party empty-handed?

"Your presence is your present," she said.

What a cute phrase, but I don't believe it. Who doesn't want presents? What if I show up and am the only one who hasn't gotten her anything?

That settles it, I can't go. It's a terrible idea for so many reasons. What will the kids do all weekend? Leesh has a big science project to work on and it would be selfish of me to ask her to keep an eye on Bobby while I'm off partying and eating s'mores. There's laundry to do, and I was going to try to dust and vacuum this weekend.

Plus, other than Nate, who has to leave at ten o'clock because he's a boy and isn't allowed to sleep over, I don't know any of the other kids who will be there. I mean, I know them because we all go to school together, but I'm not friends with them. Probably, most of them wouldn't even recognize me, much less know my name if I ran into them at the store. When I think about being surrounded by cool, beautiful, rich kids, it makes me want to climb into my closet, curl into a ball, and never come out again. It terrifies me.

I adore Cheryl and don't want to disappoint her, but going to her party simply isn't an option. Some people were built for friends and slumber parties, and others weren't. You can't argue with nature.

REAL 82

I know Cheryl means well, but for all I've told her, she still doesn't get it.

"What's the worst that can happen? You'll get grounded? That's literally no different from your life right now, so just come. It might even show your mother she can't control you forever."

"Are you kidding me right now? Do you even listen to me at all? If I go against my mother and come anyway, she'll unleash so much wrath, the Devil himself will start to worry for his job."

"Please, Zoe." She rolled her eyes at me, which made me feel about as big as a flea. "Your mother is nasty, but she's not supernatural. Besides, you thought she wasn't going to let you go to the dance, but she did. People can change."

"Not her. I don't know why she let me go to the dance, and I'm glad it all turned out fine, but I'm not about to push my luck by asking for something else so soon."

"Please come. You're my best friend, and I want you to celebrate my birthday with me. How often does a girl turn sixteen?"

I've spent the last two days so anxious about this situation, I can't even eat. I've played out every scenario I can think of, and I'm more convinced than ever I can't ask Gynger. The odds of her saying yes are only slightly better than the odds of me finding out I've been kidnapped and am actually a well-loved and horribly missed princess. If I go against her wishes, it's totally possible she'll freak out and hurt one of the kids. And if, miracle of miracles, she doesn't freak out on any of them, she's sure to bring the pain when I get home. But worse, I think it's possible she wouldn't wait until I got home to punish me. She's so messed up, I can easily see her showing up at Cheryl's and freaking out there.

I'm so tired. Tired of being trapped. Tired of being in charge of everyone and everything. Tired of having to plan my life around my mother all the time. Aren't the teen years supposed to be all about self-discovery? Isn't this supposed to be my time to figure out who I am and to have fun? My time to make stupid mistakes and deal with the reasonable conse-quences? Shouldn't mothers encourage their kids to go out and live their own lives instead of making their kids live their whole lives around them?

Sometimes, it feels like I'm never going to get out. Who am I kidding? I'll never go to college. I'll never get to live in a dorm at some fancy university. The way things are looking, I'll never even make it to community college part-time. If I can't even justify going to my best friend's sixteenth birthday party, getting out and going to college seems about as likely as Martians landing and teaching humans the ways of peaceful cooperation.

And that reminded me of the writing prompt I completely dropped the ball on a few entries back. When I think about where I'll be in fifteen years, I don't see a whole lot of differ-ence from now. I see myself still living here, still holding Gynger's hand and trying to shield everyone from her outbursts. I know in fifteen years Bobby will be an adult, but I have a hard time picturing him all grown up. I can't see anything beyond what's right in front of me, and what's right in front of me is hell. It's enough to make me want to cut out of life early.

I think the only reason I haven't killed myself is because if I did, the kids would have to handle Gynger alone. I know Leesh would do everything she could, but she's never been as good at taking the heat as I am. She doesn't know how to dance the dance, and I don't want to force her to learn. Once you learn the dance, you can wave to your childhood in the rearview mirror as you leave it behind forever. Besides, if I did kill myself to get out of here, it would kill Leesh. She's already dealing with so much and losing me would be one straw too many.

I might not be worth a whole lot to the world, or anything to my parents, but I know my sister and brother need me. Without me to be the wall between them and Gynger's wrath, neither of them has so much as a half a shot at a decent life. I'm willing to sacrifice my own happiness for them. The way I see it, I was born for Gynger to hate. Even if the others had never been born, my life was never going to be sunshine and ice cream. If I'm around, at least they have a decent shot at being happy.

Well, I made the mistake of confiding in my sister about Cheryl's party. I tried not to, but she's more observant than I give her credit for.

"You have to go. It's her sixteenth birthday, and she's your best friend, so going is mandatory." She lay on her stomach on my bed, flipping through my algebra book.

You know how in movies someone will say something important and their voice will echo around until it fades? That's what it felt like with the words "best friend." They echoed in my head until I cleared my throat to make it stop. It's true. Cheryl is my best friend. Well, one of them. Nate's the other.

"Don't worry, I'll cover for you."

"Are you insane? There's no way I'm letting you cover for me."

"I have a plan. Trust me." She studied a page with a bunch of graphs we hadn't covered in class yet. "I wish my math was as interesting as this. I'm so bored with what we're doing."

"A plan? Since when do you come up with plans? And since when are you interested in algebra? It's hard, and it doesn't make any sense. Who are you and what have you done with my sister?"

"You have English, I have math. Anyway, do you want to hear the plan or not?

"Fine but let me be clear. Just because I'll listen doesn't mean I endorse whatever you're about to say. There's roughly a two-hundred percent chance you're wasting your time."

"Wow, you really aren't good with numbers, are you?"

I tossed a pillow at her. "Let's hear it."

"It's so simple, it's brilliant. I'll make sure Mama gets so drunk she passes out."

"You mean a regular Tuesday night? I hope there's more to your plan."

She shot me a dirty look and continued, "You can sneak out after she's asleep and sneak back in before she wakes up. I'll make sure to leave the back door unlocked for you. It's so perfect, we could even take turns going out on weekends this way. Why didn't we come up with this ages ago?"

"Because one, it's stupid." I held my fingers up one by one as I counted. "Two, it's dangerous. Three, you absolutely cannot leave a door unlocked all night. What do you think this is? The eighteen-hundreds?"

"Those aren't reasons. I think you're looking for excuses not to go to the party."

"You know as well as I do the odds of her being a mean drunk are every bit as high as her lying on the couch dozing."

"Yep. So, we'll get her started earlier than usual. That way, she'll get her nastiness out of her system early on and by the time the party rolls around, she'll either be firmly in lazy-drunk land or she'll be out cold."

"Your plan makes a little sense, but I'm still not convinced. Are you going to sit up with her all night to make sure she doesn't barf in her sleep? Do you even know what to do if she does?"

"Of course, I do. It's not like you're the only one in this family who deals with her, you know. I've watched you take care of her so much, I could do it in my sleep."

"Let me think about it, okay?"

"I don't know what there is to think about, but you do you." She slammed my book shut and walked to my door. "Just let me know. I'm here if you need me."

When the hell did my sister get so sneaky?

————

SAFE 36

Dear Diary,

I'll give you three guesses who's home and the first two don't count. Yep, it's Daddy! He was only gone a few days this time, so we were all surprised, and happy, to see him. Especially Mama. She's like a flower and he's the sun. When he's not here, she curls up, and when he comes back, she blooms again and shows the world how beautiful she is. I hope I can find a love like theirs someday. It's so romantic.

"Zuzu, why don't you come sit with me for a bit?" he called from the front porch.

It's been a long time since we sat on the porch together, and I tried to figure out what I did to get in trouble with him. I didn't say anything as I sat next to him on the top step.

"Your sister tells me your friend is having a birthday party tomorrow and you aren't planning to go." He was so matter of fact, like he was talking about the weather or the color of my shirt. "Why not?"

"I don't know. It would have been fun, but I didn't know you'd be home so soon, and I didn't think it was fair to abandon Mama so I could go to some silly party. Family first."

He took a long drag from his cigarette and exhaled slowly. "Do you know how proud of you I am, baby girl? You're the glue keeping this family together, and I don't know what we'd do without you."

I tried not to, but I smiled anyway. Everyone likes to hear they're appreciated sometimes. "Thanks, Daddy, but I really don't do all that much. I just do what I can to make sure Mama's not too overwhelmed. It's nothing any daughter wouldn't do, and it doesn't feel like enough most of the time."

"I can understand that." He flicked his cigarette ashes off the side of the porch. "Sometimes, it feels like you're barely making a difference, even when you are. Trust me, you do a lot of good around here."

I could only nod because what do you say to something like that?

"Anyway, a girl only turns sixteen the one time. If she's really your friend, you can't miss her party. Me and your sister can hold down the fort. You go and have fun. I'd say you've more than earned a night off."

Then, he did something absolutely mind-blowing. He took twenty dollars out of his wallet and held it out to me.

"I want you to take this and go and get your friend a proper present."

"Oh, no! I can't take your money! Cheryl told us not to bring gifts."

"Well, that's plain nonsense, isn't it? You can't show up to a sweet sixteen party without a present." He put the money in my hand and closed my fingers around it.

"But we're out of cereal and we're almost out of sandwich meat again. And there isn't even enough laundry soap for one load."

He put his heavy hand on my head and ruffled my hair like

when I was little. "Don't you worry about that stuff, Zuzu. There's more where this came from. Things are finally looking up for our little family."

I wanted to ask him what he meant, but I didn't want to butt my nose into his business. Instead, I wrapped my arms tight around his neck and thanked him about eleventy-trillion times.

I'M GOING ON MY FIRST SLEEPOVER!

REAL 84

I don't even know what's going on, but I don't really care. All I know is I'm going to Cheryl's and I'm so excited, I feel like I could float away like a balloon. Part of me wonders what Joel meant when he said things are looking up for us, but I don't want to get my hopes up. He says those kind of things sometimes, and then nothing changes. This time, though, he gave me money, which he's never done before, so maybe things really are looking up. Maybe he got a raise or even a better job where he won't have to be gone all the time. Whatever. Best not to think too much about it.

Instead, I'm going to let myself be grateful Leesh and I don't have to get Gynger stupid-drunk so I could sneak out for the party. Not that I would have gone along with such a dangerous plan. Way too many things could have gone horribly wrong. I've probably thought of every possible way shit could blow up if I snuck out. As much as Leesh thinks she's capable of handling things, I didn't want to put her in the position of having to.

I heard Joel telling Gynger I'm going to the party.

"Absolutely not. There's no way she's going." Her voice

was sharp as broken glass. "There's too much for her to take care of for her to take a vacation."

"Oh, honey, she does a lot more for our family than most kids her age. The house won't burn down without her for one night."

"Don't you 'honey' me. If anyone deserves time off, it's me. I spend twenty-four hours a day dealing with that little shit, and does anybody ever think of me? No. I never even get so much as a thank you from her."

An icy hand squeezed my heart. I've never been under the impression she cared about me in any meaningful way, but to hear her talk about me like that when she thought I wasn't listening about broke me. It was like hearing what someone really thinks about you while they're talking in their sleep. Some things shouldn't be heard, you know?

Leesh sat on the couch, flipping through the channels faster than I could make out what was on.

"Hey, I'm gonna walk up to Walmart to look for a present for Cheryl. Do you and Bobby want to come?"

"No, we're good." Flip, flip, flip.

"Are you sure? It might do you good to get out of the house."

"Walmart never does anyone good. We'll stay here. Bobby asked me to teach him to make a grilled PB&J, anyway."

"He did? I would have been happy to teach him."

I'm so embarrassed to admit my feelings were hurt that Bobby didn't ask me. It made me feel needy, which made me wonder if that's how Gynger feels when one of the kids asks me for help instead of her.

"I'm sure you would have, but he knows you have a lot on your plate. He didn't mean anything by it. Anyway, you'll have more fun picking out a present if you don't have to worry about us. Go on. We're good."

Just like that, the hurt feelings floated into the atmosphere.

I looked at Leesh and the cold hand squeezing my heart let go as I realized she's okay. The worst of whatever was going on with her had passed. How had I not noticed she stopped wearing long sleeves? At some point, while I was caught up in my own world, she had stopped hurting herself. Not only that, but she was out of her room, offering to keep an eye on things and to teach our brother to feed himself.

"If you're sure, then. Can I bring you anything?"

"Nope, I'm good. Have fun." She stopped flipping the channels and settled on a makeover show.

I wandered up and down the aisles and wondered what you get a girl who has everything. I don't know anything about makeup, so I didn't even try to find a lipstick she'd like. Same with clothes. And anyway, even if I could find something I thought she'd like, there's no way she'd ever wear anything from a big box store. She's a mall girl through and through. Just as I thought I'd never find anything, I saw it.

A heart-shaped *Best Friends* necklace. I know, I know, how sixth grade, but it was so perfect, I couldn't put it down. I also got her a pair of *Wonder Woman* socks with little gold capes attached because I think she's pretty wonderful. Butterflies bubbled around my stomach as I imagined helping her put on her necklace. Maybe my childish gift is cheesier than a grilled cheese sandwich, but I don't care. It came from my heart, and I think Cheryl will love it.

I figured Gynger would be in a mood when I got home, and she was—just not the mood I expected. She insisted I show her what I got, and she made a big deal of oohing and ahhing over them. After a few minutes, she told me I'd better go and get my stuff together unless I wanted to be late. It was still a couple of hours before the party, but I didn't dare contradict her. I don't know what Joel said to her, but whatever it was, put her in the best mood I'd seen in months. As I packed my bag I wondered if this is what winning the lottery feels like.

———

SAFE 38

Dear Diary,

Cheryl's party was great. Better than great, actually. It was everything I imagined a party should be. Pizza and s'mores and so much candy and different types of chips that I had to stop eating, or I'd throw up all over her ginormous basement. I counted fourteen kids, and we never felt crowded down there. Cheryl's parents popped in a couple of times to make sure we didn't need more soda or whatever, but we hardly saw them.

When I first got there, I was so nervous, I could hardly even look at any of the other kids. After a while, though, I warmed up. Thankfully, Nate and Cheryl kept me close and made it a point to bring me into conversations. It's incredible to me how easily small talk comes to some people. I didn't really click with any of the other kids, but they've seen me with Cheryl and Nate at school plenty, so they accepted me into the fold.

Before I left, Mama warned me they'd probably talk about me behind my back, if not make fun of me right to my face, but nothing like that happened. I'm so glad they didn't, but I'm glad Mama warned me. She knows so much more about how people work than I do, and I'm lucky she's willing to give me advice. These kids must be way nicer than the jerks she grew up around, so I guess I dodged a real bullet. Once the awkwardness disappeared, we all got along fine. I even scared everyone when it was my turn to tell a ghost story.

As much fun as I had, I wish I hadn't gone.

Bobby got hurt again. Leesh says he was up in a tree and fell. On his way down, he hit a branch. We don't know if he dislocated his shoulder and broke his leg on the branch, or when he hit the ground, but when he finally hit bottom, he passed out cold. Nobody even knew he had broken anything until Daddy picked him up. Leesh said his arm dangled there, like a giant gummy worm. Daddy didn't say a word or think twice. He put Bobby in the truck and high-tailed it to the hospital.

I'm so angry nobody called me to tell me what happened. I know there's nothing I could have done to help Bobby, but at least I could have helped my sister. Leesh said Daddy took off so fast, nobody had time to react. Leesh wanted to go with them, but it was too late, so she stayed home with Mama.

Understandably, Mama was so upset, she went straight to her room, where she screamed and cried and threw things at the walls. I can't even imagine how scared my poor sister must have been, but who could blame Mama for being out of her mind? Her baby fell out of a tree and had to go to the hospital. Any mother would rightfully freak out, but the more Mama screamed, the more convinced Leesh was Bobby died.

By the time Daddy and Bobby came home, it was so late, nobody wanted to call me. The doctors said he'll be okay. A dislocated shoulder, a broken leg, and a concussion. They let him go with strict instructions not to let him sleep for a few hours and to get plenty of rest over the weekend.

I'm never going to leave the house for anything but school again. None of this would have happened if I had been home. Thank God Daddy was here. I hate to think about what would have happened if he hadn't been.

REAL 85

I knew it would happen someday. I knew that bitch would land one of us in the hospital, but I never, ever dreamed it'd be Bobby. After she hurt him the last time, I tried to convince myself it was a fluke. He was still the baby and still safe. I tried to pretend she's not as dangerous to the others as she is to me. For the most part, she leaves them alone, but it was stupid to trust they'd be okay.

As far as I'm concerned, I'm the one who beat the ever-loving shit out of him. I'm the one who picked him up and body slammed him into the ground. I'm the one who beat his head against the floor until he passed out and then left him for dead. After all, I'm the one who left when I knew she could do something like this. THIS IS ALL MY FAULT. Dammit, I should have known better than to think I'd won any kind of lottery.

Leesh says it's not my fault, but what else could she say? She doesn't know why Gynger did it, but I do. She was jealous. Of what, I'm not sure. Maybe because I got money from Joel. Maybe because I'm making friends and living my life and she's mean and alone. Maybe she felt like I abandoned her by going to Cheryl's, or maybe she read my diary entry about Joel giving me money and she had more sick thoughts about me. I'll never know what threw her over the edge and I'll never know what really went down.

What I pieced together is right after I left, she got nasty. As soon as she started slamming cupboard doors, the kids did what they always do and scattered. They hid wherever they could until the storm could die, like always. I guess they didn't realize the storm always dies because I'm always there at the epicenter. She focuses her wrath on me and by the time the wind has gone out of her, it's safe for them to come out and pick through the pieces.

But this time I wasn't here. I was off eating crap and telling stupid scary stories about ghosts who cry and steal children, pretending to be a normal kid when *I know better.*

Since I wasn't around to absorb her destruction, she went looking for someone to whale on. I don't know if she happened to come across Bobby first or if she had her sights set on him all along, but that's who she turned on. Nobody could tell me what crime she accused and convicted him of. There was just screaming—hers and his.

Joel was working on the van's AC and had the radio turned way up, so he didn't even hear anything for a while. By the time he clued in something was wrong, Bobby had already passed out. Joel didn't say a single word to anybody. He picked Bobby up and took off in his stupid, huge truck, leaving Leesh alone to deal with the fallout.

"Leesh, why the hell didn't you call me?" I demanded.

"I was too afraid. I knew if you came home, she'd kill you. After Daddy and Bobby left, she destroyed her room." Leesh's voice shook as hard as her body, and I wrapped my arms around her.

"I know she usually tires herself out after wrecking a room, so I figured I'd be safe enough here. I already thought Bobby was dead, so the only way I could protect you was not to tell you." My sister angrily wiped her tears and then pulled her hair. Hard. "I hate myself. I should have done something. This is all my fault."

Panicked, I grabbed her hands to stop her. "Leesh, stop it. This isn't your fault. *She* did this to Bobby, not you. Please, Leesh. Stop hurting yourself. She hurts us all enough."

Leesh let go of her hair, threw her arms around me, and cried harder than I've ever seen her cry before.

Somehow, I managed to keep my shit together while I was with her, but I'm shaking and crying now. I can see it all so clearly, like I was there. I've never known Gynger to destroy her own things before, and I can't wrap my head around what it means. Leesh said most of her screams were incoherent roars, but every now and then she'd scream something like *My baby! What happened to my baby?*

Is she so delusional she didn't remember hurting him? God, my poor brother and sister. I can't believe they were alone. I should have been there. It should have been me.

Gynger must have had a bottle hidden somewhere in her room. By the time Joel and Bobby came back, she was passed out on the bedroom floor. Leesh was on the couch watching TV with the sound low and Sam curled up next to her. The only ones awake after the storm. The only one to hear the truck rumble up the drive. The only one to see our baby brother carried in, heavy cast on his leg and his arm in an itchy-looking black sling, his face covered in bruises and scratches.

Joel carried Bobby to his room but couldn't leave him there, thanks to Hurricane Gynger. Instead, he settled him into my bed while he and Leesh cleaned up his room. That's when Daddy Dearest told Leesh *The Official Story*.

Bobby fell from the tree and hit a branch coming down. Nobody thought to tell him to come out of the tree because he loves to climb everything and spends every waking second in a tree. It's a wonder he hasn't hurt himself this bad sooner.

Joel made her repeat the story over and over, making sure every detail was perfect. After a while, she even started to believe the story herself. He told her to make sure I learned the story and could repeat it in my sleep.

"He told me if the truth ever got out, they'd take Bobby away from us. Not only that, but they'd probably take all of us away. Separate us, put us in different foster homes, and we'd never see each other again. It's the same thing he always says after you get hurt, but this time I really understood what he meant. I can't lose you, Zoe." She cried then. And the more she tried to keep herself together, the harder she cried.

I know the story well. The foster care story. They've been telling it to us our entire lives. It's the story they used to keep me afraid and quiet.

Not anymore.

REAL 86

Cheryl and Nate were already in the cafeteria when I got to school on Monday morning.

"I need you to come with me to talk to Mrs. Thomas," I said without bothering to sit down. If I sat, I might not have the strength to get back up.

"Is everything okay?" Cheryl asked.

I noticed her half of the Best Friends necklace dangling from her neck. "No. No, nothing's okay and I can't keep this all to myself anymore. It's never going to get better."

Nate stood up and wrapped me in a hug, right there in front of everyone, not even a little worried about what people would think. I pulled away from him. If I let him hug me, I'd break down, and if I broke down, I'd never stop crying.

"When?" Cheryl got up from the table, took my hand, and squeezed it.

"The sooner the better." I inhaled deeply and stood up straight. "Now. Before I chicken out."

We went up to the teacher on duty and asked for passes to Mrs. Thomas's room. My mind completely blanked when he wanted to know why all three of us needed to go at the same time, but Nate had my back.

"We're all in Mrs. Thomas's Honors class and we have a test today. We want to ask her some questions about it. My parents will kill me if I don't ace it."

The teacher gave us some heavy side-eye but wrote out three passes anyway. "If Mrs. Thomas doesn't let me know you made it within five minutes, you'll all end up in ISS, got it?"

And easy as that, we were alone in the hall. They tried to get me to tell them what happened, but I couldn't talk. I knew I only had it in me to tell this story once, and I needed to tell it to someone who could actually do something.

"Hey, guys. What's up?" Mrs. Thomas smiled as she looked up from a stack of papers.

I froze just inside the doorway. Cheryl took one hand, Nate took the other, and they pulled me gently into the room. I tried to make my voice work, but the words were a wool ball in my throat.

"Hi, Mrs. Thomas," Cheryl started. "Zoe has something she needs to talk to you about. We're here for emotional support."

My heart swelled with gratitude at the words *emotional support.*

Friends, I thought. *I have friends.*

"Well, aren't you good friends? Zoe, what's going on, honey?"

I opened my mouth to tell her I needed help, to beg her to do something, but the only sound I made was a squeak. She got up from her desk and came around to hug me, and I lost it. I cried harder than I've ever cried in my life, and she held me without saying a word.

Finally, I pulled back and dug through my backpack until I

found what I was looking for. My *real* journal. The only thing in the world that knows my truth. I held it out to her, and she took it, not quite understanding what she was supposed to do with it. I forced myself to be strong and stop crying. I took a deep breath.

"It's about my mother," I said. "She's horrible and my father doesn't do anything about it. When he's even home, he acts like everything is fine. Like he can't see what she does to us." I wiped my eyes and swallowed the wool down. "Please read the journal," I said. "It can tell you better than I can."

She hugged my journal to her chest and smiled. "Of course, I'll read it if you really want me to, but are you sure? It's incredibly common for teenagers to go through rough times with their mothers, especially girls. Are things so bad you want me to see your most secret thoughts?"

"They're bad," I whispered. "It's not like she doesn't understand me or won't let me go to parties. I'd give my left foot for a mother who was just strict."

I sat down in the nearest desk, covered my head with my arms and chuckled at the image that popped into my head. Clear as day, I saw a huge, black, smoky spirit hovering over me, sucking all the energy out of me through a red and white striped straw. The more it drank, the less I was able to control my own body.

"Never mind," I said into the desk. "I'm sorry to bother you."

I willed myself to pull my head up. To slide out of the chair, stand up, and walk out of the room, but I couldn't even wiggle my fingers. I closed my eyes and prayed to the soul-sucking spirit to finish me off already. No way was I strong enough to keep going.

Mrs. Thomas's knees popped as she squatted down next to me. I flinched when she touched my head. Stroked my hair.

"You know, I've had a lot of kids come through my classroom over the years. Some have been total jerks. Some have been dream students. I've had kids who clearly didn't want to be here and kids who desperately wanted to be here but couldn't keep up. Every one of those kids hold a special place in my heart."

Why was she telling me this? I wanted to ask, but my mouth wouldn't open.

"You're different from all of those other students, Zoe." She moved her hand from my head and rubbed large, slow circles on my back. I wondered if she had a kid whose back she rubbed.

"There's something special in you. A kind of strength and determination most kids don't have. You're no stranger to hard work and tough odds, and I admire you."

The black spirit stopped drinking and I lifted my head out of my arm cave.

"You admire me? Why? I'm nothing."

"Oh, Zoe. You're not nothing. You're so much more than nothing. You are everything. A good sister. A good friend. A good student. And my guess is, an incredibly good daughter. Do you want to tell me a little about what I'll read in this journal, so I'm not surprised? Sort of a trigger warning, maybe?"

My nostrils tingled and I could feel the snot wanting to escape. I sniffed and rubbed my nose with the back of my hand, trying to find a way to explain that Mrs. Thomas would understand but wouldn't sound made up.

"She hurts us," I finally blurted out. "Well, mostly me, but she hurts all of us. This weekend, she dislocated my little brother's arm and broke his leg. She gave him a concussion. Joel, my father—" My voice got stuck on the word *father* and it came out hard, like spitting a cherry seed across the room. "He took Bobby to the hospital and covered for my mother like he always does. He made us practice a story about how Bobby fell out of a tree until we could all repeat it without any mistakes."

The more I talked, the more I had to keep talking, but do you know how hard it is to talk when your teeth won't stop chattering? When your body won't stop shaking?

"Last night, I was sitting on the toilet, and he hammered on the door and demanded I repeat the story right there. I tried to tell him I was pooping, but he said he didn't give a shit and I'd better tell it. He said I always have to be prepared to tell the story, no matter what I'm doing, because if anyone ever found out the truth, they'd take us away. Put us in different foster homes where God knows what will happen to us. He says they'll probably rape me and Leesh and Bobby would get beat up every day if we got put in foster homes. I don't want us to be split up, but we can't stay at home anymore. Maybe we'll get lucky and can stay together. Maybe we'll end up in a home with nice foster parents. Or at least parents who won't use us as punching bags. I'm scared to death, but I have to protect them the only way I can. So, I'm asking for your help."

I bit my lip and wiped tears and snot from my face. I must have looked totally unhinged. For the first time since I started talking, I glanced at everyone. They weren't looking at me like I was a maniac or a liar. All three of them were crying.

"I'm sorry to drag you into this, but I don't know what else to do. We need help, right now. I honestly believe if we stay, one of us will wind up dead."

Mrs. Thomas, Nate, and Cheryl hugged me then. All three of them at once. And even though I was more afraid than I've ever been in my life, something told me everything would be okay. Maybe not right away. Maybe not for a really, really long time. But eventually, everything would be okay.

A FRESH START

We were all down in the basement. Me, Leesh, Bobby, Nate, and of course Cheryl. Bobby and Nate teased each other as they played *Mario Kart* together. Nate looked over at me and flashed his patented million-kilowatt smile. Butterflies danced in my stomach and for a moment I wondered if I was absolutely insane for not going out with him. When I told him I wasn't ready for that kind of thing, I absolutely knew he'd get mad and stop talking to me. Instead of getting mad, he hugged me tight and told me he'd wait until I'm ready, even if it's forever.

Leesh sat on the floor while Cheryl sat behind her on the couch and did up her hair. When Cheryl looked over and stuck her tongue out at me, the butterflies danced even harder. For the longest time, I thought the butterfly feeling was a regular part of friendship, but now I understand that I like Nate *and* Cheryl as friends and as more than friends at the same time.

Cheryl loves me like a sister, and that's enough for me. Even if she did get the same butterflies around me that I get around her, I wouldn't want to change our relationship any more than I want to change my relationship with Nate. For the first time in my life, I'm learning who I am, and I don't have room for much else.

Everyone laughed and talked over each other, and my whole body felt warm and fuzzy as I sat in the fancy massaging chair, watching my brother and sister, and stroking Sam's soft orange fur as she purred in my lap. It's been six weeks since Gynger put my brother in the hospital. Six weeks since I decided enough was enough and, as Lady Macbeth said, screwed my courage to the sticking place and told Mrs. Thomas what our life was like. Six weeks since we moved in with Cheryl.

I still can't get over how lucky we were. Her parents wanted to take all of us in, even Sammycat. When Cheryl told me her parents had their foster care license for ages, it never even dawned on me they'd be willing and able to let us live with them as long as we needed—even permanently.

It blows my mind how much things have changed in less than two short months. For example, time has changed. It used to be that time felt like walking down a long hospital hallway with no doors or windows. No matter how many steps I took, I never got any closer to an exit. Every minute seemed to take an hour and every hour seemed to take a day. A week was more time than I could even begin to measure. But now, time is moving the way it should. Some days seem to slog on, and others blur past, but mostly time doesn't feel like a trap anymore.

Leesh and Bobby are different now, too. They've put on some weight. In fact, all of us have, even Sam,—and it looks good on them. I never realized how thin they were before. How dark the circles under their eyes were. I never realized how rarely they laughed or played. I always thought I did a pretty good job of shielding them from the worst of Gynger's wrath, but I couldn't see how much they were affected by it.

How wouldn't they be, though? You can't live in a toxic

swamp and expect not to get poisoned. All three of us are seeing a therapist to help us understand not only what happened to us, but what the future holds. Talking to someone has been good for all of us, but especially Leesh. She doesn't hurt herself at all anymore.

I haven't written in the *safe* diary since we came here, and I'm totally at peace never writing in it again. At first, I wanted to keep the diary, so I'd never forget how I had to pretend to be someone I wasn't to keep myself safe, but last night Cheryl's dad built a fire in the fire pit. When he went back inside, I pulled that diary out of my waistband and tossed it into the flames.

Cheryl held one hand and Nate held the other as we watched the pages burn and curl in on themselves. Leesh and Bobby laughed as they chased each other around the yard, and my heart felt like a balloon with too much helium. It wanted to float up out of my chest and soar straight up to space.

For the first time in forever, I feel like I'm allowed to think anything I want to think. I'm not afraid of writing something that'll get me in trouble, and I have to say life is a hell of a lot less confusing now that I'm not juggling two lives.

"Hey," Cheryl nudged me as the last traces of the diary crumbled into ash. "I have something for you." She handed me a small, velvety green box.

"What's this? You've already done too much. You shouldn't have gotten me a gift." I opened the lid and gasped. A gold necklace shaped like a sunflower lay nestled in the box.

"It's actually from me and Nate. We agreed you absolutely had to have it. Open it."

I hadn't noticed at first, but the sunflower had a line running down the middle of it. My hands shook as I pulled the sunflower halves apart until it looked like butterfly wings. Instead of a body, a shiny silver medallion with the words *You are a BADASS* shimmered in the firelight.

Tears prickled my eyes, and I didn't even try to hide them as Nate and Cheryl each scooted closer to me and put an arm around me.

"Whenever you forget what a badass you really are," Nate whispered, "open that necklace and remember."

Cheryl nodded. "Seriously, Zoe. You're the baddest badass who ever badassed in the history of badassery. I can't even begin to understand what you see in peons like me and Nate."

The tears fell freely as Cheryl attached the necklace around my neck and kissed my cheek.

"That's not all," Nate said. "I'll be right back. Don't go anywhere." He ran up the back porch steps and into the house.

"What's that all about?" I asked Cheryl. Instead of giving me a real answer, she did her weird eyebrow wiggle again and stared at the burning diary.

"Here." Nate handed me a gift wrapped in yellow paper. "I've been waiting for the right time to give this to you. This seems as good a time as any."

I nudged him with my shoulder and flipped the gift over to tear open the seam.

"Nate, it's beautiful." I didn't even try to hide the tremor in my voice as I freed the brown leather journal from the paper.

He rubbed the back of his neck with his hand and blushed. "I figured since you have a new life here with Cheryl, you should have a new journal to go along with it. Somewhere for you to share your deepest thoughts, good and bad."

Without even an ounce of self-consciousness, I threw my arms around his neck and hugged him tighter than I've ever hugged anyone before. "Thank you," I whispered. "It's perfect."

Even though I got my real journal back from social services, I haven't been able to stand the thought of opening it and reliving what we went through. Maybe someday I'll be able to, but not yet.

I don't know how long we'll stay here. Mrs. Martinez, our caseworker, says the goal is what she calls *reunification* with my parents. That means, if we get reunified with Gynger and Joel, Beth and Michael won't be in charge of Bobby anymore and he'll have to move back in with them. Because Leesh and I are teenagers, we get to choose if we want to move back with them or stay here, but Leesh and I already talked about it.

If Bobby has to live with them, we're sticking together and going with him. But that's a long way off. There are a lot of steps Joel and Gynger have to take before we'll be allowed to even visit them without Mrs. Martinez there. *Supervised visitation,* they call it. At the last visitation they actually made it to, Gynger let me know exactly how pissed off she was about it.

"I don't even know why we bother to show up to these things," she said to Joel as they came into the room. "Obviously, Zoe doesn't want us here, and the state thinks we're unfit parents. I bet it would make Little Queenie happy if we stopped coming altogether."

That old, familiar icicle stabbed my heart again. It's a feeling I haven't had even once since moving in with Cheryl's family, and it hurt more than ever. Maybe because I wasn't used to it anymore.

"Easy," Joel soothed her like she was an angry horse. "Let's try and enjoy our time the best we can." He looked at Bobby, smiled big, and ruffled his hair. "There's my little man! How's your leg feeling?"

Gynger watched as Mrs. Martinez jotted something down in her notebook. Without so much as glancing my direction, she bustled over to Bobby and wrapped him in a hug. Since he didn't have to wear the sling for his shoulder anymore, he was able to hug her back. He seemed genuinely happy to see her, but I couldn't help wondering if he was pretending. After what she did to him, how could he still love her? Then again, if I'm totally honest with myself, there's a part of me that still loves her, too. She's my mother, and I think nature hardwires children to love even the worst parents.

For an hour, Joel and Gynger played *Happy Family* with Leesh and Bobby, acting like loving parents. A couple of times, Joel tried to get me to play air hockey with him, but every time, Gynger said Bobby should keep playing since he was too little to understand taking turns yet. I wish I could say her public shunning didn't even faze me, but it hurt. Actually, it was humiliating. She didn't even try to hide how much she hates me from Mrs. Martinez.

In fact, the more notes the caseworker took, the worse Gynger treated me. Eventually, I excused myself and hid in the bathroom—just like I used to do at lunch—and wondered if Gynger was right. Maybe I deserved to be punished. After all, I did break Wilkes Rule *numero uno:* Never tell anyone about family stuff. Maybe, if I can get to the point where I don't love her even a little, it won't hurt so much when she's nasty to me.

Joel came to the next visit alone. He said Gynger was sick, but I didn't believe him. She obviously hated me so much, she sacrificed her time with Bobby and Leesh just to avoid me. I tried my best to smile and enjoy spending time with him, but something felt off. He was quieter and didn't laugh so much. When he smiled, his eyes didn't light up the way they usually did. I wondered what his life was like without us there. Did she go with him when he was on the road? Was it hard on him to be alone with her all the time? Was she treating him the way she treated me? Was he finally getting a taste of what my whole life has been like?

At the end of the visit, he hugged all of us longer than usual.

"I'm proud of you, Zuzu. Even though I don't agree with what you did, I'm still real proud of you. You did what you thought was right by your brother, even though you knew it'd tear our family apart and break our hearts. That couldn't have been easy for you." It was the first time he acknowledged me blabbing my mouth.

Mrs. Martinez wrote something down.

"I'm sorry." My voice cracked, and I bit my lip to keep from crying. "I…"

But I didn't know what else to say. I couldn't tell him I was both sorry and not sorry. I'm sorry he feels like I betrayed the family. I'm sorry I broke us so badly we'll never be the same. But I'm not sorry I told. I'm not sorry we don't live there anymore. As much as it hurts to think about all the ways life could have been different if I had kept my mouth shut, it's way better than living in a state of emergency all the time.

We haven't seen him or Gynger since. Neither of them came to the next visit or the one after. They didn't even call or give some sort of excuse. They just didn't show up. Both times, Mrs. Martinez and Bobby played with Legos, and she reassured him they were on their way, but I could tell he didn't believe her.

At this point, I can't decide if I hope Joel shows up for the next visit in two weeks or not. I can say, I hope I never have to see Gynger again. I hate myself for missing her, but I'm starting to love myself enough to see I never deserved the things she did to me.

"Kids," Beth shouted down the stairs. "Dinner's on. Make sure you wash your hands."

Bobby paused the game, dropped the controller, and thundered up the stairs. Leesh looked at her new hairstyle in the mirror behind the couch and smiled at herself. She looked good, and I told her so.

"Thanks, Zoe." She hugged me, kissed my cheek, and brushed her finger across my sunflower necklace. "So do you."

THE END

—

Don't miss your next favorite book!

Join the Fire & Ice mailing list
www.fireandiceya.com/mail.html

ACKNOWLEDGMENTS

They say writing is lonely, but nothing could be further from the truth. While it's true that I tend to write my first drafts in a vacuum (I don't even let my partner of 20 years read Draft 1 before it's done), there's nothing lonely about writing a novel and turning it into an actual book that total strangers can pick up and read. It takes more than a village to bring a book to life, it takes an entire community.

First, I need to express all my love and gratitude to my husband Stirling. Thank you for giving me the time I need to turn writing from a hobby into a dream job. Thank you for your unending support and the regular pep-talks when things got so difficult I wanted to hide under my desk and never come out again. And most of all, thank you for sharing this journey with me. You will always be my first and favorite reader. I love you.

To my son, Ethan, thank you so much for your enthusiasm and sharp as hell insights that helped me stitch up more plot holes than I can count. I'm so lucky to have you on my side! My most sincere hope is that one day I can make you as proud of me as I am of you.

I owe a million thanks to my wonderful agent, Tina Schwartz. Not only for taking a chance on me and my quiet, niche book, but also for your vision and warm support. Thank you for going to bat time and again, and for being the champion both Zoe and I needed.

Without the tireless work of the team over at Fire and Ice YA, Between Safe and Real would still be a pipe dream on a hard drive. Endless thanks to Nancy Schumacher for seeing the potential in this story as well as your keen eye during copyedits. Sybelle Maloney, thank you for pointing out inconsistencies and making sure all my loose ends wrapped up nicely. I also need to thank Caroline Andrus for the incredible cover on the front of this book. My third biggest fear when I found out I was going to be published was that I'd hate my cover. Thank you, Caroline, for keeping my fears in the dark!

To all the supportive and kind people I met through the Dallas Fort-Worth Writers Conference, I'm forever indebted to you. Seriously, this conference is a one-of-a-kind experience overflowing with incredible seminars, workshops, and most importantly, people who were happy to give selflessly of themselves. Thank you to everyone who sat with me in the hallway and helped me practice and refine my pitches. You all showed me what a community can look like, and I'm so thankful to have had so many wonderful experiences with you.

Along those lines, I also need to thank DFW Writers Workshop. I'm honored that I got to spend some of my Wednesday nights learning from people far smarter than I am!

Thank you to my incredible team of beta and sensitivity readers: Cynthia Wall, Adam Jones, Emily Stanley, Lisa Hicks, and Elise Hoffman. Your insights were invaluable and I owe you all a debt of gratitude for the rest of my life. Thank you for being such fierce allies and dear friends.

Jay Whistler, thank you so much for the early developmental feedback that helped me land my agent and get this book into the world!

To the wonderful writers in AZ YA/MG Writers, thank you for welcoming me to the fold, showing me the ropes, and being a constant source of support and kindness.

To Solange Hommel and Lesley Henderson. I fucking love you. You're more than my writing friends, you're my soul sisters and I couldn't have come this far without you.

On the topic of found family, I have a whole bunch of found family to thank:

Ben Ferrufino and Lizann Croft, there's way too much to thank you for, so I'm just gonna settle with thank you for being family and loving me and mine unconditionally.

Dana Swift, thank you for talking me off the edge!

David Goodner, thank you for your steadfast support and kind words.

Eric Warren, thank you for being such a supportive friend!

Nikolai Wisekal, thank you for talking me through fear and anxiety!

Kate Angelella, dear. What can I say other than I love you?

Jennifer Dwyer, thank you for always being there for me and my family and for patiently walking me through the foster care system over and over again. Your love, support, compassion, and empathy inspire me.

To my TWSS and HH sisterhoods, thank you for being a safe place and continuing to show up for me over the years.

To everyone in my adult survivors group—which will remain unnamed for privacy—thank you for reminding me how important this book is, for cheering me on when I wanted to quit, and for helping me rebuild myself piece by piece over the years. I love you all and am immeasurably proud of your courage and strength.

Sherry Futral, Doug Thompson, Jimmie Stephens, and

John Bales, thank you for getting me through high school. I may not have expressed my gratitude then, but each one of you helped me through more than I could ever express or adequately thank you for. Mary Polk, even though we weren't close then, I'm so thankful I have you in my corner now. I wish I could go back in time and foist myself on you, because we were meant to be friends!

And finally, to everyone who picked up this book and felt seen for the first time, thank you for giving me and Zoe a chance. It may not seem like it now but take it from me. You are worthy of love, you are worthy of friendship, and you are badass.

THANK YOU FOR READING

Did you enjoy this book?

We invite you to leave a review at the website of your choice, such as Goodreads, Amazon, Barnes & Noble, etc.

DID YOU KNOW THAT LEAVING A REVIEW…

- Helps other readers find books they may enjoy.
- Gives you a chance to let your voice be heard.
- Gives authors recognition for their hard work.
- Doesn't have to be long. A sentence or two about why you liked the book will do.

ABOUT THE AUTHOR

Except for that brief time in fourth grade when Dannie M. Olguin wanted to be either a tight-rope walker or a bounty hunter, all she ever wanted to be is a writer. She even scratched out Danielle Steel's last name in magazine ads and replaced it with her own. Reading and writing were her escape, and she fully credits books and writing with surviving her childhood.

She is a member of various online and in-person writers and critique groups and attends conferences regularly. In 2019, she co-taught a class at Dallas Fort Worth Writers Conference. In 2018, she was chosen to share a narrative nonfiction piece in front of 500 strangers at a true storytelling event. As an introvert with a fear of public speaking, this tops her list of Scariest Things She's Ever Done—and she taught her kid how to drive in Dallas! She also once took the watch off a dead man and gave it to her mother. She swears no laws were broken and that taking the watch wasn't nearly as badass as it sounds

———

www.dmolguin.com
www.tiktok.com/@danniemolguin

facebook.com/DannieMOlguin

twitter.com/DannieMOlguin